KILL: FOUR
AN OMEGA THRILLER

BLAKE BANNER

Copyright © 2025 by Right House

All rights reserved.

The characters and events portrayed in this ebook are fictitious. Any similarity to real persons, living or dead, is coincidental and not intended by the author.

No part of this book may be reproduced in any form or by any electronic or mechanical means, including information storage and retrieval systems, without written permission from the author, except for the use of brief quotations in a book review.

ISBN-13: 978-1-63696-345-7

ISBN-10: 1-63696-345-5

Cover design by: Damonza

Printed in the United States of America

www.righthouse.com

www.instagram.com/righthousebooks

www.facebook.com/righthousebooks

twitter.com/righthousebooks

THE OMEGA SERIES
Dawn of the Hunter (Book 1)
Double Edged Blade (Book 2)
The Storm (Book 3)
The Hand of War (Book 4)
A Harvest of Blood (Book 5)
To Rule in Hell (Book 6)
Kill: One (Book 7)
Powder Burn (Book 8)
Kill: Two (Book 9)
Unleashed (Book 10)
The Omicron Kill (Book 11)
9mm Justice (Book 12)
Kill: Four (Book 13)
Death In Freedom (Book 14)
Endgame (Book 15)

ONE

I lay still in bed, feeling an indefinable disquiet: the stillness of the small hours, hazy beams of moonlight leaning silent through the open window, lying in limpid, twisted oblongs across the foot of my bed, an owl calling for a mate, far off across the dark fields, the steady croaking of the frogs in the pond near the black woods outside.

I rose and went to the window. Everything was motionless. The almost turquoise glow of the full moon lay luminous over everything: the blacktop on the driveway, the softly glinting leaves on the trees, the rooftops and the chimneypots silhouetted against the translucent sky. There was nothing there—nothing visible.

I stood a while, not looking for objects but for movement, and eventually it came: a shifting of the dark among the trees that bordered Concord Road, then the muted cones of headlamps and the hum of an engine retreating toward Weston.

At breakfast the next morning, as Kenny set down my bacon and eggs and poured my coffee, I said, "Check the CCTV footage for last night, will you, Kenny? We had a prowler, somebody in a car parked on Concord Road. I want to know who it was."

His eyes searched my face for less than a second. "I'll do that right away, sir."

He withdrew and I sat alone, eating my eggs and bacon, more aware of the lawns and woodlands beyond the leaded windows, behind my back, than I was of the food and the coffee on the table in front of me.

At seven thirty I rose from the table, slipped my Sig Sauer p226 under my arm and stepped out for a walk along Concord Road. It was a fresh, bright morning. The early shadows were long, dense and cool among burnished light, but the sky was vibrant blue. Fall was just a few weeks away, and you could smell it in the air.

I walked slowly, scanning the blacktop and the verges of the roads. There wasn't much to see but grass, meadow flowers and an occasional fallen leaf. Above my head and deeper in the woodland there was sporadic birdsong, or the sudden flap of wings, but aside from these small, desultory bursts of activity, there was no movement. Nothing stirred.

I came to the spot where I had seen the headlamps, and hunkered down to examine the soil. There were impressions. I photographed them with my cell, but I was pretty sure I recognized the tread as belonging to a Range Rover.

I stood, moved in among the trees and made my way back to the house through the woods, exploring one by one all the spots where you could get a good, clear view of the house without being seen. My search was inconclusive. There might have been someone there, or not. But if there had been, they were good. They didn't leave tracks.

At nine thirty, Kenny knocked on my study door and came in, closing it behind him.

"Sir, we do indeed seem to have had a visitor last night. A dark blue Range Rover parked on Concord Road. It was captured by one of the cameras you had installed in the trees beside the road. In the footage, the driver does not exit the vehicle, so his face does not appear. Nor are his plates clear enough to make out in detail. It seems he was there for a couple of hours from two until four. Then he drove away."

I leaned back in my chair and sighed, gazing out at the luminous green lawn and the tree line thirty yards away at the back of the house.

"This was why I was reluctant to come home, Kenny. I didn't want to visit this on you and Rosalia. But I thought it was over. I thought we were done with this. I really thought we were done. I'm sorry, Kenny."

His expression was pained. "Sir, if I may speak freely, Rosalia and myself, we have known you all your life, and your father before you. It is no comfort for us to survive and live, if you are killed or hurt in some distant part of the world. This is your home, and ours, and we defend it together."

I smiled at the old guy who had been more of a father to me than my father ever had. "I know, Kenny. We're family. I'll see to it, don't worry. Stay on high alert, double check the security systems and see what you can hear on the grapevine about a dark blue or black Range Rover in the neighbourhood. I'm going to go into Weston."

I took the Kuga because it was inconspicuous, I opened all the windows and drove the mile and a bit to town, through dappled shade at a leisurely twenty-five miles per hour. On the way I scanned every front yard, every parking lot and every car that came my way. I didn't see a dark Range Rover.

I dropped the Kuga at Walgreens and took a stroll around the town, visiting every shop in turn and scanning the parking lots outside each of them. I even visited the Catholic church.

I eventually found the car at the dentist's. I guess even international hit men get trouble with their teeth. So I strolled up to the green beside the hot dog stand, where I had a good view of the dentist's parking lot, and sat myself down at one of the benches there to take the sun and wait for the driver to show.

He showed after half an hour, holding his cheek, and climbed into his car, where he sat without moving for five minutes before pulling out and driving slowly away. When he'd gone from view, I strolled down to the dentist's and pushed through the door. Peggy on the reception desk smiled up at me.

"Lacklan, we haven't seen you around here for a while. How are you?"

"All the better for seeing you, Peggy. How's Dave?"

"Can't complain. The practice is going well. Nothing much changes around here, does it?"

"Say, I must be wrong, but I am pretty certain I just saw an old colleague of mine come out of here and drive away in a dark blue Range Rover. I called out to him but he didn't hear me..."

Her eyes widened at the prospect of possible gossip. "This last guy who just left?"

"About five minutes ago."

She rattled at her computer. "From your time in the military?" I made an affirmative noise and she tapped a little more. "He had a kind of military air about him all right... He was not an American, I can tell you that. I think he was Australian or maybe British. Here we are, Mark Philips, just visiting the U.S. from South Africa. Broke his tooth last night eating a salted almond. Is that your friend?"

I frowned. "You know, I think it might be. It was a few years ago. I think I'll look him up. Where's he staying?"

"At the Arabian Horse, in Wayland."

I smiled. "Sure, where else?"

I stepped back out into the late morning sunshine and made my way slowly back toward my car. When I got there, I climbed in and sat for a while with the windows open, listening to the gentle sounds of late New England summer —and thinking. After ten years serving with the British SAS, there was no shortage of people in the world who might want me dead, but most of the ones I could think of were either from the Middle East or Latin America. I couldn't think of a single one from South Africa. And the name Mark Philips, apart from being the first husband of Prince Charles' sister, meant nothing to me.

Was I becoming paranoid? Probably, but that didn't mean they weren't after me, it just meant I knew about it.

I hit the ignition and pulled out of the parking lot, but instead of heading for home I turned east, as though I were going into Boston. At Conant Road I turned north and started cruising slowly through the woods. I figured the chances were better than good that if this guy was watching me, and had found my address, he also had my cell number and was tracking my GPS. So I followed Conant Road for about a mile through the forest until I came to Sunset Road on my left. There I turned west and followed that road for half a mile or so till I came to the grounds of Weston College. At the college, I turned left into Merriam Street and drove for a couple of minutes through the dense cover of the trees until I found a lay-by. There, I pulled off the road, left my phone in the car and sprinted back through the woods to the intersection, where I dropped on my belly among ferns and waited.

I waited five minutes, and was beginning to think I might have made a mistake and read too much into what was, after all, just a guy parking on a wooded road for a couple of hours, when his blue Range Rover nosed up to the crossroads. Then I felt a sinking feeling in my gut.

It wasn't over; not yet.

He waited a long time at the intersection, maybe a full minute and a half. Finally he slowly pulled onto Merriam Street and crawled at no more than four miles an hour along the black top until he caught sight of the Kuga. Then he stopped and backed up a bit.

There was no doubt in my mind now that he was tailing me. The question had become, what for? The fact that he was watching my house between two and four AM suggested he was planning either to break in and steal something, or break in and kill me, and anybody else he happened to find in there—the only purpose in watching a house at that time of the morning is to see what obstacles you're going to find when you force an entry.

I gave him another minute to see what he did. He didn't do anything, so I backed up in among the trees and took a circuitous route back toward my car. I allowed him to see me walk out of the forest, cross the road and climb into the Ford. Then I drove back to my house at a leisurely pace. He was professional enough to stay out of my rearview mirror. But by that time I was pretty sure I knew who he was.

I got to my house, left the Kuga out front and crossed the hall to my study, where I stood a moment, looking around at the familiar room. Kenny had, as he had every morning since I had returned home, set and lit the fire and opened the French doors onto the lawn at the back. It was a quirk of mine, I enjoyed having a fire burning with the windows open.

I went to the sideboard and poured myself a Bushmills from the decanter, then lit a Camel and stood with my back to the flames, looking around the room. Throughout my childhood and my teens, it had been my father's study. I had been punished in this room more times than I could remember. It was in this room as much as any other that I had grown to hate him—long before I had learned about his membership of Omega.

It had been two years now since his death, and in that time I had spent very little time in the house I had inherited from him. I had not made my mark on it. I had not taken possession of it. I had spent all my time and all my energy destroying the organization he had been a part of.

And I had thought, after Mexico, that the job was done.

I took my drink and my cigarette to the desk, dropped into the large, leather chair and called Jim Redbeard in L.A.

"Lacklan, it's good to hear from you. It's been a long time. Sole asks after you. You know, Sole, my wife?"

"Hi, Jim. Would that be Sole, your ex-wife? Apart from discovering jealousy for the first time, how are you?"

"I am sensational, as always, and I am not jealous. I just hope your intentions are honorable. I'd hate her to meet another bastard like me."

"Right now I have no intentions, Jim. I just need to run something by you."

"Shoot."

"My house is being watched by a South African in a Range Rover. I get the impression he is a pro. He doesn't make sloppy mistakes, he's patient, he's meticulous and I am pretty sure he is here to assassinate me."

"Ah..."

"What do you mean, 'Ah...'?"

"South Africa has been popping up on the radar lately."

"Yeah? How?"

"Is your line secure?"

"As secure as any line on the planet at the moment."

"OK, I'll give it to you in general terms without buzzwords, but we should meet, soon, and discuss this."

"OK."

"I've received information about something, some kind of building, a structure, it's massive, that's being put up along the border with Namibia, on the South African side of the River Orange. I don't know what it is, and none of my informants knows what it is."

"What does it look like?"

"It's in its early stages, but it looks as though it's going to be a huge pyramid."

"A *pyramid?*"

"That's what I'm told. I haven't been able to get photographs, video—nothing. Just oral testimony. Which is in itself telling you something. It is being kept strictly under wraps. There is no official record of it, no licenses granted, no requests submitted. The thing does not exist officially, it is being built in one of the remotest parts of the globe, and it is vast. Estimates I have heard are in the region of the apex being up to a thousand feet high. That would give it a base in the region of two thousand feet across, or more."

"What the hell would they want to build something like that for? That's the size of a small city."

"I know. But there is more."

"What...?"

I asked him, but I knew what he was going to say, and he said it. "Your friends seem to have become active."

"Shit..."

"They seem to be organizing a reunion."

"Don't say any more. That's who my visitor is. A messenger."

"I'm afraid so."

"We need to meet. Soon. In the next day or so."

"What about your visitor?"

"I'll take care of him."

"Good. Let's meet in Seattle. I'll send you the details. I'll be in touch in the next twenty-four hours."

"Good."

I hung up and called Kenny. A couple of minutes later, he came in and closed the door behind him.

"Any development, sir?"

"Yes, I'm going to take a walk, cross country, to Plimpton. When I get back, I'll need to pack. I'm going away for a couple of days."

"Will you be back, sir?"

I stared at him, not sure for a moment what he meant. Then I smiled and relaxed. "Yes, Kenny. I will be back, for sure."

"Rosalia will be very relieved, sir."

"While I'm out, I want you on lock down, Kenny. Nobody comes in and nobody goes out. Anybody tries to force their way in, you shoot them."

"I understand, sir."

He closed the French windows and locked them. I cocked the Sig, slipped it into my waistband where it was less visible than under my arm, and stepped out into the front drive. Behind me, I heard Kenny lock the door, and knew that he was engaging all the house's security systems: the one my father had installed, and the ones I had added. Then I set off around the back of the house, through the old fence that separated our property from Marni's, and into the deep forest that stretched for over a mile between our small hamlet outside Weston and the village of Plimpton.

I walked like a man without a care in the world. The tall, ancient trees closed in about me, leaning in to form a translucent green cathedral over my head. Each footfall, rustling on the leaves or cracking on a dry branch, created a dull echo through the woodland, its sound bizarrely both muffled and amplified by the trees. I didn't follow a path. I meandered in a vaguely north-westerly direction, guiding myself by the familiar landmarks of the forest I knew so well. This had been my playground as a boy—mine and Marni's.

I knew, for example, that at the halfway point there was a steep slope, and at the bottom of that slope there was an ancient fallen tree, lying in a shallow trough, and that tree was what I was heading for.

I got there after about fifteen minutes of apparently aimless wandering and stood a moment in the diffuse green light, gazing down the slope, listening to all the sounds of the woodland. Then I took a step forward and screamed.

I hit the ground on my right shoulder and cried out again, rolling fast and out of control down toward the tree. At the bottom of the steep slope, I hit the tree. I had a million small aches, cuts and bruises all over my body, but I ignored them and crawled under the huge fallen trunk, over to the far side where there was a clump of tall ferns. I worked my way in among them, then pulled out my cell and tossed it over, under the tree, then lay and waited.

I didn't have to wait long. After no more than a minute, he appeared at the top of the slope. At first it was just his head peering over. He was cautious, but he saw my cell and concluded that I must be nearby, under the massive trunk. He stood and half-ran, half-scrambled down the slope to the tree. As he bent to peer under it, I stood and walked over to him, with my Sig held out in both hands. He sensed me before he saw or heard me, went very still and straightened up. I said, "Put your hands on your head. Turn to face me. Let me get a look at you."

He did as I said, speaking, as he turned, in a strong South African accent. "Look, friend, I don't know what this is about. I heard a scream and came to help..."

I studied his face and decided I'd never seen him before. "Cut the crap, Philips. Is that your real name?"

A flicker of surprise. "Yes, of course it is. But how did you...?"

"Turn around and get on your knees."

"Now look! This has gone far enough!"

"Right now you have two options, Philips. I shoot you in the face or you turn around and get on your knees so we can have a conversation."

The fear in his face was no act. He turned his back on me, but paused before getting on his knees. "Look here, mister. I don't know what idea you've got into your head, but I was just going for a walk when I heard a scream. I came to help, and find you brandishing a gun at me."

"What were you doing parked outside my house last night?"

"What?"

"I am not the most patient man in the world, Philips. Stop bullshitting me. You're not doing yourself any favors."

"You live on Concord Road?"

"Come on, Philips!"

He was swallowing hard and his skin had gone a pasty gray color. "I was shagging a hooker. I picked her up in Boston. It's impossible for a man to get laid out here! I phoned and picked her up. I couldn't take her back to the bed and breakfast, could I? So I shagged her in the Range Rover."

"What the hell are you doing out here anyway?"

He almost turned to face me. I snapped, "Stay put!" and he stopped, but he was craning his head over his shoulder.

"You fucking Americans! I'm sorry, but seriously! Where

else on the face of the planet is a foreigner held at gunpoint because he is a tourist in a place where you don't get many tourists? What fucking century are you in? This is one of the most beautiful places on the planet. I am here because I want to see it, try the seafood, wander in the woods! And what do I get for my troubles? Some gun-happy fucking Yank pulling a gun on me! And why? Because I am visiting a remote part of his country! You are a real piece of work, friend! I came here to help you because I thought you were hurt!"

"So you're not tracking my GPS?"

He half turned again. His face was creased with incredulity. "*What?*"

"So if we walk back to your truck now, we will not find a tracker locked onto my cell phone?"

"Friend, you seriously need help. I'm not being facetious. You are seriously paranoid. I mean it."

"Take your jacket off."

He went very still. "Why?"

"Because if you don't, I'll shoot you in the leg and take it off you myself."

"What is *wrong* with you?"

"I don't like people trying to kill me, Philips. Now take your jacket off before I run out of patience."

He was good. The movement was smooth and fluid. He didn't fluster and he didn't fumble. He took hold of his lapels, like he was about to take off his jacket, then his right hand slipped in under his arm and simultaneously his left leg slipped back and across to the right, so that as his Glock came out of his holster, he had already spun and was facing me. He was too good. He didn't give me a chance to wing him or wound him. I double tapped and both slugs went through his chest. He winced and coughed, his legs failed and he crumpled to the ground.

I knelt beside him and felt his pulse in his throat. He was dead. I searched his pockets for his ID and found a passport and a driver's license in the name of Mark Philips, but no other personal information. I kept his driving license, picked up my phone and left.

THE CALL CAME forty-five minutes later, as I was stepping out of the shower.

"Yeah, Walker." I wiped the water from my eyes with my fingers.

"Lacklan, it's Jim. I'm on a burner, but I don't want to stay on too long. How did you get on with your stalker? Any news?"

"We didn't get to talk."

"OK. Cape Coral. Book into an hotel. Day after tomorrow I'll call you. We'll meet and talk."

"Cape Coral. Florida?"

"Is there another?"

"You said Seattle?"

"And if anybody was listening in, that's what they are thinking right now."

"OK."

"Drive, and use something less conspicuous than that machine from hell you usually drive, will you?"

"See you in a couple of days, Jim."

I hung up and began to towel myself dry.

TWO

I booked an apartment at the Westin, a holiday complex on the Glover Bight, and drove down in my Zombie, despite Jim's request that I leave it behind. The Zombie 222 is, as he described it, a beast from hell. The chassis is an original 1968 Mustang Fastback, in matte black, but under the hood it has twin lithium ion batteries that deliver eight hundred horsepower straight to the back wheels. It will accelerate from naught to sixty in about one and a half seconds with enough G-force to spread your face like a pancake across the rear windshield. It has a top speed of two hundred miles an hour, and because it runs on lithium ion batteries, it gets there almost instantly, and in absolute silence.

It was a twenty-two hour drive from Weston to Cape Coral, but I don't sleep much—I figure I'll have plenty of time to sleep when I'm dead—and with the help of the Zombie, I got there in just under eighteen hours, at five thirty PM on the following day, nineteen hours after I had spoken to Jim on the phone in my study.

I parked the car in the parking garage beneath the apartment block, checked in to my apartment at reception and rode the elevator to the fifteenth floor. There I threw open the terrace and stood a while under the Florida sun, taking in the view of the Glover Bight, Sanibel Island and, beyond it, the immense sweep of the Gulf of Mexico, wondering when Jim would show, what he would have to tell me, and where and when the Omega story would end.

If it would ever end.

After that, I dumped my case on the bed and stood under the shower for fifteen minutes, switching from scalding, steaming water to cold and back again, trying to wake myself up and wash away the long drive from the north. Then I toweled myself dry, called down for a Martini and dialed Jim's burner. He answered as I dropped into a chair on the terrace. He didn't waste time on preliminaries.

"You're there already?"

"I just checked in. I'm at the Westin, Cape Coral."

"You either flew or you drove down in that machine from hell."

"Where are you?"

"I'm on my way. I'll be there in the morning. I'll pick you up from Pier Two at nine AM. Forgive me for asking the obvious, but were you followed?"

"I'm pretty sure I wasn't."

"OK, get a good rest after your long drive."

"Yes, Mom."

He laughed noisily and hung up.

I sat a while and watched the evening gather in the sky

above the sea, wondering why it's so much easier to be decisive about killing and destroying than it is about offering peace and creating life.

My bell rang and I opened the door to admit a young man in a burgundy uniform with a tray holding a bottle of Martini, Beefeater gin and a dish of olives. He mixed me a cocktail, I gave him twenty bucks and he left. I took my cocktail out to the terrace, sat and called Marni in Oxford.

"Lacklan... I didn't expect to hear from you."

"Everything OK with you?"

"Sure..." She was hesitant. "Why?"

"Just touching base."

There was a pause, then the hint of a smile in her voice. "It's nice to hear from you."

"How's life? Any news?"

"Like what?"

"Career, love life..." I let the words hang in the air and heard her laugh softly at the other end of the line.

"Well, since I gave Gibbons his marching orders, my career has been pretty much at a standstill, and since a certain party gave me *my* marching orders, my love life has been pretty much at a standstill too. So, no, no news to speak of."

I nodded, as though she could see me. "Well, sometimes no news is good news."

"Yeah, sometimes. Lacklan, why are you really calling?"

"I don't know. I'll have to ask my analyst." She laughed and I smiled, allowing it to show in my voice. "I might be going over to England in the next couple of days. I'd like to see you, if you're free."

She didn't answer straight away, but when she did, her voice was warm. "I'd like that."

"Marni?"

"Yes, Lacklan..."

I hesitated, indecisive. My head was crowded with things I wanted to say, but in the end I just said, "I have to go, but if anyone approaches you in the next few days, anyone who might come into your life, please treat them with caution."

"Oh..." Her voice had hardened. "Does that include you?"

"No."

"I thought you were touching base."

"I was—I am. I just don't want you to get hurt. I wouldn't be much of a friend if I didn't give you the heads up, would I?"

"So it's not over?"

"Apparently not."

"Lacklan, you can't keep on..."

"Not on the phone. I'll come and see you at Oxford. We'll talk about everything. But please, Marni, sometimes I feel it's enough for me to give you some advice for you to go right ahead and do the opposite."

"I guess we're more alike than we think."

"Maybe so, but I really need you to listen to me this time. Be careful, be smart. There are people out to hurt me, and..." I paused and sighed. "I guess you are my Achilles' heel. I don't know if they know that or not, but if they do, you're at risk. That was the real reason I was calling."

She was quiet for a long moment. Then she said, "I'm your Achilles' heel?"

"Look, don't..."

"Say it again." The smile had returned to her voice. I sighed. She repeated, "Say it again. What am I?"

"You're my Achilles' heel." I heard her giggling and stared up at the pink and powder blue sky. "Be serious, Marni."

"OK, I'll be serious and I will be cautious, I promise."

"Thank you."

There was an awkward silence for a few seconds. Then she said suddenly, "I was sorry to hear about you and Abi. I know you were..."

"It was for the best. She and Bat seem to be very close now. They seem happy."

"Bat?"

"Friend of mine from the Regiment."

"So you're alone now?"

I felt a bitter twist in my gut and tried to suppress it. "Yeah, it's the way I came in, it's the way I'm going out, and apparently it's the way I'm going to be in between too."

"I'm sorry."

"Listen, I'll see you in a couple of days. I'll drop you a line when I've booked my flight."

"Yeah..." We both hesitated, then she said, "Take care, Lacklan," and hung up.

I had a steak and salad sent up at seven thirty, then read for a couple of hours and had an early night. The next morning I rose at five-thirty, went for a run, trained for a couple of hours, showered and had a breakfast of bacon, pancakes and maple syrup, and at nine o'clock I was on Pier Two, smoking a Camel and looking like a tourist, scanning the area for Jim Redbeard. I didn't see him, but at ten past nine I saw a launch approaching through the mouth of the bite, and when I saw that, I noticed the white schooner anchored about a mile out of Big Shell Island. I smiled to myself. That was Jim all over, advising me that my silent, matte black Mustang was too conspicuous and showing up in a shiny, white, one hundred foot schooner.

Ten minutes later, I was sitting in the back of the launch and we were slapping over the small waves, with the gulls wheeling overhead under the blue dome of the morning. Soon the pitch of the engine dropped, we slowed and closed in on the steps that led down from the deck to the small boarding platform, just above the waves. Jim watched over the side, leaning on the gunwale, smoking a cigarette.

I swung up onto the ladder and he met me at the top with a warm handshake and an embrace.

"It's good to see you, Lacklan. You look well, I expected you to be heavier, putting on a spread now that you've settled as master of the manor. Glad to see I was wrong. You still looking lean and predatory."

"The war's not over yet, Jim."

He slapped me on the shoulder. "Come down to the lounge and have some coffee. Njal's down there."

"How is he? Last time I saw him, he was dying of a chest wound."

"That guy's an ox. He's indestructible."

We crossed the deck to a small structure that covered a flight of wooden steps, which led down into a space that looked more like an old world club than an oceangoing schooner. The walls were paneled in mahogany, there were chesterfields and Persian rugs, bookcases and even a bar. A short flight of steps led to an enclosed cockpit where there were two large, leather swivel chairs, a helm, and a bank of computers and electronic equipment.

Njal was sitting in one of the chesterfields, reading a book, and rose as we came in. He grinned at me, gripped my hand as though he were planning to Indian wrestle me and embraced me with his other arm.

"You still alive, huh? We thought maybe you died of middle-age boredom. What you doing now? You become a farmer or some shit, huh?"

I smiled. "Not dead, not a farmer. Just trying to stay out of trouble."

Jim laughed. "Don't go lookin' for trouble when trouble ain't lookin' to be looked for, huh? Only trouble *is* out lookin' for you, Lacklan. Come and sit down."

We sat around a mahogany coffee table as a door under the stairs to the cockpit opened and Mioko, Jim's Japanese companion, came out with a pot of coffee and three cups on a tray. She gave me a special smile, set down the tray and withdrew.

As Jim poured, I said, "So what's this about?"

Njal answered for him. "We don't know, but it stinks of Omega."

Jim handed me a cup. "It more than stinks, it is clearly Omega."

"You said that if I destroyed Omicron, Omega four and five would wither away."

He shrugged and handed Njal a cup. "Apparently I was wrong. Sometimes I am wrong. Not often, but sometimes."

"Good to know. So how wrong were you?"

Again it was Njal who answered. "We got two bits of

intel, with no obvious connection, until you dig a little deeper. First we got this building in the Northern Cape, on the border with Namibia. It is basically a pyramid the size of a skyscraper, on the Orange River, in the middle of fuckin' nowhere. It is in the desert. The nearest town of any size is Springbok, which has about twelve thousand people and is sixty miles away as the crow flies, but at least a hundred by road. Forty of those hundred miles are on dirt tracks through the desert."

"I get the idea. It's remote. But why connect it with Omega? It could be a secret government project."

Jim shook his head. "Wait and listen."

Njal continued. "Meanwhile, in parallel, almost simultaneous, we hear that Omega Four, who had been quiet for a long time, are arranging a summit. It's too much coincidence, right? So Omega Four covers all of Africa, Middle East—except for Israel, which fell under Omega One—Iran, Kazakhstan, Afghanistan…"

"I'm aware…"

"OK, right down to Pakistan and India."

"I was the one who gave you that information."

"Breathe, drink your coffee, chill, listen. Their areas of competence, what they specialized in, were Islam, mind control through indoctrination, the economy of war, unregulated research and development, especially in weaponry, biology and chemistry. So we were trying to get some idea: if this is the areas of special competence of Omega Four, what the fuck is this giant pyramid, right?"

I shrugged. "Right. And?"

"We still got no fuckin' idea, man. But, at the Omega Four summit, we got Pi and Ro, father and son, Ruud van

Dreiver and Jelle van Dreiver, both South African and both directors of the Van Dreiver Corporation. Ruud is the CEO, Jelle is his second in command. Then we got Sigma: Prince Mohamed bin Awad, resides between his Awadi palace, London and New York."

"I know him."

"Of course you do. Then we have Tau: Ameya Dabir, Brahmin woman of ancient lineage. If India was still a monarchy, she would be a princess. Her father was a very powerful industrialist, but she established her own business twenty years ago and made her way into the Forbes five hundred richest people on the planet. "And finally Upsilon, George da Silva, President of King Felipe, a small island republic in the Gulf of Guinea, between Cameroon and Nigeria, total population one hundred thousand inhabitants. All five of them are meeting in Knysna, South Africa, at the van Dreiver mansion on the Knysna lagoon, to eat fresh oysters and drink South African wine. What else they gonna do, we don't know. But it is the first time Omega Four have got together in a summit for over two years."

Jim drained his cup and set it down on the table. "I can't believe it is a coincidence that a hit man came looking for you at precisely this time."

"He was South African." I pulled his driver's license from my pocket and dropped it on the table. "It has his prints on it, I don't know if you can do anything with that."

"Yeah, we can."

"So you are making the assumption that their meeting is connected with this massive construction."

Jim nodded. "You're right. It is an assumption. Which is why we need to confirm it. We need to confirm it's an

Omega project, we need to confirm what kind of project it is, and then, if we are right about it, then we need to destroy it."

I laughed out loud. "You want to destroy a pyramid the size of a skyscraper? What do you plan to use, a tactical nuclear device?"

Njal was examining his thumbs. Jim watched me until I had finished laughing, then said, "If necessary, yes."

I stopped laughing. I studied his face and went cold inside. "You have access to that kind of hardware?"

"If necessary, yes. But the pyramid is not built yet. The point is, Lacklan, we may have to stop it ever being built. We may need to destroy it, whatever it is, and you need to find out if we do or we don't. Once that decision has been made, we'll find the way to do it."

I gave a single nod. "I shall consider myself told."

He smiled but without much humor. "We are defined by our limitations, Lacklan. But we also get to choose our limitations."

"Point taken. Don't quote your self-help books at me, Jim. So we are going on a recon mission to the Northern Cape. What about the summit in Knysna?"

Njal answered.

"That's in three weeks, the first weekend of September, from Friday through Monday. Ruud van Dreiver's mansion is on the southwest side of the lagoon, on a headland overlooking the Dylan Thomas Holiday Resort, half a mile away across the water. Security will be high and they will have a lot of well armed personnel. Knysna is in the Western Cape, about three hundred and fifty miles east of Cape Town."

Jim took over. "We book you in to one of the log cabins

in the holiday resort. From there, you make the five hits. It will require fast planning and execution on the hoof. You may find that a bomb is your simplest option. That is your department and Njal's. However you decide to do it, you execute them, and then get out of there."

"That simple."

"Not at all. It will be anything but simple."

"That was irony, Jim. You are giving us three weeks in which to develop and execute two plans that are practically impossible."

He sighed. "Lacklan, how can I put this to you? Maybe you don't like the fact that the sky is blue, but it is blue. Maybe you don't like the fact that we are bound to the Earth by gravity, but we are. This pyramid has appeared on our radar and it could potentially signify an incalculable danger to us—*all* of us, and the Omega top brass have chosen this time to meet for the first time since you destroyed their American branch. I didn't choose for it to be that way. I only noticed it was happening. Now it is up to you to investigate and take action." He shrugged. "If you feel you are not up to it..."

"Untangle your panties, Jim, and get off your high horse. Maybe you should come along and show us how it's done before you start asking stupid questions about whether I'm up to it."

"Maybe I should, but my point is I don't choose the targets. I just spot them."

"OK, point taken. So we are going to need a lot of hardware for these jobs, and a lot of high explosive. How do we get that into South Africa? Or have you got suppliers there?"

He shook his head. "No, we'll deliver you by ship to Elizabeth Bay, in Namibia."

"How?"

"A tanker departing Cadiz in a few days' time. You'll take on supplies in Dakar, Senegal, including a couple of Land Rovers and other hardware that I am arranging. Then you'll proceed on to Namibia. In Elizabeth Bay there is an old, abandoned factory which still has a functional jetty where supplies were delivered and goods were loaded onto ships. You'll be put ashore there, with your Land Rovers and other cargo. From there you will drive to the South African border, about one hundred and fifty miles south. There are not many roads. Much of the time you'll be driving along desert tracks, but you shouldn't find it too difficult." He glanced at us each in turn, then went on. "You'll cross the River Orange at Oranjemund and pick up the R382 at Alexander Bay. What you do after that is for you and Njal to decide amongst yourselves."

I nodded. "What about the extraction?"

He shrugged. "First, decide how you are going to execute the operations, then tell me what you need for your extraction and I'll organize it."

I looked at Njal. "You got anything to add?"

He shook his head. "No. Until we know what's at the pyramid site, we don't know what we gonna need."

I thought a moment. "We may have to split up. We're on the clock and the time is short. You got maps?"

He smiled. "Yeah, we got maps. We also got satellite images and we got a printer."

Jim stood. "I am going to leave you guys to it. I'll talk to the master of the *Annie Rose* and give you a departure date. Meanwhile, start laying the foundations of your plan."

We worked all day, studying satellite imagery and maps, and digesting what little eyewitness information we had. In the end, we concluded that all we could do was hide the Land Rovers in the rocky hills that bordered the river and proceed on foot by night, until we had a visual on the construction site. If we couldn't make out what it was from watching it, then we would have to snatch an architect—or at least somebody at the site wearing a suit—and get them to tell us what the damn thing was. The workers, foremen and architects would have to be living either onsite or nearby in the small town of Steinkopf or the village of Goodhouse, so snatching them would not be impossible. Once we had that information, we would decide what to do next.

We played with a few alternative plans, left them as potentials to be developed, and, stretching and crunching our joints, we went up on deck and found Jim as the sun was turning to molten copper a few inches above the horizon. There, Njal presented him with the shopping list we had prepared. He examined it, sucking on his cigarette and trailing smoke from his nose.

"OK," he said, "you have four days. Put your affairs in order. You board the *Annie Rose* in Cadiz on Tuesday 20th. On the 23rd you will stop at Dakar to take on freight, including your two Land Rovers and the stuff on this list. A week after that, you will disembark at Elizabeth Bay."

"A week? That is one hell of a waste of time, Jim. That's nine or ten days sitting on our asses doing nothing."

He nodded. "I know, Lacklan, but what's the option? You want to fly military hardware into South Africa? Organizing such a thing would take months. And buying the kind of stuff you need in South Africa without Omega getting to hear about it..." He shook his head. "It's not realistic. You're on their radar. They are looking for you. Believe me. I have thought about it. It's the only way—and even so it is high risk."

"OK, I'll take your word for it."

"The skipper is a Norwegian..."

"Of course he is."

"His name is Daag Olafsen. He's a friend. He'll ignore you, like you're not there, unless you need help. But I can't see that you should. You eat on your own, don't get into conversation with the crew and they'll ignore you too; and stay in your cabins. I want you to be as invisible as possible."

He handed me a large manila envelope and another to Njal. I took mine and leaned against the gunwale to open it while he continued talking. "You have in there a passport and a driver's license which will pass muster in Spain when you board the ship. Lacklan, you are Richard Sinclair. Njal, you are Thomas Jansen. After you have crossed the border from Namibia into South Africa, Njal, I recommend you destroy them. You, Lacklan, will need yours for Knysna. But aside from that, once there you do not exist, you're just ghosts. If they find you, you're better off going down fighting than getting caught."

Njal sat at the table and Jim handed us each a slip of paper. "Memorize this number. It's a burner. You can use it once, then it will be destroyed. I'll have it with me at all times. You call me when you need to get out and I will arrange it, if I can."

I memorized the number, set fire to it with my Zippo and dropped the smoldering ash over the side.

"OK, I'm going." I turned to Njal. "I'll see you in Cadiz. Jim, I'll see you when I get back." I paused. "Thanks." I offered him my hand and we shook.

"Sure. Take care of yourself. I'll have José run you back."

I STOOD on the quay and watched the small lights of the launch disappear into the gathering dusk, heading back toward the yacht. Then I walked back to the apartment block and booked myself onto a British Airways midnight flight to London. After that, I had a shower and went down to the Nauti Mermaid to have some grilled shrimps and a burger, with a couple of martinis, dry.

At nine, I climbed in my car and took Route 41 to Miami, through the dark wilderness of the Big Cypress National Park. All the way, the tall trees made black walls on either side of the road, which loomed overhead and pressed in from the sides, like living walls. I ignored them and called Kenny.

"Good evening, sir."

"I'm going to be away for a couple of weeks, Kenny."

"I rather thought you might, sir."

"I need you to come down to Miami International Airport and collect the Zombie."

"Of course..." He hesitated a moment. "This won't be the last, will it, sir?"

"I don't know, Kenny. We thought after Mexico..."

"In Spanish they say that bad weeds never die."

"Yeah, I'm no philosopher, Kenny, but maybe that's why we're here. Maybe we're already in hell, and we need to work our way out."

"Perhaps you're right, sir. Stay safe, and I'll see you in a few hours."

"Yeah, you too, Kenny. Say hi to Rosalia for me."

I hung up and sped on through the pressing walls of the dark.

THREE

I landed at Heathrow at one forty PM the next day, collected my rental car and drove north and west through warm, green fields under blue skies dotted with distant clouds, like Spanish galleons in full sail on an invisible ocean in the air.

It took me a little over an hour to get to Oxford. I parked at a meter outside Marni's apartment and rang on the bell. She buzzed me in and I climbed the narrow stairs to her door, remembering the last time I had been there, climbing those same stairs with a hot twist in my gut, to confront her with the fact that she had betrayed me, lied to me and passed secrets to my enemies. That had been then. Now things had changed.

I hoped.

I came to the landing and saw the door open at the top of the next flight. Her silhouette was in the doorway, backlit, looking down at me. I couldn't see her face or her expression. I heard her voice, disembodied.

"Hi."

It didn't tell me much, but I smiled and climbed the rest of the way. When I got to the top, I saw she was smiling too.

"How are you doing?"

She shrugged, leaning against the jamb. "Negotiating the challenges." She gave herself a little push off the doorframe. "Come on in. You want a beer?"

"Thanks."

She led me into her living room. She had tall, narrow windows open onto a small, cast iron balcony overlooking High Street. Wedges of warm sunshine were lying across the rugs on the bare boards, and drooping over her armchair like Dali clocks. On the floor by the sofa, she had a steel bucket full of ice, with half a dozen bottles of beer stuck in it. An open one stood on a lamp table beside her armchair.

She pointed at the bucket. "Help yourself."

I pulled out a bottle and cracked it with the opener she had hanging beside the bottles. She dropped into the chair and watched me. "You want some lunch?"

"I ate on the plane."

I sat and took a swig.

"Last time you were here, you were pretty mad at me."

I gave a small nod. "You could have got me killed. Not just me, but me and another guy who was with me."

"I apologized. I broke off all contact with Gibbons."

"I'm not here to bring that up again, Marni."

"Oh. Then why are you here?"

"I'm going to China."

She frowned. "What's in China?"

"One of the last two remaining chapters of Omega: Omega Five."

She sighed and closed her eyes. "You're going to kill them."

It wasn't a question, but I nodded and said, "Yes."

There was anger in her eyes when she opened them. "They are still human beings, Lacklan. I learned that from your father. I'm surprised you didn't. He was number three in the world, yet he came to realize that what he was doing was wrong. I killed him, and his murder will live on my conscience for the rest of my life. He was misguided, wrong about many things, but he was basically a good man, yet I robbed him of his life, and you of the chance of making peace with him. How do you live with all the men you're killing, all the children you've robbed of their fathers?"

I waited till she'd finished. "I came to talk to you, Marni, not to be lectured at by you."

She sighed. "I'm sorry. I just... I wish you would stop. I have lost the man I loved—the man I love—to a relentless, unforgiving need to kill. Stop, already, Lacklan. Please."

"They are coming after me. They sent a man to kill me. How do you suggest I deal with that threat? Call the cops? Or perhaps attempt a meaningful dialogue?"

"If you hadn't gone after them in the first place..."

"Seriously? We are going to have this conversation? Seriously? This is your new, enlightened philosophy of life? Back down in the face of despots and tyrants? Don't upset them and maybe, if you're lucky, they won't hurt you? And as for the men, women and children who *they* are murdering, torturing, enslaving and forcing to work on subsistence wages in mines, well, we'll form committees to talk about them, shall we?"

"Who's lecturing whom now, Lacklan?" She sighed. "Besides, you know that's not what I meant."

"What did you mean?"

Another sigh. "I don't know. But if there's anything in karma, you sure have a lot of blood on your hands. I just wish you'd start bringing some peace into the world, instead of violence."

"Yeah, I'd like that too, Marni. And if you ever come up with a way of doing that, that doesn't involve wishful thinking about sadists, murderers, drug traffickers and slave traders turning out to be nice guys at heart, I'd love to hear it. Can we start again, please?"

She stared at me for a moment. "Boy, you don't pull your punches, do you?"

I shook my head. "No. The last time I was here, I had lied to you about where I was going and what I was going to do. I was testing you because I believed you would tell Gibbons what I was going to do, and I was right. This time I am here for the opposite reason. I know you don't like what I am doing, but in spite of that I trust you. I want you to know where I am going, and what I am going to do. I am asking you not to tell anybody, least of all Gibbons. For the first time in years, perhaps in my life, I am trusting someone who is not a brother in the Regiment. That is hard for me. But I want to trust you, Marni. You were always the one person in the world I believed in. I want to believe in you again. I want to believe that you are true, and you have my back. If I am wrong, tell me and I'll leave."

She was quiet for a long time, gazing out the open windows at the cars and cyclists passing below in a lazy, desultory procession. After a while, she passed the heel of her hand across her eyes.

"You're not wrong, Lacklan. I'm wrong. I've been wrong about you for a long time. But I can't keep apologizing forever. At some point, you either have to accept my apology or tell me to go to hell."

"That's what I'm doing." I smiled. "Not telling you to go to hell, I am offering you my trust, Marni. I want you to know where I am going and what I am doing. I..." I hesitated. "I would like you to be more a part of my life."

She frowned. It was a small, confused frown. "You want me to be more a part of the killing?"

I gave a small laugh that wasn't very humorous. "Not exactly, no. There is more to my life than just killing people." I hesitated a moment. "There was a time when we were both devoted to bringing down Omega, remember? Now Omega is all but finished." I shrugged. "When they are gone, if I survive, I still want to have a life that has some meaning..."

"What are you saying?"

I stood, went to the window and leaned on the frame, looking down at the people milling in the street below, among those ancient stone temples to the human mind. What was I saying? I wasn't sure myself. I chewed my lip a while and turned to face her again.

"I guess what I am saying is, I'd like us to rebuild the trust we once had. More than that, we can't go back, but we can go forward and we can build a trust that is deeper and stronger than what we had before. And maybe, with time..." I shrugged. "I'd like you to be a part of my life, in some way..."

She gave a small sigh and stared at my belly for a

moment. She said, "That's nice, Lacklan." Then she looked down at her hands. "But you say this to me as you are about to embark on a journey to murder five people, in cold blood. I don't know how I am supposed to deal with that. You turn up and you say to me," she gestured at me with her open hand, "'Hi, Marni, I'm just off to kill a bunch of folk, but when I get back, I'd like you to be more involved in my life!' Neat."

I leaned on the jamb of the tall window, feeling the sun warm on my back, and smiled at her. "You're funny." I gave a small shrug. "Would it be different if this was 1945 and I was a pilot in the British Royal Air Force, and I was going on a bombing mission over Germany tonight? I'd be going to kill a bunch of people, many of them arguably less guilty than my targets in China, but when I got back, you would not see me as a killer; you'd see me as a hero fighting to protect his country."

"Come on, Lacklan, that's sophistry! It's totally different."

"No, Marni. Only the way you see it is different. Omega is real, as real as the Third Reich was. Hell! For all I know, they may be connected. Their aims are not so different. Omega murders and exploits and enslaves people every day, and if they ever achieve their ends, countless millions will die." I laughed, a harsh bark of a laugh. "It wouldn't be the first time a small elite wiped out millions of people to serve its own, peculiar vision of how the world ought to be, would it?"

"You're preaching to the choir, Lacklan. I know they exist."

"All I am doing, like that RAF pilot, is fighting them in

the only way I know how. You and Gibbons said my way was wrong. I should talk and reason and negotiate; but while you tried to do that, they grew in power until they were ready to plant a nuclear device at the United Nations, wipe out half of New York and slaughter a quarter of a million people. But now, because of those methods you disapproved of so much, New York is whole, those people did not die and Omega is almost finished. They are broken." I sighed and shook my head. "You label me a killer, Marni, but maybe you should think also about all the lives I've saved by killing these bastards and destroying their organization."

I put my bottle down on the lamp table. "I'm sorry, Marni, I am wasting your time. This was a mistake. I'll see you around."

I had gotten to the door when she said, "Lacklan, wait." I turned with my hand on the handle. "Please come back and finish your beer. Don't overreact. You want us to trust each other, so you should allow me to express my feelings, not just my opinions. They are not always the same, you know."

I walked back and sat on the arm of the sofa, looking at her. She met my gaze and went on.

"I know you hate what you do. I know it troubles you and it haunts you, and I know you left the SAS because you were tired of killing. So if you are conflicted about what you do, can't I be? For me, it isn't just the killing. If it were some anonymous entity killing these people, maybe I'd feel better about it. But it isn't. It's the man I love. We both knew it, Lacklan, from the time we were twelve, fourteen: it was us, *contra mundum*, you and me. And to think of you doing this stuff…" She shook her head. "It breaks my heart."

"I hadn't thought of it like that."

"Maybe we should talk more."

I raised an eyebrow at her. "Well, that was kind of what I was suggesting, if you recall."

She gave a snort that might have been a snigger. "Yeah, I guess it was, huh?"

I became serious. "When they are gone, then people like you and Cyndi McFarlane can talk your asses off, negotiate till you're blue in the face and find the way to make the world a better place. But before that, Omega has to be destroyed completely."

She wouldn't look at me. She just gazed out the window, with the sunlight on her face. "I know," she said at last. "I just wish it didn't have to be you."

"Yeah, well, on that at least, we can agree."

Now she looked at me. "I know. I know you feel the same."

She rose from her chair and came and sat on the sofa. I slid off the arm and dropped beside her, then put my arm across her shoulders and pulled her to me. "Do you ever think about going back to Weston?"

She slipped her arms around me and rested her head on my shoulder. "Sometimes I miss it. I remember playing in the woods with you, and our holidays in Colorado. Lately, I have found it hard to imagine going back, but I do miss it." She looked up at me. "And I love it here too."

"My mother lives near here."

"I know. I've visited her a few times."

My eyebrows told her I was surprised. "You have?"

"She asks after you. She says she gave up writing to you."

I stroked her cheek with the backs of my fingers. "Yeah. It's a long way back."

"What do you mean?"

"From where I am, to normality, to writing to your mom and visiting her, to visiting a country to see the architecture and the museums, or as she would say, the musea, and try the local cuisine, rather than toppling a regime or assassinating a drug lord. It's a long way back."

"Is it a journey you want to make, Lacklan?"

"You know it is, but I want to make it for a reason. Kenny and Rosalia are my family and I love them. But that house is so big and empty, and it still reeks of his pipe and his cigars, and the rooms still echo with his humiliating put-downs and insults. I need somebody to make the journey for. Otherwise…"

I left the words hanging and gazed out at the beautiful façade opposite.

"Otherwise what?"

"Otherwise I will probably follow Jim Redbeard and Njal, and my greatest ambition will be to fall in battle and get taken up to Valhalla by a Valkyrie, to spend the rest of eternity wenching, boozing and brawling."

"Wow, can I come?"

"No. You'd probably fall for one-eyed Odin and bear his children, and then I'd have to fight him too."

"Silly Lacklan."

"Will you be there, to help me come back?"

She nodded.

"Even though you know I must finish the job I started?"

She nodded again.

We stayed like that, talking quietly together, remembering the past and wondering about the future, watching the light turn to burnished copper on the ancient walls across the road, as the sky moved from blue to pink. Then the air seemed somehow to shift and turn grainy, and the sound of the traffic took on a nocturnal quality as the room slipped into darkness, and neither of us rose to switch on the light. Shortly after that, I picked her up in my arms and carried her to the bedroom.

In the morning, I rose at six and went for a run. When I got back at seven, she was up, making coffee in the kitchen. I showered and dressed and joined her at the table. She looked a little shy and that made me smile.

"We talked a lot last night," she said. "but it was all about feelings in the abstract. What did we actually conclude?"

I grunted a laugh. "Scientists! Always chasing facts..." I hesitated for a second, suddenly conflicted at having lied to her. "Let me do this job..." I held her eye a moment. "Marni, I..."

She shook her head. "Don't tell me anything about it, Lacklan. I don't want to know. Just come back alive and whole. And promise me this will be the last. And after that, you will leave this life behind."

I thought about it for a long moment, then nodded. "All right. I promise you that. I'll be away for a couple of weeks. When I get back, I'll come and see you, and then we'll talk in more concrete detail."

She grinned. It was a happy sight, and nice to see. "OK," she said. "I'll be waiting."

Twenty minutes later, I left and drove back south and east along the M40, toward London. There was somebody in East Acton I needed to see. It was a forty-five minute drive to his house on East Acton Lane, opposite the Alfayed Muslim School.

It was a classic, 1930s English semi-detached, with a front lawn and a big bow window. I parked my rental car in his driveway, blocking the exit for his TVR Cerbera, and rang on the bell. I hadn't phoned ahead, but I'd sent him a message saying I'd be shipping out in a couple of days, and he knew that meant I'd be showing up sometime soon.

He opened the door and looked at me without expression. He hadn't changed. He was short and wiry, his hair was grizzled and he had a mustache that would have looked more at home on the face of a Mongolian barbarian of the fourteenth century. When he spoke, the accent was Edinburgh: Scottish, but intelligible to the rest of the English speaking world.

"Look what the cat dragged in," he said. "By the looks of ye, you'll be needing a cup of tea."

"Hello, Ian. It's good to see you too."

"I never said it was good to see you. What have they been doing to you over in Wyoming? You look a mess. Come on in."

I stepped in and he closed the door, then slapped my shoulder with a hand like a girder. "How've you been, Lacklan? I heard you were fixin' fuckin' cars or some shit like that."

He led me past a living room and a dining room to a kitchen at the back of the house with a view of a large backyard with a lawn and a couple of vegetable patches.

"Tea or coffee?"

"Coffee. You settled down, huh?"

He grinned. "In a manner of speaking."

"You left the Regiment..."

He made a noise like sandpaper on petrified nicotine,

which was his way of laughing. "In a manner of speaking. I keep my hand in, unofficially. Know what I mean?"

"I know what you mean."

We were quiet while he spooned coffee into a percolator. "You see any of the lads?"

"Bat's over in the States."

"I heard. So what do you need?"

"I'm going to South Africa."

He put the percolator on the heat and pointed to a pine chair at a pine table. "Sit doon. You're not a fuckin' tree." I sat and he sat opposite. "You fixed for hardware?"

I nodded. "But I'm not sure about the route back."

He frowned at me like I'd spoken to him in classical Greek. "You're goin' in with no extraction plan? Tha's nuts."

"I know. That's why I'm here."

"I'm not followin' you, pal. How can I fix you up with an extraction?"

"You can't. And we're not without an extraction plan, I just don't much like the plan we have, so I'd like a plan B. Have we got any friends in Central Africa?"

"Guys?" He thought a moment, then nodded. "Aye, Billy. You remember Billy Beauchamp? Posh lad, Eton, dropped oot of Oxford, joined the Regiment. Nice lad, real gent."

"I remember him. He's in Africa now?"

"Aye, he got a job with the government, if you know what I mean. He's lookin' after some of Her Majesty's interests in Cameroon. You want me to get a message to him?"

I nodded. "We may have to pay him a visit on the way home."

"Who's we?"

"A pal. A good man."

"One of the guys?"

I shook my head. "No, but close enough."

"Can he be trusted, Lacklan?"

"I owe him my life several times over."

He made a face. "Good enough for me."

The coffee pot started to gurgle. He stood and made for the door, pointing at the pot. "Help yerself. There's some real whiskey in the cupboard, not that Irish muck you drink, real Scotch. I'll be back in a mo'."

I poured the coffee and laced it with Scotch, then stood at the back door, looking out at the lawn and the sycamore tree that shielded the backyard from the road at the back.

He returned five minutes later, as I was placing the empty cup in the sink. He picked up the pot and poured himself a cup.

"That's OK," he said. "He's given me a number for you to call if you're in trouble. He'll see you OK. But there's a problem."

"What's that?"

"I talked to Fido…"

"Major Crawley?"

Major Reginal 'Mad Dog' Crawley was affectionately known to the men as Fido. Ian nodded. "Aye."

"Why?"

"Because even though you're a Yankee bastard, you're a pal and I'd rather you didn't get killed. Your name has popped up on the bush telegraph a few times lately, and I thought I'd ask the major if he had any intel that might be useful to you. Seems Sgt. Bradley has been trying to get a hold of you in Wyoming, but nobody's had sight nor sound of you in a couple of years back there. What have you been up to?"

"Why was he looking for me?"

"Word is, there's a contract out on you. There's a price on your head, me old mucker."

FOUR

I sighed and rubbed my face.

"I knew that."

"I thought you might. The contract originates in South Africa. I figured that's why you were going."

I nodded. "Did he know anything else?"

"Nothing solid, but word is the contract was awarded to a couple of independent operatives. It's not an in-house job, so no clue as to who issued it..."

"I know who issued it. Who are the operatives?"

"Two South African guys, late of the Recces. One of them is in London at the moment, name of Bandile Bhebhe. No idea where his partner is..."

"His partner was Captain Mark Philips, and he is now feeding the pines in a New England forest."

He grinned and chuckled. "You always were a fuckin' psycho. I have no idea where this feller is right now. Chances are he's parked outside in an unremarkable car, watching you. My guess is that his job is to stop you from getting to

South Africa, so if you're going to do anything about it, you'd best act fast."

I nodded. "Thanks, Ian. I owe you."

"Nay worries, lad. I'll just add it to your tab."

Fifteen minutes later, I stepped out into his front yard and made my way to my car. I spotted my tail parked on the other side of the road, fifty yards down the hill. I was mad at myself for not having spotted him earlier, but I figured that, like his pal, Captain Philips, he might have been tracking my GPS.

I got into the car and drove up the hill to the roundabout and there took the first exit into Bromyard Avenue. I knew that further down, close to the Acton Vale, there was a Virgin gym on the right with a parking lot. The parking lot was flanked by evergreen hedges that largely concealed it from the road, and at that time of the morning, just after ten, I figured the place would be largely empty.

When I got there, I pulled into the lot and found a spot tight by the hedge, killed the engine and waited. He followed about two minutes later and parked a few spaces away from me. I kept my head down, like I was reading something, opened my Swiss Army knife and waited for him to kill his engine. Then I got out and made like I was walking toward the doors of the gym, but at the last moment I stopped, turned and made for his car, smiling at him through the windshield. I knocked on his window and it slid down.

He was big, with a neck like a tree trunk and a skull like a boulder. His eyes were small and unfriendly. I leaned down, smiling, like I was going to ask him a favor as a fellow gym-user, and smashed my fist into the side of his chin. I heard his jaw crack under his ear and saw his small eyes glaze with pain.

I didn't pause. He had his right shoulder to me, so I leaned in, pushed his forehead back with my left hand and, with my right, slipped the blade of the army knife down behind his left collar bone. He gave a small gasp and went into spasm, making a 'dzzz' sound, kicking his feet and drooling through his teeth. I yanked the blade left to right a couple of times, gave him a second for the spasm to pass and removed the blade. I had severed his carotid artery and his jugular and he had bled out in a couple of seconds, but all the bleeding was internal. There was no mess.

I wiped the blade on his pants, returned to my car and left the lot. I drove back up Bromyard Avenue and joined the A40 at East Acton, headed for Gatwick via the M40 and the M23, to catch my flight to Malaga.

Pretty soon, I had left London behind and I was among green hills and abundant hedgerows that threaded through the fields in a lush patchwork of oak, holly and ash. As I drove, I felt ill at ease in my own skin. Thinking back to Marni in Oxford, I didn't like what I had done. I hadn't liked lying to her the first time, back when we'd made the hit on Timmerman[1], but this time had been uglier. Any fool could have seen that she was sincere and she believed in me. But the lie had been necessary, necessary to ensure that Njal and I were safe. I didn't know how close she still was with Gibbons, or how many mutual friends they had who might be in bed with Omega. A small slip of the tongue could cost

---

1. See *Kill: Two*

me or Njal our lives. My gut told me to trust her—my brain told me to keep that base covered, just in case.

But I was also aware I'd had another, deeper motive. I wasn't only covering my back and Njal's, I was testing her. What I wasn't sure about was why. Was it because deep down I suspected her? Or was it that I wanted to prove to myself conclusively, for once and for all, that my faith in her, back in the day, had been well founded?

I asked myself the questions, but I didn't know what the answers were.

I dropped off my rental car in the parking garage and made my way through the teeming masses at the airport, through passport control and along endless clinical passages of tiles and glass, to gate C sixty-three, where they were preparing to board. As I arrived, my cell phone rang. The screen told me it was Bat Hays.

"Bat, everything OK?"

His rich, cockney baritone came back at me: "Yeah, yes, sir. You all right?"

"I'm good."

"Look, um, this a bad time?"

"I'm about to board a plane. We have a couple of minutes. What's the problem?"

"Did you get the papers? We got them this morning."

"What papers, Bat?" But even as I was asking the question, I knew what the answer was.

"The divorce, sir. The decree, it's final."

"Oh." Me and Abi, we were divorced now. Our marriage was over. I said, "OK, I…" I foundered for a moment. "I haven't been at home…"

"Thing is, sir…"

"Don't call me sir, Bat. We're not in the Regiment anymore. We're friends."

The silence was a little too long. "Yeah, that's the thing. Me and Abi, we've got pretty close. She's a wonderful woman."

"No argument from me."

"Thing is, sir... Lacklan... we're thinkin' of gettin' married."

The line was beginning to move through the gate. I went to speak, but nothing came out of my mouth. He went on.

"I was wonderin', I know it's a lot to ask, would you give us your blessin' sir, and maybe be my best man?"

I found my voice, taking a breath to steady it. "I can't think of a better woman for you, Bat, or a better man for her. I'd be honored. I'll call you when I get back."

"That means a lot to me, sir."

I hung up and headed for the desk.

THE ONLY CONVERTIBLE I could rent at Malaga airport was a Mini. To my mind, a Mini is a girl's car, but the drive from Malaga to Cadiz was two and a half hours, and I figured if I was driving for two and a half hours along the Mediterranean coast, at 120F, it might as well be in a convertible, even if it was a Mini.

As it was, with two hundred and thirty bhp and a top speed of one hundred and fifty MPH, it was a gas to drive, and as I sped high up into the mountains above Benalmadena, with the ocean stretched out, sparkling on my left, I found myself smiling.

Abi had been a dream: the dream that maybe I could leave this life of eternal fighting and killing behind me and become a normal man with a wife and a family, go shopping, go to the movies, go on family holidays. It had been a beautiful dream, but it was only ever that—a dream. I was glad for Bat. He was a good man and deserved a woman like Abi, and Abi deserved a man like Bat. I smiled some more and ignored the hot twist in my gut. After all, the talk I'd had the night before, and that morning, with Marni was a reason for hope, a reason to move on, a reason to start leaving the past behind and build a new future.

I shifted to the fast lane, peeled off onto the almost empty toll road and hit the gas. The Mini took off like a quarter horse with a jalapeño pepper up its ass.

At Algeciras I turned north, away from the Mediterranean and started to climb into the Sierra de Cadiz, among dense pinewoods under a scorched white-blue sky.

When I was an hour from Cadiz, I called Njal. He answered his cell in classic Norwegian style.

"Hey, where are you?"

"Good afternoon, Njal. I'll be arriving shortly. Where are you?"

"I am at the Senator on the street Rubio y Diaz, it's right on the port, by the Plaza de España. You eat yet?"

"No."

"OK, we gonna have lunch here, then we gonna sail at six this evening."

"Good. Any news?"

"Nothing. Everything is quiet."

"See you in an hour."

I dropped the car at the railway station and walked the

six hundred yards across the ancient port to the Senator on Rubio y Diaz. It was in a narrow cobbled alley that looked and felt like it dated back to the Phoenicians, and though the Senator was only four star, it had a kind of grandeur to it that the Spanish have a special knack for.

The building was an old palace with ochre walls that were six feet thick. The reception was located in a central patio with a fountain and a colonnade festooned with potted ferns and palms, overlooked by small balconies on the upper floors. Njal was sitting in a large, soft leather armchair at a low table by the fountain with a gin and tonic in front of him.

I dropped my bag beside the table and lowered myself into another soft leather chair. He grinned.

"How you feeling? You feeling good, yuh?"

A waiter in a black waistcoat appeared and I told him I'd have a martini, dry. He made a face like I'd made an admirable choice and went away.

"I feel like I need a meal and a sleep."

"You gonna get your wish. We are leaving ahead of schedule. We need to board between four and five this afternoon. We sailin' at six. It will be good to be on the sea. Dakar in two days. How was England?"

I nodded. "Good." Then I shrugged. "We'll see."

He picked up his glass and sipped, watching me, then shook his head. "You complicate your life with women. You cannot fall in love with women, Lacklan. They fuck with your head. You have fun with women, play, laugh, fuck. That's good. But never fall in love. That is bad. That is crazy."

"That's your advice?"

He nodded. "It is good advice."

By the time we'd finished our drinks and had lunch, it was time to walk the short distance to the docks where the *Annie Rose* was moored. We showed our fake passports to the port authority and were waved through to the empty expanse of hot, sunlit concrete that was the freight port. The *Annie Rose* was not big. She was a small freight ship that looked like she belonged in the first half of the 20th century, running guns to Third World rebels and Latin American revolutionaries. For all I knew, that was what she did, and had done. Her black hull was peeling and the foredeck was loaded with crates and containers that were lashed down with ropes that didn't look like they would stand the challenge of a high sea. She stood alone at the empty quay and I muttered to Njal, "Where are the other ships?"

He shrugged. "Spain don't have much exports no more. What they export they send from Barcelona, Bilbao… And ships coming from Europe to Africa go right on by. They don't need to stop here no more, Cadiz is a small port now."

"Thanks for the lesson in socio-economics. You reckon that's our skipper?"

"Yuh, that's him."

He was at the open door of the bridge, leaning on the steel rail that formed the banister of the stairs that led down to the deck, smoking a cigarette. He was a big man, clean-shaven, with platinum hair and a black shirt with the sleeves rolled up to his biceps. He watched us approach and climb the gangplank, then flicked his butt into the sea, turned and clattered down the steel steps.

Captain Daag Olafsen met us on the deck as we reached the top of the gangplank. He had a face that looked as though it had never laughed, and eyes so pale they looked like they'd been frosted over.

"You are Jim's boys?"

I wasn't one of Jim's boys, so I didn't answer. Njal said, "Yuh."

Captain Olafsen jerked his head that we should follow him and he took us through a steel door on the far side of the bridge and down a flight of steel steps to a cabin with two berths, a small table and a single bentwood chair.

"You sleep here. Somebody will bring you your food. Six AM is breakfast, one PM is lunch, six PM is dinner. You eat alone and you don't talk to the crew. They don't talk to you."

Njal nodded.

The captain went on. "Two days we arrive Dakar. We take on your cargo. When it is onboard, you inspect it and you sign for it. You remember to use the name in your passport, OK?" Njal nodded. "Then seven days, six if we are lucky, I drop you in Elizabeth Bay. Any questions?"

Njal shook his head. "No."

The captain jerked his head at me. "You don't talk?"

"Yeah, I talk, but I have no questions."

"Good." He turned back to Njal. "You are Norwegian."

"Ja."

He slapped him on the shoulder and jerked his head at the cabin, "*Jeg har forlatt en flaske snaps for deg, skoll!*"

Njal gave his head a small sideways twitch. "*Takk.*"

The captain nodded once and left. I said, "What?"

"He left us a bottle of Schnapps. He also said you have no manners. You did not greet him or say thanks."

He stepped into the small, cramped cabin and I followed

after him. "I'll remember to send him flowers when we get to Namibia."

"He would like that."

The next couple of days passed without incident. It was good to be at sea, and though we sailed just a few miles off the coast of North Africa, after we had passed the Atlas Mountains, the coastline was not visible and we had the illusion of being thousands of miles from anywhere. That was a good feeling. I am never happier than when I am at sea, and the ocean breeze eased the stress and the anxiety from my mind and brought some measure of peace.

Apart from having our food delivered three times a day to our cabin by a surly Afro-Caribbean guy with a blue, woolen hat, we had virtually no contact with the crew, and spent most of our time in our bunks, reading, or walking and sitting on the foredeck, staring at the sea.

On the second day we sighted land again, and shortly after that rounded Les Almadies and sailed into Dakar. It sprawled, shabby, noisy and dilapidated under the scorching afternoon sun, across the Cape-Verte Peninsula. To the north and west it was bounded by the Atlantic Ocean, to the east and the south by the Baie de Goree, and everywhere you looked you saw the flash and sparkle of the sea.

Slow and lumbering, yet dwarfed by the giant tankers that lined the quays, we headed for the vast cranes that lined the wharf, while overhead the gulls wheeled and laughed in raucous mockery.

It would have been good to go ashore, stretch our legs and explore the city, but we were not there long enough, and neither the crew nor we were given leave to disembark. Instead we stood on the deck smoking, leaning on the gunwale, watching as they winched a large, rusty blue container onto the deck, while the captain exchanged words, and a thick manila envelope, with a guy in uniform from the port authority.

As soon as the container was lowered onto the deck and secured, Captain Olafsen strode up the gangplank, shouting orders to his first mate for the moorings to be released and to take us out of the harbor. He then approached us and handed Njal some keys.

"You have ten minutes to inspect the goods. Then we are at sea." He gave something that looked almost like a leer and added, "But if you want to reclaim from these sellers, unless you got an arsenal of AK-47s, I recommend you settle for what you got."

Njal smiled with his mouth but gave him the dead eye. "You know Jim, right?"

"Yuh, I know Jim."

"Then you know we got the AK-47s and anything else we need. If they screwed us, I hope they're not friends of yours, because you'll be attending their funeral."

The captain made a show of not being impressed and climbed the steps to the bridge. We went and opened the container to inspect the contents. The heat inside was intense, as was the smell of oil and petrol. We gave it a minute to cool off and then went inside.

There were two Land Rovers. The tanks were full and there were four full, one gallon gas cans in each truck. The keys were on the dash.

But the real treat was in the back, in a large wooden case under a large, green tarp. If these suppliers were crooks, they had feared—or respected—Jim enough not to play smart with him. They'd supplied everything we had asked for, and in good order. In my truck, there was a Heckler & Koch 416 assault rifle fitted with the AG-HK416 grenade launcher and infrared telescopic sights. There were two Sig Sauer p226 with extended magazines, my gun of choice, a take down orange osage bow with twelve aluminum arrows, a couple of cases of ammunition for the HK 416 and for the grenade launcher, plus a couple of hundred rounds for the Sigs and a dozen hand grenades. On top of that, there were a couple of cases of C4, containing a total of thirty pounds of plastic explosive. In addition, there were night vision goggles and binoculars with night vision capability.

As I was inspecting the stuff, Njal leaned in the back of my truck and spent a moment looking at the arsenal. After a moment, he nodded.

"Yuh, mine is the same." He pointed at the Sig in my hand. "But I got the Glock 19 instead of the Sig. I don't like the Sig. I don't use the bow and I have also an M202 FLASH."

"Seriously? Those things are not reliable. If I'm going to fire rockets, I'd rather a bazooka."

"Yuh, I agree." He grinned. "But those TEA rockets burn hot, man. They are real destructive."

"If you manage to hit the target."

He made a 'maybe' face. "In a situation like this, maybe accuracy is less important than destructive power."

I made a 'maybe' face of my own. "How many rounds have you got?"

"Eight clips."

"Thirty-two rockets." I shrugged. "It might come in useful. What else you got?"

"Same as you, rope, spade, pick, water... everything we put on the shopping list." He watched me as I jumped out and slammed the door.

"It's gonna be a long week," he said.

I nodded. "Yeah, it is. Lots of toys and nowhere to play."

And it was. The days passed with a grinding slowness, punctuated only by the roll and wash of the ocean, and the occasional explosion of foam over the bow or the sighting of a distant pod of dolphins. As we approached the equator, the temperatures grew steadily higher, making it impossible to stay in the claustrophobic, steel-walled cabin, but equally difficult to tolerate the sweltering temperatures on the steel decks. There was no bar, and in any case, even if there had been, the captain had made it clear we were not to fraternize with the crew. So we found what little shade we could on the decks, sweated profusely and counted down the days.

On the fourth day, we sighted the dense, tropical coasts of Guinea Bissau and Sierra Leone on our port side and followed it, changing our bearing from south to south-east until we had rounded Liberia and the Côte d'Ivoire. Then we abandoned the coastline and, following the new heading, cut diagonally across the Gulf of Guinea toward Namibia and Elizabeth Bay, at a good rate. I figured our speed at some twenty-five or six knots, which, when you weigh one and a half thousand tons, is a lot of knots. Something told me Captain Daag Olafsen was keen to get us off his ship.

Another three days rolled by and on the afternoon of the fourth, we sighted land again. As we drew closer, it was clear that this was very different land from the tropical abundance of Guinea and Sierra Leone. All that was visible here was the white glare of scorching sand and, as we drew closer still, the stark, parched reds and grays of the desert highlands further inland. This was Namibia.

By early evening, we had pulled into Elizabeth Bay and moored at the long, dilapidated pier that projected into the sea from the crumbling, abandoned factory which sprawled over the low, dusty headland. Njal and I gathered our stuff from our bunks, went on deck and solemnly shook hands with Captain Olafsen. He wished us luck and we descended the gangplank to await the container on the jetty. The intense heat of the day was fading and a cool evening sea breeze was picking up.

The grinding whine of the ship's winch echoed suddenly across the bay as the container rose unsteadily off the deck and swung out over the rail, then lowered in steady jerks to a few feet above the pier. There we gripped it and guided it into position before it landed with a loud, jarring clatter. Njal unlocked it and we drove the two Land Rovers out and down to the concrete forecourt of the factory, where we stopped and climbed out to watch the container winched back onto the deck, and the small ship reverse its engines, pulling its own massive weight out into the still, turquoise bay. Finally, it lumbered slowly around and sailed out into the fading light of the evening, silhouetted briefly against the crimson horizon in the west.

Njal spoke suddenly.

"Night is gonna come in quick, and it is gonna be fuckin' cold. We should take shelter in the factory, make a fire, eat and rest. Then set out early, with first light."

I nodded. "Yeah. Let's do it."

The factory, or whatever it had been in its day, consisted of a number of crumbling structures with shattered windows and doors hanging off their hinges. Beside the main building, we found what looked like a warehouse, with vast, double doors that stood half open. We drove the trucks into the dark interior and spent the next half hour or so gathering up broken pallets and fallen, wooden roof-beams from the floor of the warehouse and the surrounding buildings.

"We could do worse than store some of this wood in the Land Rovers," I told him. "We're going to be a few nights at least in the desert. We'll be lucky to find any wood or kindling out there."

Njal gave me the thumbs up and, as the dark closed in, he built up our store of wood while I made a fire and cooked a meal of canned stew and dry biscuits. Then we sat and ate, and talked about the mission ahead. We didn't talk much though, because we both knew we were going into the unknown, which, according to all my years of training and experience, was the quickest and simplest way to get yourself killed. So most of what we discussed centered on how we were going to deal with the unexpected, when it came.

Njal's last words to me before he lay down to sleep were, "We can't plan ahead, because we ain't got no intel. But, because we got no intel, we gotta make sure we plan ahead each step before we take it. It's not good."

I nodded, but he'd already lay down his head and closed his eyes. I lay down too and looked up at the high, crumbling ceiling above, and remembered Sir Walter Raleigh's last words, before they cut off his head.

"'Tis a sharp medicine, but it will cure all that ails you."

He was talking about death.

FIVE

There was a dirt track that would have led us north, to Kolmanskop and Lüderitz, on the B4 main road, which in turn would have led us to a secondary road, just past the tiny village of Grasplatz, which would have taken us all the way down to the South African border at Oranjemund. But on reflection, though the risk was small, we decided that it would be better to stick to the cover of the desert and follow the network of dirt tracks that wound through the sand and the dust, and would render us virtually invisible, from the land and from the air.

It was a one hundred and fifty mile drive. It should have taken three hours at most, but the demands of the terrain, and the condition of the tracks we were on, meant that we rarely rose above twenty-five miles an hour, and often we had to drop as low as fifteen or even less. Fact was, we were lucky it was not the rainy season, or we might not have made it at all. It was a cruel, unforgiving environment. Though the temperatures were not so high, there was no shade to be had anywhere, the air was dry and the fine, powdery dust crept into every nook and cranny, caked the engines, interfered with the electrics, and dried out your mouth and your eyes until you felt that every ounce of fluid was being sapped from your body. It was.

In the end, it took us close to eight hours to reach the border crossing with South Africa. At four PM, we finally joined the asphalt road, five miles outside the border town of Oranjemund, heaved a sigh of relief and covered the remaining distance in a little over five minutes. We skirted the town and, after following the River Orange upstream for another four miles, came to a series of huts that fronted a barrier before the road became a bridge that crossed the river into South Africa.

The border crossing looked pretty sleepy, but even so I was acutely aware of the cargo of weapons we had in the back of the trucks. Jim had told us it had been taken care of, but in my experience, things are only ever taken care of when they are in the past.

I rolled up to the first of three barriers outside a hut with a red roof and a small garden out front with red geraniums flanking an open door. A guy in what looked like military uniform stepped out and strolled over. He looked through my window, glanced in the back and said, "Papers."

I handed him my passport and driver's license. He handed them back to me and there was a glint of hostility in his eyes.

"Where is your import license?"

I felt my gut twist and said, "I wasn't aware I needed an import license."

"For the merchandise you have in the back."

"I was told..."

"Whatever you were told, you need an import license for the merchandise. If you do not have one, you must pay a fine of two hundred U.S. dollars."

"Two hundred U.S. dollars? In U.S. dollars?"

"That is correct."

We'd expected something like this and had come prepared. I pointed back at Njal with my thumb. "What about my colleague, will the fine cover him too?"

The expression on his face became crafty. "If your friend has no license, then he must pay another fine also."

I nodded and gave him four hundred bucks. He took the money, stepped back and smacked the side of the Land Rover, like he was slapping a horse. The barrier lifted and we snaked our way past two more huts and onto the half-mile bridge that spans the river into South Africa. I still had the twisted knot in my gut. I had the irrational feeling that for some reason, the border control in South Africa was going to be tougher, and harder to bribe than in Namibia.

At the far end of the bridge, we came to a cluster of yellow huts with corrugated roofs. Ours were the only vehicles there. The place was desolate. We pulled up at the barrier and a woman in a blue uniform, wearing soft, white canvas shoes, came out of the yellow hut chewing and wiping her mouth. She leaned in my window and spoke to me in what I assumed was Afrikaans. I smiled.

"I am sorry, do you speak English?"

She shook her head. "Pepah."

She held out her hand. I gave her my passport and driver's license. She glanced at them, then glanced in the back. She pointed and said, "What is it?"

I cursed Jim in my mind and said, "Photographic equipment."

She shook her head. "No, must pay import duty. Two hundred U.S. dollar."

I concealed a sigh behind a smile and jerked my thumb at Njal behind me. "I'll pay for me and my friend."

"Four hundred dollar, U.S."

I handed over the money and we pulled away from the huts into sandy scrubland. In my rearview, I could see her walking back into the hut, counting the money. The scrub soon faded away and became nothing but sand as far as the eye could see, ranging through a variety of hues, from white through gray to red and black. It was warm, but the heat was not oppressive, and the dust and dryness were tolerable.

I figured we had two choices. Option one was to take a dirt track that branched off to our left, four hundred yards from the border control, and follow it along the course of the Orange River, two hundred miles through desert and rocky highlands to the east, trusting in the satellite images we had that the tracks would be clear enough to follow. If we took that option and made fifty miles an hour, it would take us just four hours to reach our destination. But we both knew the chances of the satellite images being accurate were slim, and we were more likely to be doing fifteen miles an hour than fifty—if we could make out the tracks at all in the windblown sand.

The second option was to follow the R382 fifty miles south, along the coast, then follow it inland, east, for another fifty miles until we came to Steinkopf, and there pick up the National Route 7, headed back north for about twenty miles, having made a big 'U'. After that, we would veer off the road for forty miles along desert tracks toward the black, rocky hills that bordered the river. There, among those massive rocks, on the banks of the Orange, was our objective.

Though that route was longer, it was also easier and faster, but it had the major drawback that we were exposed and highly visible. However, after discussing it, Njal and I had both agreed that the risk of getting lost in the desert, among the hills and the invisible tracks, was too great. We needed to act and act fast. So we would take the main road and as soon as we had left Steinkopf behind, we would lose the trucks among the sand dunes and the black rock hills.

We reached Steinkopf in a little under two hours, just as the sun was beginning to settle on the horizon, having encountered practically no traffic on the road. We didn't enter the town. We bypassed it on our right. Viewed from the windows of our Land Rovers, it seemed to consist mainly of wooden prefabs with corrugated roofs and walls patched with blue tarps and wooden pallets. Each house seemed to have its own plot of land, but the land was little more than parched ochre dust, and what trees and shrubs grew there were stunted and gnarled, more wood and bark than leaves.

We picked up the National 7 just beyond the town and accelerated north. Then, after twenty minutes, as dusk was shifting to dark, we pulled off the empty blacktop and, keeping our headlamps off, drove east into the gathering darkness of the desert.

Pretty soon, the darkness was all but impenetrable. There was no moon and what little light there was came from the stars. If we had put on our headlamps, they would have been visible for miles around. So we drove slowly, no more than ten or fifteen miles an hour, negotiating the rocks and small potholes as best we could. There was no road to follow, only the knowledge that we had to head north and east, and that before long, the flatlands we were crossing would narrow into a valley between the sandy highlands to the south and the black, rocky hills in the north, which bordered the river.

Finally, after fifteen minutes of slow, grinding, bumping progress through the night, we came to a place where massive, dark silhouettes began to rise up ahead to block out the stars, leaving only a narrow 'V' of luminous sky in between. We drove on, heading for that 'V', and soon found that we were enveloped, bound on both sides by steep walls of rock and earth.

There we slowed and searched for some kind of hollow, cave or ravine where we could conceal our vehicles till first light. We eventually found one: a deep, winding gash in the rock wall on our left. We pulled in, keeping as close as we could to the cliff face, and killed the engines.

Using the Land Rovers' roof racks and the tarpaulins, we improvised a kind of shelter where we could make a fire with no risk of being seen. There we cooked a meal of canned beef stew again, with dry crackers, took turns to keep watch and slept four hours each.

At four the following morning, we scouted the area on foot, with the help of the light from a late moon, and found a deeper crevice between two massive rocks that must have towered to at least a thousand feet out of the sand. There we were able to hide the Land Rovers in the cover of overhanging boulders, so there was no chance of being spotted either from the ground or from the air. After that, before the sun had risen, we took an HK416 each, plus our sidearms, binoculars and night vision goggles, and set off on foot, guiding ourselves by our satellite maps, across the soft sand among the sheer black stone walls, to take our first look at the monolithic structure they were building beyond, by the river.

We followed the winding paths, like a maze, for about fifteen minutes, making slow progress. Then, as we drew nearer the target, we began to ascend into the towering rocks, climbing high among the jagged peaks, but taking care never to make a silhouette against the translucent, pre-dawn sky. The going was slow and painstaking, and it took us a full two hours to cover three miles, winding through steep gorges, clambering up sheer walls of smooth, volcanic rock, and crawling, inch by inch, along hard stone surfaces at a snail's pace.

Eventually, at four after six AM, at the darkest hour before dawn, and just as the moon was setting into the western horizon, we came to the top of a huge, smooth rock. We lay flat on our bellies and peered down.

What we saw, maybe one and a half thousand feet below, was a flat, sandy plateau bordering the south bank of the thick black snake of the Orange River. The plateau was enclosed by a horseshoe of the black stone hills in which we were lying, with its apex in the south, about one and a half miles from the river, and about a mile across at its widest point. Sitting in the middle of this sandy plateau, measuring about two thousand feet across at its base, was a square, concrete structure that tapered gently as it rose to about forty or fifty feet, which was faintly luminous in the fading moonlight.

I fitted my night vision binoculars and had a closer look. It was hard to make out much detail, but from what I could see there was a massively thick, tapering outer wall with a gaping maw that might have been an entrance in the eastern wall. At the center there was a vast, hollow, concrete circle, as though they were allowing space for some kind of tower, or vast cylinder at the center. It must have been a good twelve or thirteen hundred feet in diameter.

As we lay and watched, we saw spotlights and arc lights snap on, and within a minute or so, the place was flooded with Jeeps, trucks and a couple of hundred people. And five minutes after that, work had started again on whatever it was they were building.

While Njal set about photographing and filming it, I tried to make sense of the construction. I tried to estimate the height of the outer wall by judging it against the people and then vehicles. I confirmed what I had thought: it was fifty feet high, and, from where we were, the walls did seem to be tapering in. It was looking like the base of a pyramid.

I spoke under my breath. "You make that six hundred and fifty yards across?"

Njal nodded. "Yuh."

"So if that's going to be a pyramid, it's going to be the height of the Chrysler building, about nine hundred feet."

"That is big."

"What the hell is it?"

"I don't like that ring in the center."

I looked at him. "Why?"

He shook his head. "I don't know. But it's telling me something that is not good. It is to hold something, contain something. Something so big. That is not a good thing, Lacklan."

I grunted and turned back to watching the construction.

The sun rose in the east and soon the spotlights and the arc lights were doused. Now we could make out a row of buildings a couple of hundred yards to the east of the building site. They were little more than wooden shacks, two and three stories high. They looked more like administrative buildings than dorms or sheds. The row of five coaches parked nearby seemed to confirm that the workers were bussed in, and didn't sleep there.

Just short of those buildings, maybe a hundred yards from the construction, we could also see a perimeter fence. It was made of a series of concrete towers, twenty or thirty feet high, with crows nests on top occupied by a guy with an assault rifle. Between one tower and the next, there was a chain link fence, bound on either side by barbed wire. Along this fence, men with rifles were on patrol.

Construction continued at a pace. It was hard to estimate accurately how many people were working there, but on several counts I made, I always came back to roughly two hundred or two hundred and fifty men. Njal estimated the same.

They worked in teams of between ten and twenty men, and each team was supervised by a guy in a hardhat. The workers themselves wore all kinds of things on their heads, but none of them was a hardhat. As well as the supervisors, I also spotted four guys in pale jackets and ties who appeared in a Range Rover and strolled around talking to each other, looking and pointing and consulting clipboards.

I elbowed Njal and pointed at them. "We need to talk to those guys."

"It's not gonna be easy. You seen the perimeter fence?"

"Yeah, they seem as keen to stop people getting out as they do to stop them getting in. But the workers don't sleep on site. You saw the coaches?" He shifted his glasses, found them and nodded. I went on, "The workers are bussed in, and I'd lay you twenty bucks that those guys in the Range Rover don't sleep here either. There must be a town nearby."

He made a skeptical face. "Steinkopf?"

I shook my head. "No. At least, not the workers. This is a secret operation. With security like that, they don't want people shooting their mouths in a town with major roads running through it. Uh-uh." I pointed down river. "Didn't we see a town east of here on the satellite pictures?"

"Goodhouse. It's like a mile upstream, behind those hills. But it is abandoned. There is nobody there anymore."

"Two gets you twenty, Njal, the town has been revived as a dormitory for the construction site. That's where these guys are sleeping and eating."

"Could be. But the guys in suits? I don't think so. What you wanna do?"

I lay for a while watching and thinking. Eventually I pointed at where the rocks formed the apex of the horseshoe.

"We circle 'round till we have a good view of the town, Goodhouse. We watch, and see when the Range Rover comes in and out, what route it takes, how much security there is in the village, what we're dealing with. When we have enough intel, we make a plan. We need to snatch those guys and find out what this place is."

He sighed and nodded. "Yeah, OK. It's the plan."

It was a six mile trek through extremely difficult terrain. Sometimes we walked along deep gullies with sandy floors, and that was easy and the going was good, but at other times we had to scale rock walls that were smooth and almost vertical, or crawl through narrow, rocky gullies over a loose, slippery mix of sharp stones and sand, and then the going was agonizingly slow and difficult. In the end it took us almost six hours to cover the distance, and by the time we got there, we were exhausted and our hands and knees were raw and bruised.

We found a hollow in the rocks about a half mile from the village and lay down to watch. The first thing that struck me was that the place had, as I had suspected, recently been revitalized. There was a hotel in the main square that was reminiscent of a saloon in an old cowboy movie. The streets were broad and dusty, and the houses were made of wood, with corrugated roofs. Some houses had yards where there were goats tethered, and nearby, at the riverbank, there were allotments where canals had been dug and vegetables were being cultivated.

Njal stared for a long while and eventually nodded. "Yuh, it's a dormitory town, but not only a dormitory town. People are living here also who do not work at the site. They are growing crops, keeping animals. You see? There is also a hotel. Which means people are coming and going."

"Laborers from neighboring villages, attracted by the work?"

"Maybe."

"OK, here's what we do. We make provisional camp here for the next twenty-four or forty-eight hours. We watch the town. We want to know to what extent it's a part of the construction site, and to what extent it continues to function as a normal town."

"OK."

"But our primary objective is the Range Rover and those four guys in it. It is a short drive from here to the construction site, so we need to see if they go anywhere else. Do they go to Steinkopf? Maybe you're right and they're making the commute there. Or are they staying at the hotel in Goodhouse? Maybe they're even going to Springbok. We need to know. If we are lucky, they drive to Steinkopf or Springbok in the evening to stay in a decent hotel, and drive back in the morning. If they do, we set an ambush for them where the rocks begin, near where we left the Land Rovers."

He nodded. "Yuh, it's good, but as soon as we do that, we gonna put the whole place on red alert. What we gonna do then?"

"We have two options, Njal." I held up a finger. "One, we make it look convincingly like an accident."

"You mean we interrogate them and kill them, then make it look like an accident."

"Yes."

He looked skeptical. "That is gonna be hard to pull off. What's the other option?"

"We make it stage one in a comprehensive attack on the whole site. We take out their communications so they can't call their HQ, take out their cars and trucks, and then blow the whole damn place to hell."

He grunted, still looking skeptical. "No third option?"

I shrugged. "Something halfway between, maybe."

SIX

For the next twenty-four hours, we took it in turns to do four hour shifts during which one of us dozed or ate and the other made detailed notes and observations about what went down in the village of Goodhouse: who came in, who left, where they came from and where they left to; was there any nightlife or did they all just go home to bed? Were there women, and if so, were they wives or prostitutes?

The following evening, we sat around a small fire in a hollow formed by two rocks and compared notes. Njal had taken the last watch.

"The hotel is working like a bar, like a saloon. There were people going in there until midnight, and the last one was kicked out..." He checked his notepad. "Three forty-eight in the morning. Some of the guys who are workin' at the site are living with women. I marked five guys and followed their movements, where they live, where they went, what they did. Three of them have women living in their houses. I saw one of the women hang out washing in the backyard. Some of the washing was women's clothes."

I nodded. "Good. I saw the same thing."

"Also, twenty of the houses have at least one goat in the backyard. Most of them, and..." He hesitated, shrugged and splayed his hands. "It's hard to tell in just twenty-four hours, right? But there are at least ten houses where you got this combination." He held up his thumb. "There is a guy with a woman, there are animals in the yard and the guy does not work at the site, he works on the fields by the river. Some of those guys have also kids in the house."

I nodded again. "I counted twenty houses where I saw kids."

"So if you ask me, is this a dormitory village for the site workers? I'm gonna say yes and no. It is a village that used to live from the orchards and fields by the river, it was becoming a ghost town, and the constructors have taken it, revitalized it, and used it as a dormitory."

"I agree. I noticed a couple of other things. Twice during the afternoon I saw small groups of guys arrive—three guys on foot and a larger group of six in a pickup truck. The truck came from the direction of the N7, southwest. The guys on foot came from the east, along the river. They wandered into the village and made for the hotel. I didn't see them leave and I am guessing they were looking for work."

Njal consulted the satellite maps we'd printed. "Two miles west you got Haksdoorn, on the Namibian side of the river. It's a farming community, by the looks of the fields, but it is a fair guess a young guy can make more money in a couple of months on a building site in South Africa than all year on a farm in Namibia. And who's gonna stop you swimming across the river, right?"

"How many white guys did you see?"

"OK, I was coming to that. I saw the guys in the Range Rover. Three of them are white, the fourth is black. They did the same thing yesterday and today. They spend an hour at the hotel, then they get in the truck and leave toward Steinkopf." He shrugged. "Or at least toward the N7. Beside them, I seen five guys who are not so black. At this distance you can't say if they are white with a tan or mixed race. If we need to, we can turn up looking for work and explore the place, but that is a high risk option."

I grunted. "OK, so so far as the guys in the Range Rover are concerned, I think we've got two options. Ambush the Range Rover tomorrow morning on its way back, or go and look for it tonight. I don't know what impression you got of Steinkopf when we drove through, but I don't figure it has a huge catering trade going on. There can't be that many hotels. If there aren't any, we'll need to move on to Springbok and look there. But maybe we'll get lucky and find them in Steinkopf."

"I like that option. We go look for it now. If we find it, cool, if we don't, we go for plan B and set an ambush in the morning."

"Good, let's go."

The way back was quicker. We scrambled down the south side of the rocks and then ran the distance, through gullies and open spaces, to where we'd left the Land Rovers. It was an eight mile run, but we made no effort to stay hidden now. Dusk was falling and we were pretty confident we would be virtually invisible; plus we knew where our enemy was now, and what they were doing. Speed was now the imperative, not concealment. We made it in just under two hours, transferred my crate of weapons from my Land Rover to Njal's, clambered in, and pulled out of the cover of the rocks and onto the track, headed back toward the N7. I checked my watch; it was nine PM.

The only light we had was from the rising moon, which was waxing toward full. I knew it was about twenty miles to the N7, and I planned to make it in less than an hour, so I put my foot down and it was an uncomfortable ride for the next forty minutes, bouncing over ruts and small holes, skipping over rocks and furrows. It rattled our bones and shook our teeth loose in our skulls, but forty minutes later, we rolled onto the blacktop, turned south and covered the next sixteen miles in fifteen minutes.

The darkness of a desert at night is hard to describe. Even with the moon almost full, the light and the shadows are deceptive and misleading. But it is also true that you see things at night in the desert that you might miss in the full light of the sun. That was what happened to me, less than half a mile outside Steinkopf, when I saw bright lights thirty or forty yards from the roadside on my right, flooding out of what looked at first like some kind of compound.

I slowed and saw there was a turn off from the road onto a track leading to a cluster of huts surrounded by a kind of wooden palisade. Then the cones of light from the truck caught the sign. It was small, which was why we had missed it before, but now in the light of the headlamps I read, 'SELF CATERING, HOTEL RONDA'.

I muttered, "Son of a bitch!" under my breath and turned in. Half way down the track, Njal said, "Stop here."

I pulled up and before I could ask why, he had the door open, had swung down and was peeing into dirt by the side of the road. I sighed. "Seriously? Now?"

He ignored me, did up his fly, then crouched down and did something in the dirt for a moment. After that he stood, with something in his hands, and went to the back of the vehicle. After a moment, I saw him pass my window and crouch in front of the grill. Then he stood, wiped his hands on his pants and climbed back into the truck, slamming the door.

"OK, now the plates cannot be identified. We can go."

After a moment, I grinned at him and we drove on into the compound.

It didn't take long to spot the Range Rover. It was the only one there and it was parked outside the largest of the huts. I pulled in beside the main compound gate, forty feet from the cabin, and killed the engine. Then I grabbed my assault rifle and we crossed the compound quietly toward their hut. The lights were on and there was the muffled sound of music playing inside. We stood at the door a moment, listening. There were voices, too: talk, male voices and female. I made a question with my face. Abort or go? Njal shrugged, pulled his Glock and knocked. I pulled my Sig and cocked it.

A voice called through the door. It sounded like he said, "Who uzut?"

I put a smile in my own voice and said, "Hi, we're your neighbors. We're here from California? And my wife wondered if you could use another bottle of vodka at your party!"

Njal sighed, closed his eyes and shook his head. I heard a

small laugh inside and the door opened. The guy was in his late forties, wearing chinos and an open shirt over a distended belly. He was barefoot and had a glass of what looked like gin and tonic in his hand. I put the muzzle of the Sig in his face and said, "Only trouble is, my wife looks like a big, ugly killer. Back up."

He took a step back and I moved in, shoved him hard so he staggered back and fell on his ass, spilling his drink. Njal stepped in behind me and closed the door. There were a couple of small screams. The music was Brazilian jazz.

There were two guys sitting on a leather sofa. They both looked to be in their late forties. One of them had a Saddam Hussein moustache and the other was black and bald. Each of them had a girl on his lap. Both girls were half undressed. A third guy, maybe ten years younger, with brown hair over his collar, was in a leather armchair with another girl who had most of her clothes on the floor beside her. I scanned the room for the fourth girl.

I saw polished wooden floors, a zebra skin, a coffee table with a mirror and traces of powder, eight glasses. Beyond the sofa I saw a table, a kitchen, a bar with bottles on it. Two open bedroom doors, a third door closed.

I pointed at the closed door and said, "Check the john for the fourth girl."

Njal went and I looked at the seven stunned, frightened faces looking up at me. The guy I'd knocked over scrambled backward to the other armchair and climbed into it.

"What do you want?"

I was thinking ahead, about the girls. Njal had opened the bathroom door and was pulling out a pretty young girl in her twenties. Her eyes were wide and she wanted to scream, but he had his finger over his lips, pointing to the sofa and the chairs. I said:

"Sit down, behave and nobody is going to get hurt."

She crossed the floor, staring at me, and sat on the floor beside the sofa. I turned to the guy I'd knocked down.

"How much cash have you got in the house?"

He swallowed, glancing at his friends on the sofa. The big, bald guy gave a small shake of his big, bald head. Saddam Hussein said, "Tell the truth, Ken. It's not worth the risk. It's only money. They'll find it anyway." He turned to me. "We got a hundred thousand rand. That's a lot of money. You take that and you go. OK?"

Njal looked at me. "That's seven or eight thousand dollars."

The guy looked mad. "That's two fuckin' years executive salary, you lazy fuckin' thievin' bastard!"

The bald guy said, "Shut up, Ken."

I gave Ken the dead eye and said, "Yeah, Ken, shut up." To the bald guy, I said, "Go with my friend and get the money."

He got to his feet. I saw his hands were shaking. He held them up to shoulder height and crossed the floor to one of the bedrooms, with Njal just behind him. They went into the bedroom and I said to the girls, "Get dressed."

As they started pulling on their clothes, I said to Frank, the guy I'd knocked down, "Where are the keys to the Range Rover?"

He looked like he might get sick and pointed at a linen jacket hanging on the back of a chair at the table. I jerked my head at the girl sitting on the floor, who was already dressed. "You know how to drive?"

She nodded.

"Go get the keys."

Frank said, "What the hell are you playing at?"

"Shut up, Frank."

From the bedroom I heard Njal's voice. "Nice and slow and easy so I can see what you are doing." Then, "OK, now take it out to the living room."

They came back from the bedroom and the bald guy was holding an attaché case with a lot of money in it. The girl who'd been in the john was standing behind the sofa, holding out a set of car keys toward me. Her pose and her expression had something tragic about them, like a scared little girl who wants to please Daddy. I said to her, "Take the case, take the Range Rover, get the hell out of here, go to Cape Town, don't ever come back. Go, now."

Ken was half on his feet. "Now wait a minute!"

I leveled the Sig at his head and Njal pressed the muzzle of the Glock against the back of the bald guy's head. Everyone went very still. I looked at the girl and said quietly, "Do it now."

She hurried around the sofa on small feet, took the case, looked into the bald guy's face for a second and said, "Sorry," then she and her friends were hurrying toward the door. As they opened it, I spoke, without taking my eyes off Ken, "Never talk about this. If you do, I will come and I will find you, understand?"

There was absolute silence from the door, then they wrenched it open, ran out, and slammed it closed. We heard them squealing lightly as they clambered into the Range Rover outside. More doors slammed and a moment later, we heard the engine roar and the car speed out of the compound.

To the bald guy I said, "Sit down."

He sat and Njal walked behind the sofa. I waved my gun at Frank and at the younger guy with the daringly long hair. "Turn your chairs to face me, so I can talk to you better."

They both glanced at Njal, knowing that if they turned to face me, none of them would be able to see what he was doing behind them, and he'd have all four of them at his mercy. I smiled. It wasn't a friendly smile.

"Now, you can all see that my friend and I have no interest in money, and no interest in women. We are interested in only one thing: information."

For the first time since we'd come in, I saw real fear in their eyes. I gave them a minute, studying each face in turn. I didn't see a really big willingness to cooperate. I sighed.

"This is really simple, and you boys need to take a moment to assimilate exactly what is happening here, and what kind of situation you're in. When my friend and I leave here tonight, we will leave with the information we came for. That is not in question. The only question is, what state will you be in when we leave?" Frank had gone the color of yesterday's mashed potato. Ken was sweating, his hands were shaking badly and the bald guy and the young guy didn't look any better. I held up three fingers of my left hand. "You can finish this night in one of three conditions: alive and well, dead, or, if you're really unlucky, alive and not well at all. Am I getting through to you?" I turned to the young guy with the long hair. "What's your name?"

"Bob."

"How well do you think you'll stand up to torture, Bob?"

He shook his head. "Please don't..."

I turned to the bald guy. "What's your name?"

"Nelson."

"You know what always distresses me about torture, Nelson? When a guy is really brave, and he holds out and he holds out, until he has lost fingers, toes, maybe even an arm or a leg; and then he breaks and talks." I shook my head, holding his eye. He looked sallow, and there were yellowish patches under his eyes. "What a pointless sacrifice, right? Personally, I think it's a charity to kill somebody when they reach that point." I looked at Njal behind them. "You remember that guy in Vegas?"

He shook his head and sighed. "That was sad, man. It's times like that I question my job, you know?"

"Right. He was tough. I never knew anybody as tough as that guy. He held out practically to the end. We had taken off both his arms and both his legs. We were going to start on his eyes when he broke. He finally told us what we wanted to know." I spread my hands and started laughing, looking at Njal, who started laughing too. "But what's the point, right? What the hell? You're gonna talk, talk before I cut your fucking arms and legs off!" I shook my head again and sighed. "Man..."

I studied Bob's face carefully, because I'd figured him as the weakest of the four. "So here is how we do this." I pulled my Fairbairn and Sykes from my boot. "I am going to take a left thumb from each of you, just so you know I am serious and I mean business..."

Bob was already half out of his seat, holding up both

hands, palm out. "No! No, no, no! That isn't necessary! You don't need to do that! We will cooperate! Nelson, Frank, tell them! Tell them we'll cooperate, please! I *really* don't want to lose my thumb!"

His face was creasing up and I thought he might start crying. I glanced at Njal and smiled. I looked at the other three. They didn't look like they were ready to disagree. I sighed. "I always take something off to start with, to establish clearly that I mean business."

Nelson closed his eyes. He was now sweating like Ken. "You don't need to establish that. We believe you. Please. We are just employees. We will tell you whatever you need to know. You don't need to mutilate us."

"Open your eyes, Nelson."

He opened them.

I wagged a finger at him, then wagged it at the others. "I'm going to give you a chance to share everything—*everything*—with us. But the first sign of hesitation, prevarication, dishonesty... anything like that, and things will turn ugly. And I do mean ugly."

"We'll talk." It was Nelson; he glanced right to left at his colleagues. They all nodded.

Frank added, "We'll talk."

SEVEN

I pulled over a chair from the dining area, sat on it and pulled a pack of Camels from my pocket. I lit up with my old Zippo and inhaled deeply. As I let out the smoke, I said, "What is it?" Before any of them could answer, I said, "Remember, guys, prevarication or hesitation results in a lost limb. OK? Now, what is it?"

It took about half a second, but they all shifted their eyes and glanced at each other. I took careful aim at Nelson's shoulder. I saw the panic build in his face and at the same instant, Njal smashed his open palm into Ken's ear. They all screamed out and started shouting. Ken was holding his head, rocking back and forth saying, "Oh God, oh God…"

Njal grabbed him by the scruff of his neck and pulled him. I kept my gun trained on Nelson's shoulder and repeated, "What is it?"

Ken and Nelson both spoke at the same time. Nelson blurted, "It's a power station!"

And Ken groaned, "It's a fusion reactor… please don't hit me again, please…"

My head reeled for a moment. "A fusion reactor." I took a long drag and let the smoke out slow. "That's impossible. The science for a fusion reactor is all still theoretical."

Nelson shook his head. "No, no, it's not. We've been fusing atoms for years in tokamaks, but…" He hesitated.

I said, "You work for Omega, right?"

He frowned. "You know about Omega?"

"I know about Omega. I have let two hesitations pass, Nelson. The next time you hesitate, it gets ugly." I turned to Ken, who was still holding his head. "What do Omega employ you to do, Ken?"

"I'm in charge of personnel. I keep discipline among the workers, keep the job on track…"

"Who do you report to in Omega?"

"I don't…" He looked over at Frank. "I report to Frank. Frank reports to Omega."

"What about you, Nelson? What's your role?"

He pointed over at Bob. "Me and Bob, we're in charge of the architectural design. We're building the housing for the reactor."

"Frank?"

"I liaise with Omega."

I spoke to Nelson again. "You need temperatures six times as hot as the sun to create nuclear fusion. Generating that kind of heat is almost impossible, and creating materials capable of withstanding that kind of heat is impossible."

He shook his head. "It's not. We've been researching fusion since the forties. We can achieve temperatures of one hundred and fifty million degrees, ten times the heat of the sun. Fusion then occurs between deuterium and tritium. When this happens, we get a helium nucleus, a neutron and *a lot* of energy! To sustain the temperatures needed for this process, we create like a cage of magnetic fields which prevent the heated particles from escaping. This plasma..."

I held up my hand. "I believe you. What's the deadline on the project?"

Frank answered. "Eighteen months."

I screwed up my brow at him. "That is a hell of a deadline."

"That's what they want. It's up to us to make it happen."

"How do you plan to achieve that?"

He took a deep breath and puffed out his cheeks. They all exchanged glances. Frank hunched his shoulders. "Well, you know, we have the most advanced computer technology on the planet, the machinery we're using is latest generation and sometimes beyond. Omega provide us with everything..."

"That's bullshit, Frank, and you know it. We've been watching you for two days. The machinery you're using is standard. Whatever computer technology you may have used, you used it for design, not construction, because there are no computers involved in the building work you're doing."

Bob spoke up. "Don't be an ass, Frank. Risk your own fucking limbs if you want, but don't risk mine. We laid the foundations and the first few months' work in the standard way. But we are entering a new, experimental phase next week. We're pulling in more kaffas and we are feeding them steroids with their food."

"Steroids?"

Frank sighed again. "They're developed by Omega at the labs in Pakistan. They induce a state that is both passively receptive and highly excitable. Subjects can work up to thirty-six hours without rest. We've tried it on a couple of individual subjects and the results are pretty amazing. Their personal output went up by like..." He shook his head. "I don't know, three hundred percent? Maybe more." He shrugged. "It opens up the possibility of using women and children as laborers too. I'd be pretty surprised if they don't go with that."

I studied Nelson's face. "You're down with that?"

He sighed like I was being embarrassingly naïve. "These people... they are little more than animals. I mean..." He gave a small laugh. "What are their lives? You have seen the desert out here. They are born here, they live forty, fifty years, sixty at the most, they die and their bones are picked by the animals. They live in superstition, with spirits and tribal gods. They cannot read. They have no schooling. To work on a project like this, it is a dream come true for them. And for the time they are working, taking the steroids, they feel powerful and strong. It is a blessing for them." He shook his head again. "You don't understand these people like we do."

I turned to Frank. "So, what are the side effects of the steroids?"

"One in a hundred might develop tumors, not necessarily malignant. One in two hundred might get an enlargement of some organ, like the heart or the kidneys, or even the brain. But we figure it's an acceptable risk."

I smiled. "You figure it's an acceptable risk."

Bob was shaking his head at the floor. "But, in any case, I

really think you are asking all the wrong questions. As Nelson said, these..." He waved his hand. "These *folk* are barely human. That's true. They are primitive to the point of being practically simian. But, hey, you know what? I wouldn't actually treat my dog the way we are treating these workers. Nevertheless, you have to ask yourself the question: What are we doing it *for?*" He stared at me, wide-eyed, and gave a small laugh. "Have you *any* idea what this reactor is going to achieve? It will supply the *entire globe* with clean energy, for the next ten thousand years, at a cost of a few hundred thousand rand a year just to maintain the physical infrastructure and the core personnel. It means the end of coal, gas and petrol. It means the end of the internal combustion engine. It means clean air, clean oceans, a stabilized environment..." His eyes were alive with passion. "Frankly, if a few kaffas have to be sacrificed to achieve that end, I think it's a small price to pay."

Njal spoke for the first time in a while. "You think maybe that's because it's not you paying the price?"

He drew breath to answer, but then bit back the words. Instead he said, "So what do you plan to do with us?"

I still needed their cooperation, so I managed to look slightly surprised. "I plan to send you back to work." I turned to Frank. "When do you report to Omega?"

"Once a week, on a Friday, I fly down to Cape Town for a progress meeting. Usually the guys come with me."

"Who do you meet with?"

"I..." He shook his head. "I can't..."

I turned to Bob and put a 9mm slug through his right kneecap. He screamed like a fifteen-year-old girl and fell on the floor clutching his leg. His shin and foot were sticking out at a grotesque angle. I turned back to Frank, who was staring at Bob with wide eyes and a gaping mouth.

"Who do you meet with?"

He started shaking his head again. His face was distressed. Bob was still screaming. Frank kept saying, "No, no..."

I shot Bob through the head and he went quiet and lay still, except that his hands and feet twitched occasionally. His blood pooled slowly under his head. I said:

"This is because I didn't remove your thumbs when we started. Now, Frank, let me see if I can make you understand this: The way things are going, Bob is going to be the lucky one." I turned to Nelson and Ken. "You two are going to pay the price for Frank's heroism. I am going to ask him one more time. No answer, and we start removing limbs." I turned to Frank and almost felt compassion for him. His face was tight and contracted, his eyes wide and staring. I said, "How about it, Frank? Take a moment to assimilate the fact that you have no choice. Now answer me. Who do you meet with from Omega?"

"Pi..."

"Good. You know who he is?"

An imperceptible nod. "Ruud Van Dreiver..."

"Good. That's very good. You're doing well, we are almost done. All I need now is the plans for the building. I don't care about the reactor. All I want is the building."

He pointed toward the dining table. "My computer..."

"Go with my colleague. Show him your password."

He closed his eyes and sat for a full five seconds, breathing deep, shuddering breaths. Then he stood. Njal showed him a pen drive and he closed his eyes again. His face was gray. He went with Njal. They spent ten minutes on the computer and Njal looked over at me and nodded. "OK, I got it."

Frank stared into my eyes across the room. "You said if we cooperated, you would let us go."

I nodded. "I did. How much do you know about Omega's long-term plans?"

"What little they have told us in seminars..."

Nelson interrupted. "Humanity is a plague. It is destroying its host and will eventually destroy itself. Omega plans to save the planet, and in so doing, to preserve what good humanity has created: democracy, medicine, the great philosophies, science. They will build a great library..."

I interrupted him. "And the price humanity pays for this great salvation is eight billion lives sacrificed so that a small elite can move into the new Eden."

He shook his head. "Those who survive into the new age do so because they are of a higher order than common humanity. It's nature who wipes out the plague, not Omega."

I smiled. "And what makes you of a higher order, Nelson?"

He put a long finger to his head. "My mind, my clarity of vision, my understanding."

I looked up at Frank. "And you?"

He sighed and shook his head. "It is beyond your understanding. It's our ability to see beyond the petty, and understand the grand design."

I smiled at Ken. "Whose grand design, Ken?"

"Pi's..."

"Not Alpha's?"

Frank went very still. His voice was tense, wooden. "Alpha is dead."

"Is he?"

Terror and realization dawned on him at the same time. He half whispered, "You…"

"Yeah, me."

I shot him between his eyes. Njal shot Nelson in the back of the head and I put two slugs through Ken's heart. Then there was a strange stillness in the room. Stan Getz was playing the Girl from Ipanema, Nelson was sagging forward and blood was pooling on his lap, trickling down from a large hole in his forehead.

Njal said, "Now we got a problem."

I pointed at the vodka and the gin. "Grab the bottles and wait by the door."

He looked at me like I was crazy, but did what I said. When he was safely behind me, I emptied a few more rounds into the sofa and the bodies, then opened up with the Heckler and Koch, ripping the bodies and the sofa and the armchairs to shreds, and stripping kindling from the bar and the table, making the chairs spin and dance across the floor. When I'd emptied the magazine, I said, "OK, let's go."

We swung into the Land Rover and, keeping the lights off, sped out of the compound and onto the N7, accelerating north at sixty miles an hour. The moon was higher and the visibility was better, but moonlight can be misleading, and you have to be really careful, or it can lead you far astray.

At the second major bend in the road, we turned west of north and plunged into the desert. Once off the blacktop, we slowed to a steady twenty-five, trailing large, billowing clouds of moonlit dust behind us.

After a while, Njal said, "What's your thinking? Or are you just going fucking crazy?"

"The Range Rover is gone, so is the money, and so are the bottles of booze and the girls. But the computer is still there. There are three different types of rounds in the room, the predominant one being from an assault rifle, fired recklessly. When they dust the place, they are going to find prints from the girls as well as from the victims. The picture won't be crystal clear, but it will paint a picture that suggests a raid by a gang, rather than an interrogation and an execution. The victims picked up some hookers. The hookers' boyfriends or pimps showed up, killed the victims, stole their money and their booze, and left with the girls, leaving the laptop behind them. Hence, they were not interested in the computer or its contents."

He was quiet for a bit. Then he said, "That sounds like wishful thinking."

I nodded. "Yeah, but it's all we got."

We didn't return to the rocks where we had been keeping watch on Goodhouse. We returned to the gully with the overhanging rocks where we had left the Land Rover. There we hung a tarp from the two trucks, made a small fire, sat around it in silence and brewed some coffee.

When the coffee was done, Njal poured us each a cup and handed me mine.

"Wishful thinking aside, Lacklan, this is gonna put Omega on red alert."

"I know. Maybe. Either way, we need to assume it will."

He frowned at me. "So...?" His frown deepened further. "And what do you mean, maybe?"

"Every hit we have made so far has been directed against the actual members of Omega themselves."

He made a skeptical face. "That's true."

I went on. "In this case, the members of Omega are congregating on the south coast, at the other end of the country."

He made a different kind of skeptical face with a touch of 'maybe' in it.

I continued, "Also, they will be looking for the Range Rover, and when they find it, it will be in Cape Town. There is nothing in the attack that immediately and positively speaks of a threat to the reactor…"

"Except the death of the architects."

"Think again, Njal. I already told you, the laptop was left behind, which speaks to a lack of interest in the project. Plus, the four guys we killed were lower middle managers, and they were careless, taking hookers back to the cabin. They were only recently initiated into Omega, knew practically nothing of the organization and were overseeing the construction of the building, not the reactor itself. We have caused exactly zero damage to the project so far. So…"

"So?"

"So, they will increase security, they will search for the Range Rover, and they will wait. Nothing will happen. After a few days, they will conclude it was a random home invasion. The theft of the booze and the money, and the wild, erratic use of firearms will tend to confirm that view. Like I said, probably some boys associated with the girls they'd picked up."

He puffed out his cheeks and blew. "You are very confident, my friend."

"It's a front, believe me."

"What do you mean, nothing will happen?"

"We need to get the contents of that computer to Jim. He needs to analyze it and we need expert guidance, not only on how to blow the damn thing, but whether it can be destroyed at all. That is going to take a few days at least. During that time, we do absolutely nothing here at the site."

He nodded, then narrowed his eyes. "Here at the site..."

"I'm going to Knysna."

"You. You are going..."

"You have to stay here."

Now he looked mad. "*What?*"

"Think about it, Njal. Stay with me and follow my reasoning. They are going to be on high alert for a few days at least. As soon as the Range Rover shows up in Cape Town, they are going to be looking at Knysna, which is just five or six hours' drive from Cape Town, as well as being the site of the Omega summit, where the five heads of the cabal will meet. That is where they are going to perceive the threat. That is where they are going to focus. Agreed?"

"Yuh, and that is why..."

I held up a hand. "Stay with me. Now, that is going to take the heat off the reactor, at least for a while, which means that as soon as you get a reply from Jim, you can start laying the plans to destroy this place. It also means that if I don't make it back, you can at least destroy the reactor. If we both go to Knysna, we both risk getting killed there, then nobody can finish the job."

He stared at me a long time. Finally, he said, "You sent the girls to Cape Town deliberately, to deflect attention from the reactor. When you said we had two options, an ambush or go look for them, you had already planned this and made up your mind..."

I sighed. "Not exactly, Njal, but it made sense that if they were the foremen of the site, they would have cash for expenses, to pay the laborers, that kind of stuff. It seemed like a good opportunity to make the hit look like a theft. I was going to take the Range Rover to Cape Town, but the girls were a bonus and made that unnecessary."

He still looked mad. "OK, but next time, you run the fuckin' plan by me first, Lacklan. You don't fuckin' maneuver me into it. That ain't cool."

"Understood."

"So when you gonna go?"

"I'll grab four hours sleep and leave around four AM. Meantime, you send the files on the pen drive to Jim and await his instructions. Apart from that, we maintain total radio and cyber silence. I shouldn't be more than a couple of days or three. If it runs over, I'll let you know. If you haven't heard from me in five days, assume I'm dead."

He nodded. "OK." He stared at the fire a while, the small orange flames dancing on his long, angular face. After a while, he twisted his mouth into a snarl. "I don't like it. I don't like that you didn't tell me what you were thinking. The plan is OK, but you should have told me."

"I apologize. It won't happen again. But we need to move past it now."

"OK. Go sleep. I keep watch."

EIGHT

Before sleeping, I had booked an Audi A4 from Hertz at the Springbok Airport. Jim had already booked a log cabin at the Dylan Thomas luxury holiday resort in Knysna. So I prepared a small kit bag with the weapons I thought I might need, took the Land Rover to Springbok, which was a two hour drive and got me there at six thirty that morning, left the Land Rover in the airport parking lot, and picked up the Audi A4, which I figured would fit in better with the clientele at the Dylan Thomas Resort.

After coffee at the airport, I set off on the eight hour drive to Knysna, aiming to get there by three or four in the afternoon. The drive was long and tedious, and the landscape dry, semi desert and largely unchanging for the two hundred miles from Springbok to Vanrhynsdorp. However, soon after that, the road bore east and began to climb into the Boland Mountains at the back of the Cape, heading through broad, lush fields toward Worcester and the Haweqwa and Riviersondorend Nature Reserves. There the landscape changed and became greener and easier on the eye.

The drive through the mountain pass took a little over an hour, and soon I had left Cape Town and the Atlantic Ocean behind. I was out on the south coast, with the Indian Ocean on my right bringing in warm, moist air, and only a hundred and fifty miles to go to Knysna. To my surprise, here the landscape was Mediterranean, with broad, fertile fields, semi arid hills and an abundance of pine trees, the whole area dotted with incongruous village names like Heidelberg and Albertina.

Finally, at four in the afternoon, I rolled down out of the hills that looked as though they belonged in southern France and drove the last stretch from George to Knysna with the windows down and the sea air battering my face, blowing away the cobwebs of exhaustion of the last couple of days. Most of the way, the Indian Ocean lay deep and blue on my right, reflecting broken sheets of light across the white beaches and rocky headlands of the coast. And, just before I reached Buffalo Bay, outside Knysna, I noticed a small village practically on the beach, where a range of old, painted fishing boats were drawn up on the sand, strung with nets. That made me smile.

The Dylan Thomas Resort was a collection of luxury log cabins that sprawled across the steep side of a hill which led down from Knysna town to a turquoise lagoon fed by the Indian Ocean, slightly to the south, and a couple of nameless rivers in the north. The cabins were connected by a network of rambling paths that wound through scattered pinewoods and copses which enclosed the cabins in discreet privacy, and housed myriad birds including African wood pigeons, robins and golden orioles. The place was beautiful and for a short while I indulged the fantasy of coming here on holiday with Marni, instead of coming on a mission to assassinate five people I had never met.

The fantasy passed and I wound down the track to the reception building, where there was also a café, a restaurant and a cocktail bar, all constructed in African hardwood with thatched roofs over large plate glass windows allowing panoramic views of the lagoon. I parked my car in the lot and sat a moment looking at my face in the mirror, thinking about the week's growth of beard on my chin, and thinking also that it was not such a bad thing. Coupled with an English accent learned from my mother, to be used on our visits to her parents, it might serve as something of a disguise.

I climbed out of the car, crossed the lot and checked in at a reception desk where a pretty girl who said her name was Janine gave me a key and said my cabin was the Polly Garter cabin, up the path and on the right. I told her in a flawless imitation of Hugh Grant that Polly would have to wait until I'd had a martini, extra dry, and she laughed like I was the funniest man on the planet. Then she asked me if my bags were in the trunk.

"Nicked in Jo'burg," I told her. "I shall have to restock my wardrobe while I'm here. Perhaps you could lend a hand."

She winked at me. "Which one, the right or the left?"

"I'll play it safe and take both."

We made more witty yet scandalous laughter and I went

and found the cocktail bar. There I downed two stiff martinis laced with vodka and climbed the hill to my cabin, where I collapsed on the bed and slept for the next three hours.

I came to at just after eight, showered and changed into my other pair of jeans, which were slightly cleaner than the ones I was wearing. I put on a linen jacket, which I had carefully rolled inside out in my bag, and then hung for the three hours while I was sleeping, and headed down to the dining room, by way of reception, to see if my friend Janine was still there. She was and smiled when she saw me.

"You look almost human."

"You know? That's the nicest thing anyone has said to me since I woke up." She giggled and wrinkled her nose. Before she could come back with repartee, I went on in my cut glass, faultless English. "I say, is it true Ruud van Dreiver lives around here?"

She raised her eyebrows and nodded. "Right across the bay. He has a ten bedroom mansion there, swimming pool, tennis courts, stables. It's palatial!"

"My father knew him, back in the day. It would be amusing to drop in and say hello, but one doesn't want to be pushy."

She looked impressed. "Really? They have some kind of billionaire party going on this weekend. We have a table booked tonight, actually."

"Not Ruudy and Jelly? Mind you, I doubt they'd remember me."

She shook her head and tapped at the computer. "No, Ameya Dabir. They say she's a Brahmin Princess. I thought India was a republic, but what do I know?" She raised an eyebrow. "And I see she's dining alone. Maybe you're in with a chance."

I gave a single, dry laugh. "A forlorn one, I fear. On another, more interesting subject. Do you rent out scuba diving equipment, and if you do, is there anyone, like yourself for example, who could show me the more interesting parts of the lagoon?"

She cocked her hip and arched her eyebrow. "Yes, yes, and are you flirting with me, Mr. Sinclair?"

I smiled. "Would you be very upset if I said I was?"

"Not very, no."

"Then I am. Will you take me scuba diving tomorrow morning, please, Janine?"

"You're awful." She said it like she didn't really mean it, then added, "But I will."

"Actually, I'm quite delightful in a bathing costume, you know."

I left her giggling and made my way to the dining room. It was surprisingly elegant, with a high, wooden-beamed ceiling, crystal chandeliers and waiters in bow-ties carrying buckets of champagne and dishes of oysters among tables of people, all of whom glittered in the candlelight.

The maitre d' gave my jeans a frigid look and led me to a table where I would not be too visible. I ordered a dozen oysters, a glass of house white, a sirloin steak and a bottle of Diemersdal Cabernet Sauvignon. Then I settled back to observe the dining room.

Practically every table was occupied by either a couple or a group, and I couldn't see anyone who looked like a Brahmin princess, though there were a few tables empty, and one, tucked in a corner beside a palm, did have a reserved sign on it.

The oysters came, with red and green Tabasco sauce, and I took my time eating them, sipping the white Sauvignon and thinking of Njal, stuck in the desert sleeping in the Land Rover. Life is rarely fair.

She appeared at nine o'clock, just as the waiter was clearing my plate. She wasn't beautiful. Beautiful was the baseline where she began. Beautiful was boring beside what she was. She was stunning. She wore an oxblood sari embellished with gold and dark, royal blue. Her hair was thick, blue black and hung down to her waist. Her skin was olive, her eyes were black and she wore an absurd amount of gold. It should have looked vulgar and excessive, but instead it looked absolutely appropriate, as though to have any less gold on her would have been somehow a transgression of some unwritten law.

She walked with grace and elegance, and the waiters flocked to her, like bees and butterflies to an exotic flower. She smiled and accepted their bows as her due, sat and allowed herself to be served, as though it were she who was granting favors to them. I watched her and knew that this was a very, very dangerous woman.

She ordered oysters, which seemed to be the thing here, and while I took my time eating my steak and sipping my wine, I watched her eat her oysters. It was as she was slipping the last one down her throat that the guy came in.

He was in an Italian suit that probably cost as much as the Audi I was driving. He was tall and slim the way you can afford to be when you're a billionaire and have a gym, a tennis court and a swimming pool all en suite to your bedroom. His black hair was tightly curled and his goatee was trimmed short to make him look like a sultan from the Thousand and One Nights. This, I figured, was Prince Mohamed bin Awad.

He stopped beside her table and made a show of surprise that was as transparently false as her surprise at seeing him. He bowed over her hand and she gestured to a chair at her table. He graciously accepted and instructed the waiter that he would be dining with the lady.

Here was two fifths of the cabal, Tau and Sigma, alone, having a very public clandestine meeting, and I wondered why. Why the subterfuge? Was it because he was a Muslim and she a Brahmin? Or did Omega frown on intimate relationships within the cabal? A rule against office romances.

I scanned the room looking for his bodyguards, or hers, but I didn't see any.

They both had lobster, and while they had that, I ordered black coffee and a glass of Bushmills in a cognac glass, with no ice. Nothing much happened then, except that their body language spoke volumes about an unresolved mutual attraction which needed, with increasing urgency, to resolve itself somehow. I wondered briefly at the kind of crazy world where you can be among the five most powerful people on the planet and still have to keep your infatuations secret. It was a situation that intrigued me.

I signed my bill and took my drink out to the terrace. The moon was in its first waning, but still large and fat, and reflected a long, silver path across the lagoon. I set my glass on a table and lit up a Camel. The sky was dark yet translucent, and though it wasn't cold, a breeze off the Indian Ocean chilled my skin and made me shudder. I walked to the edge of the terrace and looked right, up the slope to the pinewoods where the lodges were. I saw no men standing guard, no covert security. Left was the reception building and the parking lot. There were several cars there, all expensive, impossible to tell which were theirs. Either way, there was no sign of any bodyguards there either.

I sat a while with my ass against the parapet, smoking and finishing my drink, then made my way out to my car. I climbed in and sat for half an hour, watching and waiting. Eventually, they stepped out into the courtyard that lay between reception, the café and the restaurant and stood a while, chatting and laughing softly. Then he took her hands in his and she took a few rapid steps into the shadows, toward the parking lot, pulling him with her. There she closed in, standing so close their bodies were touching, looking up into his eyes. He cupped her face in his hands and they kissed. Finally she pushed him gently away, speaking hurried words I couldn't catch. He hesitated and I heard her voice, raised for any possible eavesdroppers: "Good night, Mohamed. We must catch up soon. Bye!"

And she turned and made her way up the hill, toward the cabins. He hesitated a moment, then loped across the lot to a cream Porsche 911. He climbed in, fired up the engine and drove out of the lot at high speed. But by that time, I was out of my car and running silently up the path through the pines where I had seen Ameya Dabir disappear.

I stopped when she came into sight, and moved in among the shadows of the pine trees. The paved path came to a fork, where one branch curled away to the right, climbing the hill toward my own cabin, and the other branched left, leveled off and led to a large cabin with a veranda. This was the path she took and I watched her climb the steps, fumble for a moment inserting a key, and disappear inside. After a second, a warm, amber light came on in the window. Then a second light came on at the back. I figured that would be the bedroom.

I continued on my way up to my cabin. From my veranda I knew I would have a clear view of the back of her cabin, and the fork in the path. I settled back with my feet on the rail, lit another Camel and waited, thinking.

After ten minutes, the light at the front of the cabin went off, but the one at the back stayed on. Then there were steps, and the figure of Prince Mohamed bin Awad appeared at the fork, hesitated, looked about, and made its way up to her veranda. There might have been an exchange of whispered voices, it was hard to tell, but there was definitely the soft clunk of a closing door.

Both bin Awad and Dabir were guests of Ruud van Dreiver. They must have suites at his palatial mansion where they could meet, yet here they were, at the resort, making clumsy, ineffectual attempts at a clandestine meeting in a cabin she had hired, barely a mile from her host's house. I knew she was single because we had read up on her background. He had three wives and was entitled to have as many more as he pleased. Their difference in religion went some way to explaining why they were keeping their affair secret, but it didn't explain why they were keeping it secret from van Dreiver and the other members of the cabal. Unless the divisions between their religions were a part of Omega's own internal policies. That was entirely possible. Whatever the case, it played right into my hands.

Two hours later, shortly after midnight, he emerged

from the cabin and made his way quickly and quietly back toward the parking lot. A minute or two later, the light at the back of the house went out, and fifteen minutes after that, I watched a small light proceed steadily across the dark water of the lagoon, and the faint whine of a speedboat carried across the chill night air. The prince was going back to the van Dreiver palace.

The next morning, I was up at six. I ran down to the lagoon, went for a long jog along the sand, had a swim in the cold water, then spent an hour training in the sand and ran back up the hill to shower and dress for breakfast. A little later, I found Janine in reception. Her expression was somewhere between surprised and curious.

"Good morning, Janine. Are you going to take me scuba diving this morning?"

"You are persistent, Mr. Sinclair."

"I'm known for it."

"You realize I could be married."

"I don't want to take you away from your husband, I just want to swim with you."

She laughed out loud.

I insisted. "Will you?"

"What?"

"Swim with me."

She regarded me for a moment, still smiling. "Yes, all right. Meet me down on the beach in half an hour."

I went to the café, had a couple of espressos and a croissant, returned to my cabin to change into some shorts and met Janine down at the lagoon half an hour later. She was in a yellow bikini and looked slim, tanned and fit. She was standing by a parasol, a basket and a couple of towels. As I approached, she pointed to what looked like a boathouse forty or fifty feet down the beach.

"Give me a hand to get the gear."

I followed her over, pushing through the soft sand with bare feet, and watched her unlock the padlock on the door. "This is where you keep your scuba diving gear? Don't you worry about it getting stolen?"

She wrenched open the door and stepped in. The place was packed with rubber suits, air bottles, masks and flippers, gas tanks and a generator. There was also a stack of canoes and oars. She grabbed an air bottle and shoved it at me.

"Believe it or not, despite South Africa's crime statistics as a whole, Knysna has practically zero crime." She shoved a mask and some flippers into my arms too. "And if people do steal, they don't steal swimming gear. They steal money."

"Good to know."

"You ever used these before?"

"Yup."

"How often, once? Twice?"

I thought about lying, but shrugged and shook my head. "I lost count."

She frowned. "So what do you need me for?"

"You mean apart from the pleasure of your company? To show me around. Where are the good places to dive? The shallows, the quicksands, the deep parts where there are fish..." I grinned. "You know, the tour of the lagoon."

Her frown became skeptical. "OK..."

"I mean..." I pointed over to the mouth of the lagoon, where large waves were crashing against the reefs that secluded it from the Indian Ocean beyond, a hundred yards from where van Dreiver had his small, private pier. "Is it safe to swim over there? Are there dangerous currents... Is it beautiful...?"

She nodded. "It's beautiful. Come on, I'll show you."

I was about to start pulling on the gear, but she pointed to a small, wooden boat with an outboard motor, pulled up on the sand.

"Give me a hand."

We dumped the gear in and she climbed aboard while I pushed it out into the shallows. She yanked the cord and fired up the engine as I clambered aboard and we started a slow putter. For a good fifty or sixty feet, the sand was white and the water completely transparent and shallow, barely above my knees. Then it grew slowly deeper, dipping toward a deep channel that curved in from the mouth of the lagoon.

As we moved out toward those deeper waters, she watched me for a while, and I saw her eyes flick over my body. I saw her take in the various scars I'd collected over the years, and I guess she noticed I was in shape. Finally, she said, "So, what do you do for a living, Mr. Sinclair?"

"Call me Richard."

She waited. I smiled. "What do you do for a living, Richard?"

"I'm an instructor. I teach martial arts and extreme sports."

"Seriously?"

I nodded. "Seriously. Which is why I am a little more careful than other people might be when it comes to..." I gestured over at the mouth of the lagoon. "Situations like this one. I know only too well how dangerous currents can be in a place like this. So I prefer to have somebody like you show me around first."

She narrowed her eyes and looked away at the approaching, darker water. "You are bullshitting me, Richard Sinclair. I don't know why, but I know that you are, sure as eggs is eggs."

I ignored the comment. "So, are you married?"

"Divorced. Why?" There was a challenge in her eye, but also amusement and pleasure.

"In case I want to take you out. I need to know if I'll have a jealous husband to contend with."

"What makes you think I'd go out with you?"

I gave my head a little twitch. "I don't know. Maybe you strike me as a risk taker."

She gave a small laugh that was almost a snort and shook her head. "What are you *like?*"

"So how come you can just skive off work to come swimming with the likes of me?"

"Because I'm not skiving off. I own this place. It's my business, and despite your shabby clothes, your rental car and your wildly improbable stories, I can smell money and potentially a good, repeat customer."

The water beneath the boat had turned suddenly dark. She cut the engine and we slowed to a gently rocking drift. A quarter of a mile away, I could see the rhythmic explosions of surf against the reefs at the entrance to the lagoon, and the air was filled with a steady background roar. Janine pointed to my feet. "You've got the anchor there, just behind your feet. Drop it over, would you? We're in about six to eight meters here, there are rocks and small fish, and seaweed. But all the sharks are on the outside, beyond the reef."

"Great whites?"

"Less than before, but yeah, also raggies, silvertips, cows, duskies..." She shrugged. "We got a lot of sharks, about ten different types along the south coast."

"But not in the lagoon."

She grinned with a hint of malice. "Not in the lagoon. You're comparatively safe with me. Put your gear on and let's go swim."

NINE

We swam for an hour, going first south, exploring the rocks and caves along the southern edge of the lagoon, beneath van Dreiver's mansion, and then heading west and a little north, along the deep channel that cut through the lagoon, to where the depth dropped to little more than two and a half meters, and schools of brilliantly colored fish darted in and out among algae and rocks with rigid, startled eyes. And while Janine showed me her submarine treasures, I made a map in my mind of what lay beneath the water between my log cabin and van Dreiver's palatial mansion.

What I found was that a fifteen minute run along the beach would bring me to a dogleg in the lagoon where to the right there were oyster beds and to the left there was that long, deepening trench along which we had been swimming, which would carry me all the way to the mouth of the lagoon, past the small, private quay which the van Dreivers had had built at the foot of their hill.

After an hour, our tanks began to run low on air, so we returned to the boat and pulled ourselves out of the water. Janine sat in the stern, tossed me a towel and started rubbing dry her hair and her face. When she'd moved down to her arms and her shoulders, I said, "Did you know that your hotel was the clandestine meeting place for Prince Mohamed bin Awad and Ameya Dabir?"

She toweled her thighs, smiling, and raised an eyebrow at me. "Gossip now?"

"Hey, lay off, or I'm going to think you have it in for me. What's wrong with a little harmless gossip?"

She shrugged. "I knew she had both booked into the hotel. I didn't know they were having a clandestine meeting. Besides, it really is none of my business."

"I couldn't help seeing it. Their table was opposite mine. And when I was sitting on my terrace having a nightcap, I saw her go into my neighboring cabin, and a little while later he joined her. It was rather hard not to see."

Her face said she was impressed but trying to hide it. "Really? Did he stay all night?"

"How should I know? I wasn't spying."

She laughed. "Liar."

"He stayed two hours, then left and took a boat across the lagoon."

"You *were* spying!"

"I had nothing better to do. I need you to come and play cribbage with me at night, or snap, to keep my mind off my exotic neighbors."

"Cribbage? Doctor might be more fun."

"That could work too."

She yanked the cord on the small motor, it growled into life and we started putt-putting back toward the beach.

"So, what kind of guy is Ruudy van Dreiver? Does he come to the resort ever, or does he keep to himself?"

"I don't think he has ever come here. His guests come over sometimes. It's not the first time Ameya Dabir has dined here." She hesitated a moment and grinned.

I grinned back. "What?"

"He has rented a yacht for this afternoon..."

"He who? Van Dreiver?"

"Prince Awad."

I concealed my interest by asking an irrelevant question. "You rent yachts?"

"We have an office at the Moorings, by the Heads. We have powerboats and a few sailing yachts, which we rent by the day. Of course he might be taking a whole party out, but judging by the champagne and caviar he's ordered, my money is on him just having one guest on that yacht." She laughed. "See? You've got me gossiping like you now!"

I laughed and thought for a moment. "These waters not dangerous for sailing?"

"They can be, at that! But they won't go out far, mile or two off the heads, I'd guess." She smiled and winked. "I'm pretty sure they'll have other things on their mind besides sailing."

"Hmmm..." I grinned. "No doubt they'll be playing high-stakes cribbage."

We got back to shore, I helped her put the stuff away, thanked her for a great morning and told her I'd like to do it again sometime. She gave me that curious look of hers and said, "So what are you going to do now, Mr. Richard Sinclair?"

I shrugged. "I might go into George and buy some slightly more respectable clothes."

"Answer me a question."

"Of course."

"Where *are* your clothes?"

I laughed out loud, like the whole thing was a crazy, amusing story and a whole lot of fun. "Somewhere between Thailand and London, actually. I've just spent a couple of months in Thailand. I was flying back to London and got sidetracked when a friend told me I really had to go and visit Knysna. So I changed my flight and detoured to Cape Town, but my luggage never got the memo."

She gave a lopsided smile and shook her head. "I'm surprised you don't choke on the methane."

I raised an eyebrow and cocked my head to one side in a silent question.

She nodded. "The methane released from all the bullshit you spout."

I made an effort to look hurt. "That's a little unkind."

She stepped toward me and placed a damp hand on my chest. "I am not often wrong, Mr. Richard Sinclair, and I can tell you are actually an honest man, but I can also tell you are generating enough bullshit to fertilize the Sahara. I don't appreciate being lied to or being made a sap of, so let's call a truce. Stop flirting with me until you're prepared to be up front and honest with me. If, when you're done bullshitting, you still want to flirt with me, let me know, because I like you. Deal?"

I nodded. "Deal."

She made her way back to reception and I sprinted up to my cabin, had a quick shower, dressed and made my way to my car in the parking lot. All the while, my mind was racing. I was thinking about the fishing boats I had seen on the beach at the village of Goukamma, six miles west of Knysna on the way in from George. I was thinking of Prince Mohamed bin Awad and Ameya Dabir last night, and wondering how much of a leap of faith it was to assume they would be alone on the yacht this afternoon. My gut told me it was no leap of faith at all.

But I was also thinking that maybe the only person who could tell me for sure—about that and about van Dreiver's affairs in general—was Janine, and I had blown her as a source of information by coming on too strong. On the other hand, I didn't think I could have played it any other way with the timetable I had.

I climbed into the Audi, slammed the door and pulled out of the Dylan Thomas parking lot. I drove fast to George. There I left the car in a public parking lot, took thirty grand out in South African rand—just over two thousand bucks—and bought some clothes, a mask, a snorkel and some flippers. I also bought some bread, cheese, ham and mineral water, and headed back toward Knysna at a steady fifty MPH. Before I got there, I turned off the N2 and onto a dirt track that wound down to the coast, and the village of Goukamma, the village I had spotted from the road when I had first arrived.

Goukamma was tiny, little more than a cluster of small pink, blue and yellow wooden houses on the beach, surrounded by vast fishing nets suspended from tall, angular posts buried in the sand. Among those nets, drawn up away from the tide, were maybe a dozen boats, painted in faded reds, yellows and blues, each with a mast, a set of oars and an outboard motor attached at the back.

I climbed out of the Audi, opened the trunk and took a few moments to prepare a bag. In it I put my new swimming gear, my lunch and my Sig p226, sealed in a plastic bag. When I was satisfied I had everything I needed, I walked down into the village.

There was a handful of men, women and children standing and sitting around, not doing much, but my eye was caught by a guy in one of the boats. He was long and lanky, anything between thirty and sixty years old, and he was sewing a net. He grinned as I approached and showed me what was left of most of his teeth. I smiled back at him.

"Good morning. I'd like to rent your boat for the afternoon."

He screwed up his brow like he didn't understand, then he screwed up his nose like I was crazy and then he opened his mouth and wheezed among his tombstones.

"You want my boat. What for, man?"

I improvised. "I'm a travel writer. I write for TV and magazines, you know the kind of stuff, and I want to write about what it's like to go out on the Indian Ocean in a wooden boat."

He shook his head, laughing, and returned to stitching his net. "Crazy. Crazy people."

"I'm serious."

"You gonna sink mah boat. I don't want you to sink mah boat, man."

"No, I'm not. I'm real good with boats. But look, I'll

make it worth your while. I'll pay you five grand, up front, and if I do sink it, I guarantee I'll buy you another."

Now he screwed up his eyes and did some more wheezing. "You not gonna buy me a boat if you been eaten by the sharks, man!"

I pulled out the equivalent of five hundred dollars from my wallet, about seven grand in South African currency. He stopped sewing and regarded the money with interest and a little apprehension. I said, "I just want it for a few hours. The weather is good, the sea is calm, and I'll be back before nightfall. I'm not going out more than a mile or two, max."

"And you gonna write TV about that?" He shook his head again, but after a moment he shrugged, dropped the net and slid down to the sand.

"You know how to sail it?"

"Yeah, I'm pretty good."

He held out both hands. "Gimme the money." I handed it to him. "OK, you can take the boat now. Come back before dark. Weather can change fast."

I gave him the thumbs up. "Help me get it in the water, will you?"

Between us, we pushed it down the beach and into the ocean. He watched me swing aboard and stood scratching his head with one hand and his ass with the other while I inspected the engine. "You don't want me come you? There a lot of sharks out there."

"I'll be OK. I'm not going swimming. I'll have her back here before nightfall. Don't you worry."

He wheezed a laugh. "Your funeral at sea, man."

I pulled the cord, the engine fired up, I gave the guy another thumbs up, turned her around and started out on a southeasterly heading toward the headland that concealed Buffels Bay.

The boat was slow and the current was against me, so it was gone one PM and the sun was high by the time I reached the cliffs that marked the easternmost point of the bay. There I killed the engine, dropped the anchor and settled to a light lunch of bread, cheese and water.

The yacht emerged from the mouth of the lagoon about two hours later, at three in the afternoon. I started up the engine again and began puttering in a direction slightly south of east, toward where I guessed they were going to drop anchor and start drinking champagne.

As it was, they went farther than I had expected. They were cruising at about six knots, taking it easy, and they kept going for almost an hour. So by the time they stopped and dropped anchor, though the coast was still visible to them, they were largely invisible to anyone on shore. I figured that was no accident.

I kept going until there was no more than a mile between us, then I killed the engine and raised the sail. With the gentle southerly breeze, I was making about three knots, but having to take, and after another twenty minutes, I was less than half a mile from the yacht. Then I let her drift a little closer, lowered the sail and dropped the anchor. I wasn't surprised to see nobody on deck. I was pretty sure they hadn't come out here to gaze at the ocean. I slipped my waterproofed Sig into my waistband, pulled on my flippers, mask and snorkel and slipped quietly overboard, trying not to think of the abundant sharks.

The weather was good and the sea was calm, so I made it to the yacht in slightly over ten minutes. Aside from the lapping of the water on the hull, it was completely silent. I kicked my way from the starboard side to the stern, where there was a small diving platform with a couple of steps up to the rear deck, and pulled off my flippers and snorkel. I laid them on the platform, pulled myself gently out of the water and took the Sig from its packaging.

I waited for sixty seconds, motionless, listening. Still there was no sound but the lapping of the small waves against the hull. I took the two steps up to the rear deck. There I saw a table, two chairs beside it, a silver bucket with ice and a half empty bottle of Dom Perignon, no glasses.

Beyond the table, there was an open door and some steps going down into a spacious cabin. I stepped to the side of the door and peered in: a couple of sofas, another, longer table to one side and, at the end, steps rising to a sophisticated cockpit. Beneath and behind the steps, there was a highly polished mahogany door. Again I listened, again nothing.

I slid down the steps, looked behind me, left and right, and crossed the main cabin to the door. I took hold of the handle, counted to two, turned and pushed.

There was a bed directly ahead of me. The sheets were purple satin, rumpled and half on the floor. On either side of the bed, there were twin bedside tables in the same, high-polish mahogany. Each held a lamp and a half-empty crystal flute of champagne. Beside the sheets on the floor: a pair of cream chinos, gray socks, a pair of blue deck shoes, a pale blue shirt, a sari, a black lace bra, black lace panties, a pair of havaianas.

In the bed, tangled in each other's arms and legs among the purple satin sheets, two dark, naked bodies slept, partly covered by her long, black hair: bin Awad and Ameya Dabir. A twist of something like grief and despair clenched my gut, a certainty that what I was doing was wrong on a fundamental level. But I told myself I had no choice. This was a job that had to be done, and if my soul was to be damned for doing it, that would make no great difference. I was damned already. I spoke and my voice was loud and jarring in the confined room.

"Wake up! Awad! Ameya Dabir! Wake up!"

He raised his head, frowned, rubbed his face and his tightly curled hair. She frowned too, but opened her eyes and turned to face me, pulling the purple sheet over her bare breasts.

"What the hell...?" Her voice, her accent, were both exquisite.

Now bin Awad was on one elbow, his bare feet seeking the edge of the bed. He echoed his lover and said, "What the hell...?"

I cocked the Sig and showed him the muzzle. "Enough questions. Get up."

They sat up. She gathered the sheets around her. They both looked more mad than scared. That would change.

He said: "Who are you? What do you want?"

"I'm the man you're trying to kill. I need you out of bed in three. If you aren't, I'll blow your kneecap off. Then your lover will have to carry you." I aimed at his knee. "One, two..."

"Wait! Wait, wait..." They were both climbing out of bed, standing. She was dragging the sheet with her.

I said: "Leave the sheet. Put a bikini on if you want to."

She hesitated, then dropped the sheet. Her body, like her voice, was exquisite. "I didn't bring a bikini..."

I ignored her. "I'm not here to kill you. I'm here to negotiate. But understand me, push me half an inch and I will execute you both, like Timmerman, like *El Vampiro*, like all the rest. Do we understand each other?"

They both nodded. I waved my gun and backed up a few feet. "Up on deck."

They crossed the saloon, naked and vulnerable. I felt sick and followed them up the steps to the rear deck. There they stood watching me, now more scared than mad. I waved the Sig at the chairs. "Sit." They sat. "Where's the scuba diving equipment?"

He pointed at the wooden boards. "In the hatch."

"Open it." He stood, then squatted down and opened the hatch. "Take out two weight belts. Put one on, give the other to Dabir."

He stared up at me and now there was real terror in his face. "What are you going to do?"

"I told you. I have no interest in killing you. Do as I say and you have nothing to worry about." I waved the Sig at the two belts with their lead weights. "That's to strengthen my negotiating position. Now do it."

He pulled out two belts, handed one to Ameya Dabir and put the other around his waist. I looked at her, but couldn't meet her eye. "Stand up, put it on, then both of you go and stand on the platform."

He shook his head. "Now look, anything you want, just please, don't..."

"I won't warn you again. Do it."

She put on the belt and they both went and stood on the

platform, facing me with their backs to the sea. He drew breath to speak, but she cut him short. Her black eyes narrowed and she spat the words at me. "You want to negotiate? Here's the deal, Mr. Walker! You let us live and your death will last only a day instead of a week, and I promise not to skin you alive and cover you in salt! A deal?" She laughed. "You are *nothing!* What can you offer Omega? You think you have hurt us? You think you have made *one single move* that we did not dictate or anticipate? You are a piece of pig shit, Lacklan Walker, just as your father always knew you were. Go away and *die*, and save us all the annoyance of having to kill you, and yourself the agony of your miserable, lingering death!"

I sat in the chair she had been sitting in. I felt cold inside, as though my soul were an infinite sheet of ice under a cloudless, frozen sky. "Tell me something, Ameya, is that how you justify the murder of eight billion people? You just think of them as pig shit?"

She carefully and elaborately spat on the deck at my feet. "Little boys sob, Mr. Walker, while men get the job done."

In the silence that followed, the ocean slapped and sucked at the creamy white boat. There were no seagulls, no sounds at all but that eternal sound of the ocean; and then the stark, firecracker smack of the Sig. One round smacked through her perfect brow and erupted out of the back of her head, spraying blood and gore onto the dark surface of the sea. As she dropped into the waves, the second round punched in through his left eye and he went down too. Their bodies drifted down into the blackness and were quickly lost to view.

Soon there would be sharks, and nothing left of Tau and

Sigma but shark shit. Not pig shit like me, but shark shit. I couldn't swim back, not with the sharks congregating to eat the Arab prince and the Brahmin princess. So I raised the anchor and fired up the engine and headed at a slow chug for the fishing boat.

In the west, the sun was turning copper and sinking toward the horizon.

TEN

By the time I got back to Knysna, it was almost six PM. I took a bottle of Bushmills to my cabin, knocked back two stiff shots and stood under the shower for twenty minutes, switching from scalding hot to cold and back again, trying to wash away the image of Ameya Dabir's startled face rocking back as the slug crashed through her forehead.

I toweled myself dry, took another slug of Irish, dressed in the new clothes I'd bought and made my way to reception. Janine saw me walk in and arched an eyebrow at me.

"Good evening, Mr. Richard Sinclair."

I gave a smile that wasn't a smile because my eyes were not involved and dropped the Hugh Grant accent.

"That's not my name."

"More BS?"

"Give me a chance, will you? My name is Lacklan, and I'm from Boston. Will you let me buy you dinner and come clean?"

I watched her eyes flick around my face. Her pupils dilated slightly and she smiled. "My goodness. I do believe Mr. Richard Sinclair is telling the truth. How could I refuse?"

I engaged my eyes in the smile and said, "Cut it out. When shall I pick you up?"

"Why waste time? Let's strike while the iron is hot." She leaned through a door in the wall behind the desk and said, "Clem? I'm going out for the evening. Man the desk, will you? If you need help, call Isabella."

A muffled voice replied. She picked up her purse and walked around the desk to join me, grabbed my arm and guided me toward the door. "This is going to be good," she said, and squeezed my bicep.

She took me on a walk through a maze of twisting paths that threaded their way among pinewoods and luxury villas, until we came to a short road that bordered the lagoon, just a short distance from the mouth, where the water was a deep green among rocks during the day, an almost black in the failing light of the evening. All the way, she had her arm linked through mine and kept up a gentle chatter about everything and anything, from the oyster beds in the lagoon to nearby ostrich farms and the crocodiles at the George Crocodile Park.

The restaurant was a long, oblong wooden box with a terrace, perched on the edge of the rocks, overlooking the waves that belched and crashed through the narrow opening from the Indian Ocean, erupting in explosions of spray a mere twenty feet below. The chill air coming in off the sea made it too cold to sit outside among the flaming torches that illuminated the terrace, so we went inside where it was warm, there was a powerful smell of char grilled meat, and a pleasant buzz of conversation. We found a table by the window and sat opposite each other. A waiter in a black and white apron down to his ankles brought us a couple of plastic-coated menus and I ordered an Irish, straight up. Janine nodded at the waiter.

"I'll have the same, then tell Jaqui to find me your two tenderest sirloins. She knows how I like them, and we'll have a mixed salad in the middle, no vinegar, just olive oil and sea salt. Bottle of Alto Cabernet Sauvignon, make it a 2014 if you've still got some. Open it now, Greg, would you?"

"You got it, Janine. Coming right up."

He withdrew and she fixed me with her eye. "OK, Mr. Richard Sinclair, let's hear it."

"I told you, that's not my name."

"It's what it says on your passport and your driver's license."

"My name is Lacklan. I'm not going to tell you my surname, so you needn't ask. I am from Boston, in the U.S.A., and I am sorry I tried to play you."

"Sounds like more BS."

I shrugged. "Well, it happens to be the truth. I am not flirting with you and I am not lying to you. If there is something I can't, or don't want to tell you, then I won't. I'm done lying to you."

"You want me to believe you're CIA or NSA or some crap like that." She said it without malice, just as though she were stating a fact.

I shook my head. "The NSA only deal with electronic surveillance. I am not a member of the CIA. I'm not a member of anything. I'm retired."

"So what are you doing in Knysna, snooping on the van Dreivers? I have a good mind to alert them to the fact that you're here."

I shook my head and spoke quietly, remembering Ameya Dabir's head jerking at the impact of the 9mm round. "Don't do that." I leaned forward on the table with my elbows. Greg appeared and deposited two glasses of Irish whiskey in front of us and withdrew again.

"Janine, I can't tell you everything. Even if I wanted to, I couldn't. It would be irresponsible and dangerous. But I am going to tell you that the van Dreivers are not good people, and the reunion they are having this week is not just an innocent gathering of friends. I can't tell you any more than that, but take it from me that many, many people have died for them to get where they are, and many more will die to keep them there."

She sighed and sagged back in her chair. "Have you any idea how that sounds?"

I nodded. "Yes."

"You know, I am really tempted to cancel dinner and just go home."

"I understand. I don't blame you. But tell me, what can I do to stop you from doing that?"

She sighed again. "I'm not sure there is anything."

I smiled like she was being unreasonable. "Come on, don't be like that. Give me a chance. I *am* telling you the truth. Ask me anything."

"What's your real name—your *full* real name?"

I weighed up the benefits of having her on side against the risk of her knowing who I was, and made a decision. "Lacklan Walker. My father was an associate of Ruud van

Dreiver's. Janine, I am putting you at risk by telling you this, but I need you to believe me and trust me."

"Oh God..." She sounded almost bored. "Where to begin? A: how do I know *this* name is for real? B: why on Earth do you *need* me to believe you? You know what this reeks of? It stinks of a confidence trick or, much worse, a guy who is having an early midlife crisis and is building up a fantasy about being some kind of spy."

"Are you done?"

"I'm not sure. It depends on what comes out of your mouth next."

I reached into my jacket and pulled out my passport and my driver's license and dropped them in front of her. She looked at them and shrugged. "They look as real as the other ones."

Then I searched through the photographs on my phone and found pictures of my house, me in the kitchen garden with Rosalia, me, Abi and the kids before we divorced, the four of us with Kenny and Rosalia, celebrating our engagement, and the sunset over the trees to the east, over Weston. I handed the cell to her and she scrolled through them.

"That's my house in Boston, and those are my cook, my butler, my ex-wife and my ex-stepchildren." I watched her a moment and added, "And you can google Bob Walker, of Weston, Massachusetts. You'll find my father. He was a financier. And that really is all you need to know about me."

She handed the passport and the driver's license back, but kept the phone and gazed a little longer at the photographs. "They seem to like you," she said at last. I didn't answer and she looked up, like she was asking me to confirm it.

"We're family."

She handed me the phone and took a deep breath. "Lacklan, with all due respect, you don't get to decide what I need to know. You can decide what you're willing to tell me, but that is not the same thing."

"Point taken."

"Why are you nosing around the van Dreivers?"

I drew breath to tell her that was something I wasn't willing to tell her, but instead I said, "He owes me something. Don't ask me what. I won't tell you."

"Do you plan to hurt him?"

"I don't plan to hurt him, no, but I can't promise he won't get hurt. All I can tell you is that that is not my intention."

"He hurt you?"

"He has hurt a lot of people, Janine, he and his consortium."

"What about you? Have you hurt a lot of people you didn't directly intend to hurt?"

I took a while to answer. Our steaks arrived, and the bottle of wine. The waiter poured her a drop, she swirled it, sniffed it, tasted it and after a moment gave him the nod. He poured us a glass each and withdrew. When he was gone, I said:

"I was in the army, the British army."

"The *British* army?"

"Long story. My mother is English. I was in a special operations regiment. I was in Afghanistan, Iraq, Colombia…" I shook my head. "Many places. So I would have to say yes, I have hurt a lot of people; some I intended to hurt, others I didn't."

"And now you're on some kind of vendetta, on behalf of your father, as a way of trying to find peace for a soul that has too much blood on its hands."

She had come so close to the truth I wondered for a moment if she was Omega, but discarded the idea and tried to inject conviction into my expression when I shook my head.

"It's not a vendetta, and you should be careful about making assumptions and jumping to conclusions based on stereotypes. I am looking for justice, Janine, which I believe every person is morally entitled to do. But I am not out for revenge."

"Good, because I don't want you to use me or my resort as a platform from which to launch a campaign of vengeance. I don't want that karma, understood?"

"Understood."

She cut into her steak and I was transfixed for a moment, watching the blood ooze out onto her plate. She put a piece in her mouth and we watched each other across the table while she chewed. She spoke suddenly, with her mouth full.

"I want to like you." She shook her head. "Don't say any of the shit people say to comments like that. I'm not asking for you to reciprocate." She pulled off half her glass of wine and smacked her lips. "I haven't got a problem with you being a badass, uncompromising or even violent. I've seen enough in my time to know that sometimes that's necessary. I like a man who has a pair of balls between his legs he can call on when he needs them. But I can't abide injustice, or inhumanity."

I gave a small snort of a laugh, cut into my steak and said, "Well, I don't want to like you, Janine. I do like you. You're cool, and I apologize for having used you and lied to you." I held her eye a moment, with a chunk of steak halfway to my mouth. "But it would be a lie if I said I am sorry I did it. I didn't know you, I knew nothing about you, and I did what I had to do."

She reached across the table and held out her hand. I was a little surprised and took it in mine. We shook rather seriously and formally. "Friends," she said, "and we move on. If you want to talk and tell me about it, I'll be happy to listen."

She released my hand and carried on eating. I thought about it, chewed and swallowed a chunk of steak. Then I drained my wine and refilled both our glasses.

"Thank you." I tried to speak several times after that, but found the words sticking in my throat. Finally, I said, "Actually, talking would probably be a relief, but it's just not possible." I shook my head. "I can't do it."

She ate in silence for a while, like she hadn't heard me. Eventually, she leaned back in her chair and picked up her glass, swirling the wine slowly around. "So what's next?"

"Next?" I shrugged. "Ideally, I would like to have a talk with George da Silva, one on one."

"Da Silva, the president of King Felipe?"

"Mh-hm. He's one of the guests this weekend…"

"I know."

"But I can't exactly stumble into him while playing golf, can I?"

"No. He doesn't play golf, but he does go hunting. I'm not sure…" She reached in her purse and pulled out her phone. "This is a small community and we all know each other. A friend of my dad's…"

She held the phone to her ear a moment and started

speaking suddenly: "Clem? You remember uncle Winny was talking to van Dreivers' secretary…" She nodded a few times, then said, "Did he book it?" Another pause and, "When for…? And he booked the whole day? …Only I have somebody who'd like to tag along… Oh, OK, thanks, pet. See you in a bit."

"'See you in a bit'?"

"It's a manner of speech. My uncle Winston has an estate a little to the east of here, about fifty thousand acres…"

"Fifty thousand acres? That's about the size of Brooklyn."

"I wouldn't know, but he keeps it as a game reserve and charges billionaires extortionate prices to let them go and hunt there. Normally he takes parties, but apparently President da Silva has booked the day for himself and his cronies. I was hoping to get you in as part of the party, but it seems he was emphatic. He wanted it exclusively for himself."

"Thanks for trying, Janine. Where is this reserve?"

She grinned and then started laughing quietly. "You're not going to, are you? This is Africa. You could get shot, your body would get eaten and nobody would ever know what happened to you."

"Of course not. When is it, tomorrow?"

She nodded.

"Tomorrow I was planning on going to visit Port Elizabeth."

"Right."

"So, where is it, for maybe some other day."

"I'll give you a map when we get back. You hunt?"

"Only for food."

"That happen a lot in Boston? You have to go and hunt for your food?"

"Sometimes, if it snows a lot."

"What's the motto...?" She closed her eyes. "Who dares wins, isn't that it?"

I looked at the black glass in the window, at our ghosts looking back in at us. "I don't know what you're talking about."

"The Special Air Service, the British special ops unit. Who Dares Wins."

"Yeah. That's the motto."

"You're a fucking psycho, aren't you." It was a statement, not a question, but she was smiling.

I shrugged. "I try not to be, but sometimes you have to be."

She signaled Greg and told him to bring over two more whiskeys. When he'd delivered them, she leaned her elbow on the table and touched my glass with hers. She took a swig and as she set down the glass, she said, "It's in the Bracken Hills, about ten miles northeast of here on the N2. It's mainly dense forest, steep hills and occasional savannah. There are no lions or anything of that sort, it's mainly gazelles. The big attraction is that you can go hunting with bows and arrows. People are really turned on by that."

"Primal."

"I guess."

"So does he provide the bows and the arrows or do you have to bring your own?"

"He has a whole selection, so you can rent one from him, or you can bring your own if you prefer." We looked at each other for a long moment. She was starting to smile. "Do you travel around with a bow in the boot of your car, Lacklan?"

I shook my head. "What kind of man would travel around with an arsenal in his trunk?"

"You're a dangerous son of a bitch, aren't you."

I nodded. "Yes."

She drained her whiskey. "Come on, let's go back to your cabin and I'll get you that map. We'll pick up a bottle of Bushmills on the way."

The rest of the evening seemed to take a course of its own and there was nothing much I could do, or wanted to do, to stop it. I knew it was a bad idea, I knew it couldn't lead anywhere good, but my hunger for human warmth, for a woman who was hot and alive and loving, a woman who could counter the black, enveloping images of death in my mind, was too strong to resist.

She stopped at reception for the map, collected a bottle of Bushmills from the bar and we walked arm in arm to my cabin. There I unlocked the door and she went in ahead of me. I closed it behind us and she didn't wait. She came to me, holding the bottle by the neck, and dropped the map on the floor. After that it was a fumbling, stumbling struggle against our clothes as we staggered across the living room to the bedroom. And once there, in the bed, I sank gratefully into warm oblivion, where the whole world, the whole universe, was her arms and her legs and her skin.

I rose at six and showered. When I stepped out of the shower, she was still asleep. I made coffee and toast and carried it out to the veranda, where I studied the map. All I could see was the boundaries of the reserve and the main gate, the highlands, to some extent, the forests and the areas of what she had called savannah. Nothing else was clear, and as for his plans, I had no way of knowing what those would be.

I left Janine a note thanking her for the evening and telling her I was going to Port Elizabeth for the day. Then I walked to the parking lot, got in my car and drove out, north and east, following the N2 along the coast, as though I was indeed going to Port Elizabeth. Just after Hornlee, about half an hour into the journey, the landscape began to change. It became more hilly, more green and fertile, and dense forests of tall, straight pines began to appear, thick and massive on either side of the road, swarming up into the hills.

Eventually I came to the tiny village of Bracken, and shortly after that to an intersection where two broad, dirt tracks led off to right and left. The one on the right had no signposts and gave no indication of where it led, but the one on the left had a large, wooden sign that read: 'Uncle Winny's Hunting Reserve,' and beneath it, 'Please report to the Lodge.'

I pulled over to the right, followed the road down for a hundred yards until I was secluded by the trees, killed the engine and settled to wait.

ELEVEN

It was a long wait. Morning became noon and then early afternoon, and it wasn't until one thirty PM that the small procession of four cars appeared, slowed at the entrance of the park and turned onto the long dirt track that wound its way through the thick pinewoods which sprawled up and over the hills.

I watched them and waited till they were out of view, then climbed out of the Audi and opened the trunk. From it, I took my rucksack with the orange osage takedown bow and six aluminum hunting arrows, three inserted into the canvas on each side. I waited till the road was empty, sprinted across, vaulted the fence and ran fast across the open ground for the cover of the trees. After that, it was an uphill run through trees and ferns that grew ever thicker and taller, and harder to negotiate. The canopy overhead blocked out the sky completely, the light turned a deep green and all the sounds, including the tread of my boots, acquired a muffled echo. The ferns, as high as five feet, were like a jungle within the forest and eventually the only directional guide I had was the incline of the hill.

Finally, I reached the top of the hill, dropped to the ground and took Janine's map and my compass from my rucksack. I found my bearing and set off at a steady run for another quarter of a mile. After fifteen or twenty minutes, the trees started to thin out and I began to see sunlight ahead. Then I slowed to a walk and pretty soon I could see a broad stretch of lawn surrounding a colonial style lodge with a broad, gravel parking lot out front, bordered by gardens of geraniums and tall palm trees. In the parking lot, there were four Land Rovers and the four cars I had seen pull in earlier, down at the intersection.

There was also a large group of men out front. A small knot stood at the double, plate-glass doors, talking. The guy doing most of the talking was white, wearing jeans and a pale linen jacket. On his head he had a broad-brimmed, flat-crowned, leather hat. He was talking mainly to a giant of a man dressed in camouflage. He was easily six-six or seven feet, his skin was a deep, almost purple black, his shoulders were massive and his legs were like tree trunks. He was laughing a lot and his voice was deep and resonant. It carried across the open space in snatches to where I was lying and listening, but I could not make out what he was saying.

With these two men were a couple of others, both black and dressed in suits. They wore sunglasses and didn't speak, but kept their eyes on the surrounding territory. These were his bodyguards.

Around this cluster of four were half a dozen men and women in Italian designer safari clothes. They were groupies, smoking long cigarettes and sipping from silver flasks. And circling around them were still more men, loading things into the Land Rovers: trestle tables, foldable chairs, cool boxes, a mobile barbeque and a couple of canisters of propane. There were also rifles and several bows of varying shapes and sizes, and boxes of arrows.

I gathered the guy in the hat and the linen jacket was Uncle Winny. He was doing a lot of pointing north and east. I checked the map and saw that what he was pointing to was an area about a mile away where Janine had said there were abundant herds of springbok. It was a clearing, savannah, about four square miles and roughly the shape of Texas, with a road winding its way to the lower, southwestern corner. Two got you twenty they would establish camp there, with their barbeque, and then go hunting their prey.

I looked at the group again. The guy in camouflage with the big voice was unmistakably George da Silva, and the rest of them were either his retinue, workers on the reserve or da Silva's servants.

I withdrew carefully back into the forest, circled the lodge until it was behind me and set off at a run again. A mile in these conditions would take me about twenty minutes, if the terrain did not get too rough and there were not too many steep hills in the way. Provided they kept talking and laughing, and swigging from their flasks, I might just get there at the same time they did, or even a little before.

As it turned out, it took me twenty-five minutes to get to the spot where the winding dirt road reached the clearing. They were not there yet, but my gut told me they would arrive imminently. I found a spot among the trees, camouflaged by a thick bed of ferns, set up my bow and settled to wait.

They arrived just fifteen minutes later, in a convoy of three Land Rovers. They came in off the dirt track, leaving a slow-drifting cloud of dust behind them, penetrated about a hundred yards into the clearing and pulled up in a semicircle. As the grind of the diesels died away, the doors opened and people started to spill out and unload the barbeque, the folding tables and chairs. Linen tablecloths were thrown over the tables and out of the cool boxes came bottles of champagne, while minions started stringing the bows and loading quivers with arrows.

Winny was there organizing and giving instructions. Da Silva was in evidence, like a black sun at the center of his solar system, laughing and shouting by turns, embracing the women in his cortège and pounding the men on the back as he strode around the campsite.

I was aware that my plan, as it stood, was limited: shoot George da Silva with an arrow. That was it. I had no strategy and no plan B. Above all, I had no extraction plan. The foundation of all the training I had received at the Regiment was plan, plan and plan; and when you're done planning, double-check your plan and every step of the way. But with an operation like the one Njal and I had undertaken, meticulous planning was not an option. You take the opportunities as they present themselves and you improvise your plans as you go along.

As things stood, the shot was not a difficult one. I could feather him twice before anybody knew what had happened. That would leave me four arrows and a Sig with a full extended magazine. A quick look at the company told me there were about two dozen people there. At least half were trained hunters and two of them, at least, were trained killers.

I took a moment to think it through, and while I was doing that, da Silva approached one of the tables where the champagne was standing in silver buckets of ice among stacks of plates. There was an attractive young woman there, and he grabbed her in a huge bear hug. She squealed with laughter and he grabbed her ass in his huge hands. He was about seventy or eighty paces from me and a sure kill at his size at that distance. I nocked an arrow, but hesitated a moment.

A small guy in a white waiter's jacket approached him with a silver tray holding glasses of champagne. Da Silva looked at him a moment, with one hand still gripping the girl's ass. Next thing, his left hand lashed out, knocking the tray flying. The glasses spiraled in the air, showering the three of them with foaming, golden liquid. The tray clanged to the ground. The waiter cowered. So did the girl. Da Silva kicked the cowering man to the ground, and as he scrambled to his feet, he started slapping him. I was thinking that a slap from da Silva must be like getting slapped by a blue whale.

The waiter covered his head with his arms and stumbled away from his attacker in a failing run. Da Silva went after him, screaming at him, bending over him, pounding on his head and back, kicking him in the ass and legs. Then I felt a hot jolt in my belly and my heart thudded. Da Silva was walking away from the cowering man toward one of the Land Rovers. He was still shouting and screaming, but he was holding out his hand, demanding something. Another one of his minions scrambled into the back of the truck and emerged with a bow and a quiver of shafts. The waiter started to scream and cover his head with his arms. Everybody else backed away from him.

I looked for Winny. He seemed to be paralyzed, transfixed, staring open mouthed at what was happening.

Now da Silva turned and descended on the poor guy again, pointing out at the vast clearing, shouting, "*Go! Go! Run like a fucking animal that you are! Run! Go!*"

The guy was on his knees, begging and sobbing. Da Silva kicked him, once in the chest and again in the ass. "*We are here to hunt! So go on! Let us hunt. Run, piggy! Run, run, run!*" He turned to the others, who were watching him, frozen. "*What are you waiting for? Get your bows!*" Then he went back to kicking the waiter. "*Run or we will skewer you here! Stupid animal! Run!*"

The man ran. Da Silva's cortege stirred and were suddenly flocking to the Land Rovers, collecting their bows and their quivers. The game was afoot, and the game was called staying in favor with Crazy. Crazy was now laughing and chasing his victim in circles around the camp, while the unfortunate servant stumbled and tried to kneel, beg and run all at the same time.

I felt disgust and rage well up in my gut. And from that disgust, an escape plan popped into my head. I pulled my Sig from my waist band and lined up the valve on the propane canister. You might think anything over twenty-five yards with a hand gun is ambitious, but in my book, any decent pro should be able to achieve a group of six inches at fifty to seventy yards with a good weapon.

I fired six rounds in rapid succession at the valve. Three hit home, shattered it and sent a stream of propane gas blasting up through the flames of the barbeque. The gas ignited in a violent explosion that sent the barbeque flying and everybody froze and turned to stare. Then they staggered back a few steps, shielding their faces from the soaring flames. By that time, I had put away the Sig, picked up the bow and drawn the string back to my ear.

Da Silva was motionless, gaping at the burning canister, trying to make sense of it. He was a vast target. I loosed the arrow, there was a small rattle of aluminum on wood, the feathers whispered in the air and the shaft thudded home deep into da Silva's chest. By that time, I had nocked and drawn a second arrow, lined up one of his bodyguards and loosed again. The shaft pierced the base of his throat and burst out the back of his neck, severing his vertebrae. By now, Da Silva had gotten slowly down on his knees, while his bodyguard crumpled beside him. Only now did people begin to look away from the roaring, flaming canister at the dying men.

His second bodyguard shouted suddenly and ran to his boss. He fell on his knees beside him, drawing his weapon and scanning the area around him, still struggling to understand what was happening. My third shaft punched through his skull, sliced cleanly through his brain and burst out the far side. Then I turned and ran.

At first I thought they were not following, but then I heard the roar of diesels and, behind me, the crackle and spatter of automatic fire showering the trees where I had been standing. Now I needed urgently to know how many were in pursuit.

I did some rapid mental arithmetic as I vaulted a fallen tree and scrambled down a slope into a gully, then began scrambling up the far side. His two bodyguards were down. That might leave as many as ten men in pursuit. Some would try to cut me off in the trucks, but if Winny was running a legit operation, they would not want him or his staff to witness a murder. Clearly that had not worried da Silva, but I was willing to bet his men would be more careful. So my guess was the bulk of them would be following through the forest. But the forest was not my only problem. Before I got to the road and my car, I had a broad expanse of open land to cross, and my pursuers were armed with assault rifles. Unless I could get rid of my pursuers before I reached that open land, I was in serious trouble.

Another deep gully ahead, with ferns growing thick and dense at the bottom. It was a risk—a big risk—but I was running out of options. I scrambled down into the ferns, then scrambled up the far side. When I'd gotten to the top, I ran nine or ten feet, then turned, ran back and leapt into the ferns. It was a blind jump and I was lucky not to land on a rock or a fallen tree. I lay flat on my belly in the soft dirt and backed up slowly along the gully. Then I nocked an arrow and waited.

They were just a minute behind me, six of them. I expected them to be fanned out, but they were in a cluster, following my tracks. At a glance, three of them looked like serious trackers and hunters; the other three were Armani hunters, over excited and out for the kill. They followed my tracks down the gully and up the other side. The hunters went up first, examining the tracks; the playboys followed, the least fit lagging behind.

When he was two thirds of the way up, and his pals were over the edge, I put a barb into the back of his neck. His body quivered, but he made no sound. He just lay on his belly, slid a few feet down the slope and went to Armani Heaven.

There were shouts. They had lost the trail and were fanning out, hoping to pick it up again. I slid farther back along the gully, staying cool, keeping movement to a minimum; fifteen paces would do it. Then I could turn around and move faster. As I moved, under the cover of the ferns, I heard the shouts above, with their dull echo under the high, green canopy. They hadn't noticed yet that they were one down. They were still searching for my tracks ahead of them.

I came to a fallen tree, slipped beneath it, stood, half-crouching, and ran up the slope, in among bushes and undergrowth. There I dropped and lay again. I could see two guys, maybe thirty feet away, moving slowly, scouring the carpet of brown pine needles and leaves. I had three arrows left. I had to make them count. I dropped quietly to one knee, drew and loosed: the small rattle of metal on wood, the lethal whisper, the soft thud as the shaft drove home. I'd skewered him through the neck. The broadhead had severed his jugular and his brain had bled out before he folded to the ground.

His pal turned to look at him, frowning. Then his expression turned to alarm as he scanned the undergrowth, but he was out of time, the arrow was already whispering toward him. He saw it too late. It split his sternum, sliced through his heart and he, like his pal, died silently, folding to the ground.

I nocked my last arrow and waited. Nothing happened, so I crawled out from the cover and dragged myself a few feet closer to the bodies, so I could see where they had come from. Fifty, sixty yards away, I could see a figure searching the ground. I heard a shout, but nothing much happened. I stepped over to the nearest of the fallen men and picked up his assault rifle. It was an AK-47.

Without running or making sudden movements, I stepped back into the undergrowth and slipped down into the gully again. While they searched south, I moved west until I was a hundred yards from the dirt track that led to the lodge. There I let off two bursts of automatic fire, dropped the rifle and ran, hell bent for leather, twenty paces toward the road. There I stopped and loped, taking broad, random, irregular steps for a hundred yards south, then turned again and ran crouching at a steady, silent pace, east for twenty minutes. After that, I finally turned south again and made my way to the N2.

My three remaining pursuers would still be scouring the woods on either side of the road, convinced I was lying low there somewhere. They probably didn't realize that the difference between hunting an animal and hunting a man is that a man can be unpredictable.

I took down the bow, put it back in my rucksack with the field glasses, climbed over the fence and walked quickly back to where I had concealed the Audi. I scanned the area, but there was nothing to be seen anywhere along the road, and I was beginning to think I would get away, back to Knysna, without too much trouble. Feeling almost optimistic, I arrived at the car, opened the trunk, threw in the rucksack and slammed it closed.

That was when I saw the Land Rover at the intersection, with the guy leaning out of the window, looking at me. He shouted, "Hi!"

I glanced at him, then ignored him and opened the door. The truck turned and came down the track. The door opened and one of the guys got out. The other stayed at the wheel. Blocking the road.

The guy who approached me was white, in his thirties, with the hard look of a man used to scrapping, and hurting people.

"How long you been here, mate?"

It was a good question. I said, "Maybe a couple of hours, why? Do you work for George da Silva?"

He frowned hard. It was the last answer he had expected from me. "Yuh," he said. "Who are you?"

"I'm the guy who killed him."

I pulled my Sig from my waistband, and while he was still trying to make sense of what I'd said, I blew his brains out the back of his head. His pal was shifting from neutral to first when I double-tapped through the windshield and tore his chest open. Then I climbed in the Audi and headed back toward Knysna, with the windows open and the wind in my face, telling myself it was almost over. Three down, two to go.

Pi and Ro, Ruud and his son Jelle.

Tonight. It would have to be tonight. Because within the next few hours, the whole place would be crawling with cops; cops and Omega operatives. It would be a miracle if I made it back to the construction site.

TWELVE

She arrived three minutes after I did, as I was undressing to climb in the shower. I heard the key in the front door, was reaching for my Sig and she stepped in and stood staring at me. I thought about smiling, but her face told me there was no point.

"What have you done with Prince Mohamed, and Ameya Dabir?"

"I don't know what you're talking about."

"The yacht was never returned. The coast guard found it drifting ten miles out at sea. The police have been here, asking questions."

I studied her face for a long moment. "What has that got to do with me?"

She crossed the floor and stood staring up into my face. "What have you done with them, Lacklan?"

I scowled. "You're being ridiculous. You're letting your imagination run away with you. I thought we'd got past this kind of nonsense last night."

"Don't patronize me!"

I shouted at her, with more feeling than I had intended. "I am not patronizing you! You're being ridiculous!"

Her voice became shrill. "Are you *serious?* You come here with your cock and bull stories and your fake accent! You start nosing around asking questions about van Dreiver and his party. You find out about bin Awad and Ameya Dabir going out on a yacht together and next thing, they disappear without a trace! And *I'm* being ridiculous?"

"For God's sake, Janine! Get a grip! You don't even know whether Ameya was on that yacht! You don't even know *he* was on the yacht! All you know is that he hired it for the day!"

"I *told* you the cops were here!"

I went quiet, studying her face, wondering how to handle the situation. Eventually, I said, "What did they say?"

"Why don't you tell me?"

"Please stop it, Janine! You're jumping to crazy conclusions based on practically nothing but your own assumptions. What did the cops want?"

Her face was taut with anger, but her voice had dropped in pitch. "They wanted to know if we had seen either Prince Mohamed bin Awad or Ameya Dabir in the last twenty-four hours, because Ruud van Dreiver had reported them as missing."

I sighed and shook my head. "Look, Janine, in the first place, you know as well as I do that those two are insane about each other and having an affair. They probably set up the yacht as a ruse and now they are off having a romantic couple of days together in Cape Town. Day after tomorrow, they'll turn up with shining eyes and everybody will put it down to their being in love." I pushed open the bathroom door and paused. "And in the second place, I told you last night, I have no interest in either of those two. The person I want to talk to is Ruudy."

"What about da Silva?"

I shook my head. "I didn't bother. I was hoping he could get me to van Dreiver, but the lodge was on lockdown and they wouldn't let me in. So I went and spent the day in Port Elizabeth. I have to tell you, you're sounding pretty crazy right now. You're blowing things right out of all proportion."

She turned and dropped into a chair. "You have to admit…"

I shook my head. "No, I don't. This isn't the movies. I'm not a murderer. I'm not even an assassin. I'm just trying to get close enough to van Dreiver to talk to him."

She buried her face in her hands and sighed noisily. I gave her a moment and asked, "Were there any signs of violence on the yacht?"

She shook her head. "I went to see it. The bed had been slept in—or *not* slept in—the sheets were tangled up and stained, and their clothes were all over the place. There was a bucket of ice with champagne in it, but there was no sign of them anywhere, no sign of violence, no blood… nothing."

I sat on the sofa. "Forensics going over it?"

"All I know is that the police have sealed it and are trying to decide whether to treat it as a crime scene. At the moment, there is no evidence that a crime has been committed."

I snorted. "Billionaire rich kids, brought up to believe that the world is their oyster and they can do what the hell they like. They want to get away alone so they can have their forbidden love affair, but they want to do it in the most narcissistic, attention-grabbing way they can."

"You're a cynic."

"I'm a realist. And you should sue them for any damage that was done to your boat."

"Yeah, that would be good for business."

I shrugged. "That's how they get away with the way they behave."

She sighed again. "Look, Lacklan, I just want to run my business. I don't need all this..."

I held up both hands. "OK, but I didn't do anything other than spend the day sightseeing in Port Elizabeth, and yesterday I went shopping in George. That is the extent of my culpability, so give me a break, Janine."

She nodded and spread her hands. "OK, you're right. I'm sorry. I overreacted."

I pointed at the bathroom. "I'm going to have a shower. Let me take you to dinner this evening. We'll have a nice time, we won't talk about van Dreiver or any of that shit. We'll talk about you and me and what sights you're going to take me to see tomorrow."

She smiled. "One of these days I have to get back to work, you know. People will start talking."

"Let them talk. By the way..." I pointed at my back. "I have a spot I just can't reach with the loofah. Do you think...?"

She started laughing and stood. She stepped toward me, reaching for my face with both her hands when her phone rang. A hot twist of anxiety burned in my belly. I said, "Don't answer it."

She made a face and shrugged. "I have a business to run, Lacklan." Before I could stop her, she had it to her ear. "Yeah... Hey, Winny, what's up?"

She was quiet for a long time. I sat in the armchair, looking at the floor, thinking, trying to map out a plan in my head. She sank slowly onto the sofa, staring at me, still listening to the phone. After a moment, her eyes narrowed. "Shot with a *bow?*"

After a while, she thanked him for letting her know and hung up. We sat for a while staring at each other. Finally, she said, "You're a murdering bastard. Give me one good reason why I shouldn't call the cops right now."

I snorted and raised my eyebrows. "Well, if I am a murdering bastard, that's one reason right there."

"Are you threatening me?"

"No, Janine, I am not threatening you. What did Winny tell you?"

"You know full damn well what he told me."

I nodded, stood and took the phone from her hands. She watched me then, go and lock the door from the inside and return to my seat.

"He told you that George da Silva had been shot with an arrow, that both his bodyguards were also killed, and that five of his men were killed while pursuing the assassin. He told you that the assassin got away and nobody got a look at him."

"So it was you."

"Did he tell you anything else?"

"Like what?"

"Like what happened just before da Silva was killed."

"What happened?"

I pulled my Sig from my waistband, found uncle Winny's number and handed her the phone. "Please bear in mind, Janine, that in the last twenty-four hours I have killed ten people, and one of them was a woman. Call him and ask him to tell you everything that happened just before da Silva was killed. If you try to raise the alarm, or if you call somebody else, I won't kill you, but I will shoot the phone out of your hands, and we will have a big problem. Understood?"

She stared at me for a long time, her eyes bright with rage. Then she nodded and after a moment pressed call.

"Uncle Winny, it's me, Janine. Listen, don't ask any questions, just tell me something. What happened immediately before da Silva was killed?"

I could hear the excited drone of his voice. I saw her eyebrows come together. Her eyes narrowed. "He did *what?*"

She listened for a long while. Then, eventually, she told him goodbye again and hung up. I gave her a moment before I spoke. "He was going to hunt him like an animal. They all were. He was kicking and beating him, chasing him around the camp, and you know why? Because he offered him champagne while he was grabbing a girl's ass. He beat him to the ground, kicked him, called him a pig and an animal, took a bow and ordered his entourage to take bows and they were going to hunt that man and kill him, for sport, because he offered da Silva champagne while he was grabbing a girl's ass. That is the kind of man he was. That is the kind of people they are."

"They? Who?"

"They are part of an organization, Janine, a club, a syndicate—call it what you like. My father was a member. I am not going to tell you anything about them. If they believe you know about them, they will kill you, but you have to believe me, Janine. These are very bad people. And the best thing you can do is forget all about me, about them, about this whole affair. You had fun for a couple of days with Mr. Richard Sinclair, and he went back to England, to whatever it was he did there. You do not want to get involved in this—and Janine? You *really* don't want van Dreiver's friends coming around asking you about Lacklan Walker."

She sat in silence for a long time, staring at me. Finally, she shook her head. "You can't just go through life murdering people because you disapprove of the things they do."

I gave my head a little sideways twist. "Would it help if I told you I worked for the TAIA?"

"The *what?*"

"The Trans-Atlantic Intelligence Agency."

"I've never heard of it."

"And you never will, but have you ever wondered if the English speaking nations like Canada, the U.S., the U.K., Australia, New Zealand and South Africa cooperate on special operations?"

"No."

"Well, they do."

"So these murders were authorized?"

"Would that make you feel better?"

She thought about it and after a moment sighed and stood. "I need to get back to work."

"What are you going to do?"

"Nothing. I am going to get on with running my business. I don't want anything to do with you or your filthy operation. I want you out of my resort by tomorrow."

"I'll be gone tonight."

She moved to the door and stopped. "Are you going to go after Ruud and Jelle?"

I shook my head. "They were never the target."

"You're going—leaving?"

"I'll be gone tonight, Janine, I told you." I paused. "But, Janine? If you call anyone, I will know. Don't get involved. These are not people you should be protecting."

I threw her the keys. She caught them and unlocked the door, then paused before stepping out. "Go back to America, Lacklan. I never want to see you again. You disgust me. You all do, all of you. Just leave."

She closed the door and I watched her through the window, walking away down the path.

I had no time to feel regret. I got dressed, packed my stuff and returned to the Audi in the parking lot, where I stowed it in the trunk. I pushed into reception. Janine was not there. I paid my bill and left.

I drove fast up through the winding, wooded roads of Knysna and turned west onto the N2. I followed it, closing on a hundred MPH as far as the turn off for the village of Goukamma. There I slowed, making the tires complain, and turned down the dirt track toward the small cluster of multicolored houses where I had rented the boat the day before.

I found my friend sitting on the small, wooden stoop of a pink, wooden house and walked over to him. The sun was setting in the west and its light looked burnished on the waves, on the sand and on the pink walls of the building. Gulls were crying out over the sea, and a sudden chill touched the air.

I stopped in front of him, offered him a cigarette and he

took it without saying anything. I sat next to him on the step, poked a Camel in my mouth and we both lit up with my old, battered, brass Zippo. I inhaled deep and released the smoke through my nose. "I need a place to leave my car till I can collect it, later tonight."

He grinned and nodded a few times. "You can leave it back of my house. We can put some big fishing nets over it. Nobody will see it."

I flicked ash and asked him, "You ever go fishing at night?"

He laughed, showing all his tombstones. "Why do I want to go fishing at night, when I can be in bed with my wife?"

I smiled. "That's a good question. Maybe the fish you catch at night could be worth more money than the ones you catch by day."

"How much more?"

We talked a while longer, then I went and smeared mud and dust over the plates of the Audi and tucked it in close behind my friend's wooden house. After that, we draped folded fishing nets over it, piled whatever junk we could find on top of them, and by the time we were done, night was closing in and it was pretty much invisible.

Then I handed him five hundred bucks, which was about seven thousand Rand, and told him, "I just need one more thing from you."

"Man, you have a very complicated life. What you want now?"

"I need a shave, and a ride into Knysna."

"You just come from Knysna."

"Yeah. I need to go back."

He sighed, shook his head and led me to a shack beside where we had concealed my car. He hauled open the door and inside, he had a beaten up, old Toyota truck sitting among huge fishing nets hung from the ceiling. "I get you a razor and some water. Where you want to go in Knysna?"

Half an hour later, he dropped me just outside the town, near the Premier Hotel, and a stone's throw from the beach. I walked quickly, with my collar up, and slipped in, down the winding footpaths through the Dylan Thomas Resort. By that time of the evening, most of the villas and cabins were empty because the residents were either out for the night or at the restaurant. Even so, I stayed in among the shadows cast by the tall pines, and found my way down to the beach. The moon was not up yet and it was very dark. The only light was from the stars, and the glimmering streetlamps and windows, barely visible through the trees. It was silent too, apart from the sigh and wash of the small waves.

I crossed the cool sand and, after a couple of minutes with my Swiss Army knife, opened the padlock on Janine's swimming gear shed. I slipped in, grabbed a couple of full air bottles, a mask and some flippers, and stripped down to my bathing shorts.

Then I double-bagged my clothes and boots in plastic and tied the bag to my weights belt. Two minutes later I was sinking silently into the dark water, moving out to the deep channel that would lead me, without being seen, to Ruud van Dreiver's pier on the far side of the lagoon.

Swimming at night, without lights, is a surreal experience. You are enveloped and enclosed by wet darkness, all you can hear is the sound of your own breathing in your ears, and your only sense of direction is from the luminous compass on your wrist, which tells you to swim on, into the blind liquid blackness.

Time passed with no sense of progress or movement, other than the wash of liquid over my skin, and the gentle, occasional thud of my bag of clothes against my leg.

After fifteen minutes, I rose slowly to the surface and looked around. It was good to feel the cool air on my face. Less than a hundred yards away, I could see the faintly luminous foam of the waves breaking gently against the shore, at the foot of the black mass of the headland where van Dreiver had his mansion. Another minute and I could see the dark bulk of the landing jetty where two launches were moored, creaking and thudding softly in the swell coming in from the mouth of the lagoon.

I swam in close, took a hold of the sodden, slightly slimy wood, and hauled myself up onto the pier. There I slipped off the swimming gear and hid it in the stern of one of the launches. I dried myself off with my shirt, dressed, slipped my Sig in my waistband and started to make my way along the pier to dry land.

Then I froze and shrank down to the wooden boards. There was a shadow moving at the base of the cliff ahead. I lay on my belly, slipped my piece from my belt and held it in both hands, waiting. A flashlight came on and started to sweep the pier. I didn't hesitate. I double tapped an inch above the light. I heard a soft, "Oh, God..." and the light dropped to the ground. I pushed up and sprinted to where the guy had fallen.

There was a broad gravel esplanade which looked like a makeshift parking lot, and to the left a broad track that seemed to wind its way up toward the house. In the middle of the esplanade there was the dark bulk of a human body, and a couple of feet from it a flashlight illuminating the form, casting a long, inky shadow behind it. Beside the body, still clutched in his hand, was an AK-47. I kept my Sig trained on the fallen man, knelt with one knee on his back and felt for a pulse in his neck. He was dead. I rolled him over and saw he had a radio in his pocket with the microphone clipped to his lapel.

I switched off his flashlight, shouldered the assault rifle and moved into the shadow of the cliff. I listened for a good two minutes. There was no sound. That meant that security was going to be concentrated around the house. This guy had been detailed to watch the jetty and call in any unusual activity. I hadn't heard the crackle of his radio, so there was a chance they didn't know I was coming.

I moved to the start of the track, where it curved around and started to climb toward the mansion, keeping to the undergrowth by the side of the road. I climbed for about a minute without seeing anything, then, as the road started to level out, I saw why. As I had suspected, he had concentrated all his security around the house.

The top of the headland was largely flat. The path I had been following curved onto a large esplanade and then snaked right and opened out into a broad driveway at the front of the house: a large, colonial, Georgian mansion with a colonnade at the front, and broad steps leading up to the door. To the right, surrounded by pines and cypresses, there was a lawn with a swimming pool, and at the back I could make out what looked like a couple of tennis courts. Everywhere there were trees, evergreen hedges and rose gardens.

The front steps and portico, the pool, and the tennis

courts at the back were all illuminated with spotlights, and in the glow of those lights I could see two armed guards on the front door, two guards patrolling the side of the house, and a patrol of five guys making the rounds of the pool and the gardens. I figured there would be a very similar set up at the back of the house and on the far side. I was looking at eighteen to twenty guys before I even got inside. Putting it bluntly, I was as screwed as a two dollar whore during shore leave.

THIRTEEN

When you are badly outnumbered by your enemy, you have two options: retreat to a stronger position, or kill your enemy to even up the numbers.

I wasn't about to retreat.

I dropped and crawled, inching my way along the side of the path into the cover of some evergreen bushes. Ahead of me, about thirty feet away, I had a hedge. Beyond that laid the pool, set among lawns and trees, and ahead and to the left I had the driveway and the house, maybe three times that distance. Along the near wall of the house, on the ground floor, I could see two large sets of French windows, with light filtering out onto the lawn.

I remained motionless for an hour, observing the movements of the guards and the patrols. The guards at the front by the door remained stationary, the guards at the side of the house paced back and forth, sometimes facing each other, sometimes with their backs to each other, while the patrol made the rounds of the drive at the front of the house, the pool area and the tennis courts at the back, then started the return journey. Each round trip took them a little more than twenty minutes.

I watched them leave the third time and crouch-ran to the hedge. It was no more than four feet high and I vaulted it easily and landed silently in the shadows, then belly-crawled around the edge until I was level with the nearest guard by the side of the house.

In their pacing back and forth, there was a period of about twenty to twenty-five seconds, as they paced away from each other toward the corners of the house, when the guards had their backs to each other. What I was going to attempt was practically suicidal, but I had no other option, and I was pretty much resigned by then to not making it back from this operation.

I crawled to the gap in the fence where the gate to the pool stood, and waited for the guards to meet at the middle point of the wall. They turned their backs to each other and then began their return journey to the corners. When they were about six paces apart, I stood, vaulted the gate and sprinted silently toward the guard on my left. I slipped my hand over his mouth and rammed the knife in through the side of his neck, cutting into his jugular vein and his carotid artery, and slicing out through his windpipe. I didn't bother to lower him carefully to the ground. Instead I dropped him, turned and threw the knife. The other guard was turning to see what the bustle was and the blade thudded home through his sternum.

I now had about fifteen minutes to work with. I recovered my knife and ran to the lighted window near the back of the house. I flattened myself against the wall and peered in. It was a drawing room. There was a fire burning in a large, marble fireplace. There were antique sofas and a couple of antique armchairs drawn up around the fire. Sitting in them, I could see three men and a woman seated, drinking and talking. I recognized two of the men as Ruud and Jelle, but I had no idea who the other man and the woman were.

Suddenly, in that moment, for no reason I could identify, I became intensely and violently aware that I had no time to waste. I was up against maybe thirty men armed with assault rifles and there was no way I was going to pull this off. It was up to Njal to destroy the reactor, alone. And it was up to me to deliver what might be Omega's final death blow, even if it meant that I died doing it.

I stepped out of the shadows and put two 9mm rounds through the latch on the French windows. Then I smashed my foot into it and stepped into the room. I looked left and right. There was nobody else in the room. Ruud and his son were on their feet, shouting. The woman had jumped up and was screaming. The third guy was watching me curiously. I ignored him and took aim at Ruud, but before I could squeeze the trigger, behind him, the doors burst open and two guys in suits burst in.

I fired over Ruud's shoulder; two double taps and the guards went down. By that time Ruud, his son and the two guests were running for the door, still shouting and screaming. I should have sprayed them with the AK-47 and mowed them down. I took the weapon and aimed it. But I couldn't bring myself to pull the trigger. The man and the woman were not Omega, and I would not murder them. I cursed violently and went in pursuit.

I burst through the door into a large hallway with white marble floors and an elegant staircase curling up to the next floor. Four men in suits were descending on the fleeing bodies, shouting instructions. Two of them grabbed van Dreiver and his huddled, fleeing group, and the other two came at me, pointing their weapons. Hot lead spat past my head and smacked into the wall. I dropped to the floor, squeezing the trigger. Plaster showered around me, spattering on the tiles. My first slug tore through the nearest guy's grey cotton trousers, ripped into his thigh and sent a plume of blood showering out the other side. The second hit him in the groin, doubling him over and sending him writhing and thrashing to the floor.

I slid onto my belly, still squeezing the trigger, and put two rounds through the next guy's shin bone. His leg collapsed and folded and he went down screaming. I was already on my feet and putting a slug in the back of his head as he hit the floor. I ran up the stairs. Two shots hit the banisters and I saw the small group disappear along the landing. Behind me, I could hear shouts as men came storming in through the shattered French windows into the drawing room.

I stopped, swung the AK-47 off my shoulder, aimed at the drawing room door and counted three as I heard the shouting voices and the tramping boots growing louder. The door burst open and I opened up in three short bursts, putting twelve rounds through the door. I heard screams of pain, shouldered the rifle and ran to the landing. Rage and frustration were beginning to mount in me and I fought to control them. Van Dreiver and his son were getting away, and there were too many men on my tail. I couldn't focus and I couldn't concentrate.

I had seen the group go down a passage on the right and I made after them. As I rounded the corner, a door closed at the end of a red-carpeted corridor. I sprinted. I could hear voices behind me again and tried to make an estimate of how many men I had taken down. I figured ten or twelve all told. Which still left something in the region of twenty men chasing me, determined to kill me.

I didn't pause or hesitate. I blasted the lock, kicked open the door and spun away as a shower of lead smashed into the wall behind where I'd been standing. I dropped on my belly, leaned in and popped one of the bodyguards through the eye and the other through the throat. Then I was on my feet and through the door.

Ruud was up against the far wall, punching frantically at a keypad on the wall. I knew it was the door to a panic room. Beside him, Jelle and the woman were screaming at him to hurry up. I shot him through the hand and shattered the keypad, then shot him in the back of the knee for good measure. He went down clutching at his leg and whimpering, "No, oh God no…"

Outside I could hear boots—lots of boots—storming down the corridor. That was a bad mistake they'd made. Jelle and the woman were gaping at me. The other guy was frowning curiously. I ignored them, stuck the Sig in my belt, swung the AK-47 off my shoulder and stepped into the corridor. I knew I was going to die and I didn't care. A kind of madness had gripped my mind and I was aware that nothing mattered anymore. This was my hell and I planned to leave it in flames.

There were fifteen, maybe twenty men. I didn't count them. They were all tightly grouped and storming down the narrow corridor. Only the front two or three could open fire because the rest risked shooting the guys in front. I remember thinking that was how Napoleon had lost against Wellington. I aimed at waist height and sprayed. It was carnage. The bullets tore through flesh and bone, erupted through chest cavities, tore through bellies and guts, ricocheted off walls, punched through limbs and skulls like a giant mincer tearing through body and limb, spraying the walls with blood and gore. It was a basic lesson in military strategy that these men had learned too late and to their cost: never charge in a column into a confined killing field.

A more basic lesson was the one I overlooked: never turn your back on somebody who wants to kill you.

There was a scream, not of terror and pain, but of rage, and a brick wall collided with me, sending me crashing to the carpeted floor, knocking the wind from my lungs. I tried to lever myself to my feet, but a heavy body pressed down on me and locked its arm around my throat, choking off my air. I clawed at his arm but found only the linen of Jelle's jacket sleeve. I clawed at his face and head, but he shied away and kept squeezing. I couldn't breathe and the pressure of blood was building up in my head.

I heaved my body sideways and crashed him against the wall. His grip was like a vise and kept tightening. I bent my leg, drew my knee up to my chest and wrenched the knife from my boot. Then slamming it into his thigh by my side, I stabbed ferociously six, seven times, heard him screaming in my ear, felt the warm blood spouting over my hand, but still he would not let go.

Finally, I grabbed his wrist and thrust the blade of the Fairbairn & Sykes into the soft underside, slicing through arteries and tendons. His arm jumped and quivered and I staggered to my feet, croaking and coughing, gasping for air, as Jelle quivered and thrashed, bleeding out on the floor.

I staggered into the room, feeling the blood dripping from my hands and face. The woman was goggling at me, her mouth hanging open. The man, in his early thirties, stood looking down at Ruud van Dreiver. As I entered, he looked up, studying my face with a frown. I roared at them both, *"Get the hell out of here!"*

They didn't need to be told twice. He took her hand and they left, hurrying down the corridor, past the blood and carnage, and down the stairs. I turned Ruud on his back and scowled down into his face.

"Why did you send your men after me?"

His big, blond face twisted with rage and hatred. "You have to be stopped! You are a disease, a cancer! You are insane. You are destroying everything we have worked for, the work of decades. All you do is kill, kill, kill and destroy…!"

He sagged back. The blood was pooling under his leg. He was bleeding to death.

"I had stopped. Mexico was my last job. You shouldn't have come after me."

"You will never stop, until you are dead. But we must rise up again. Humanity, our survival, depends on it. You…" His face was distorted by hatred and contempt. "You will be the butcher of humanity. You will be the killer of mankind. If humanity is to survive, you must die."

"You're out of your mind!"

He pushed himself up on one elbow and screamed in my face. "*You have to die!*"

I stood and backed away from him. "You would wipe out eight billion people..."

"No! You fucking idiot! The plague must die! It is nature's way! We let the plague take its course. We are trying to salvage what little of worth the species has created! But you, you *fucking human animal!* You keep killing and destroying and murdering..."

I dropped on my knees beside him and grabbed him by the scruff of the neck. "Tell me! Ben, Ben Smith, is he alive?"

He sneered. "Your brother."

"I killed him."

"Then why are you asking if he is alive, you stupid fuck?"

"*Is he alive?*"

"Fuck you!"

I knew I was running out of time. Tried to focus on what Jim would need to know. "All right, Ruud, you get to choose. We can make this easy or we can make it hard. The fusion reactor, when is it due to go online?"

His face hardened. "How do you know about that?"

"Last chance. When is it due to go online?"

"In a year to eighteen months. How do you know about it?"

He had turned a pasty gray and his pupils were dilating wide. He had a minute at most.

"What's the plan? How do you plan to replace other sources of power? Is this a concerted plan? What about China? What about oil, coal, nuclear reactors...?"

He smiled, then laughed. "You know shit. You're too

late. We will win, Walker. You can't stop us. Humanity will survive and you can't stop…"

His eyes glazed, his throat rasped and he lay still.

I stepped out of the room, feeling strangely defeated, and walked down the passage. I picked my way through the half-dismembered bodies and went down the curving, marble staircase. I crossed the marble hall and went out the front door, into the night. There I stopped. From the front steps, I could see four sets of lights moving fast across the lagoon toward the headland. Cops? Omega? Both?

I forced myself to move and ran at a steady jog down the path, feeling my heart pounding and the start of a grinding headache above my left eye. I made it down to the jetty in less than a minute, but my breathing was labored and I had a sense of tight panic in my chest that I was fighting hard to suppress. I looked out across the black water. The approaching lights were about halfway and moving fast. I wondered how much control Omega had over the cops in the area, and as the question entered my mind, I heard a twin engine plane overhead and looked up. It flew low over the house and descended across the lagoon. I could see the floats underneath the wings. It was a King Air 350 seaplane.

It banked and circled, descending all the while, then hit the water away near the resort. The launches were closing in.

I threw the AK-47 in the water and slipped the Sig into my waistband. I hung my boots around my neck, pulled on the flippers, the mask and the air tanks, and fastened the weight belt around my waist. Then I slipped into the water and sank gratefully beneath the surface as the launches started to arrive. I swam deep and made for the inlet to the lagoon, where the waves were thundering and crashing over the reefs. It was slow and difficult to negotiate the inlet, but the cold water was soothing and helped to calm the panic I was feeling inside.

Once out of the mouth of the lagoon, I swam for forty or forty-five minutes, south into the ocean. Eventually, I surfaced to look around and saw the dim, glimmering light of a lantern and headed toward it. It was a small fishing lantern, hung over the bow of my friend's fishing boat. The boat was at anchor, but he was not in it. This was something he did not need to be a part of. He had made his own arrangements to return to his village, as I had told him, but he had left his boat for me, as a small beacon, a way home from the dark ocean of the night.

I slung the air bottles over the side and clambered aboard. Then I killed the lantern and noticed for the first time that there was half a moon rising in the east. I searched the boat and, in the dark, I found that he had left me a blanket, some dry clothes and a package with hot soup, rice and fish in it. There was also a bottle of whiskey. I ignored the food, but drank the soup and followed it up with a few stiff shots, then made my way under sail, back to Goukamma.

By the time I got there, it was past two in the morning. I pulled the boat up on the sand as far as I could, left no trace of my presence, and carried my stuff silently to the back of his house. There I removed the nets from the Audi, put my stuff in the trunk and climbed behind the wheel.

A wave of deep exhaustion washed over me. I was having trouble adjusting to the fact that I was alive. I took another shot of whiskey and put the bottle in the glove compartment, then I opened the windows, fired up the engine and rolled slowly down the track, toward the N2.

At the intersection, I stopped and was gripped by a fit of hysterical laughter, leaning my head on the steering wheel, which threatened to turn to convulsive weeping. I had another slug of whiskey and steadied myself, then found a pack of Camels in the glove compartment and lit up. After a couple of drags, I turned west, toward the Boland Mountains, Cape Town and the Northern Cape. It was going to be a very long night, and tomorrow was going to be a long, exhausting day.

I drove for an hour, letting the cold night air batter my face. I kept thinking about the seaplane, wondering who was in it and why they had flown in. It was too much coincidence that it had arrived at the same time as the cops were closing in, just after I had killed Pi and Ro. But who had called them? My gut told me beyond a doubt the occupant of the plane was Omega. It was the only thing that made sense of the timing. But who in Omega, if I had killed them all?

As I left the N2 at Swellendam and started to climb into the Boland Mountains, toward Worcester, I pulled out my cell and called Njal.

"Fuck me," he said without feeling. "You still alive."

It was good to hear his blunt, Norwegian voice. I said, "I'm as surprised as you are. It's done. I'm on my way back. Expect me in ten or twelve hours, maybe a little more if I sleep. Anything to report?"

"Yeah. I got mail from home. I tell you when you get here."

"Everything cool?"

"Everything cool."

I hung up and sped on into the blackness of the mountains.

FOURTEEN

I stopped after three hundred and sixty miles, when I realized I had been asleep at the wheel and didn't know for how long. I pulled into a Wimpy fast food diner at a village called Klawer, in the middle of the desert. It was three o'clock in the morning, but the place was still open. I had a pint of coffee which I laced with whiskey, and ate two burgers. Then I went out to the parking lot and slept for four hours before driving on.

I arrived at our site at just after eleven AM, leaving behind me a conspicuous trail of dust lingering in the still air. There was nothing I could do about that, except hope that nobody noticed it and conceal the Audi beside the Land Rover under the overhanging rocks. Njal clapped me on the shoulder as I climbed out of the car, gripped my hand and told me I looked like shit. Then he pointed at the vehicle. "Cops are looking for this pile of German shit?"

"Yeah, but they're looking for it in the Western Cape, not on the border of the Namibian desert."

He nodded once. "I make some coffee."

I followed him past the Land Rover into a hollow where he had made a comfortable camp. He'd even acquired some bacon, eggs and bread, which he had set out ready to cook. "Where the hell did you get these from?"

"In the supermarket, where the fuck do you think?"

We both laughed and he poured me a mug of coffee and laced it with more whiskey. Then he fried some bacon, eggs and bread. We ate in silence, and when I had finished, he debriefed me. It was a relief to talk about what had happened and explain it to somebody who was simply collating the facts, not judging my actions and my decisions. When I had finished, he said, "It was a risk to give Janine your real name."

"I know, but I was on the clock, Njal, and she was my only source of intel. Anything else would have taken time I didn't have. I had to gain her trust and the only way I could do that was by opening up."

"You might have had to kill her."

"It paid off."

He nodded. "What are we gonna do with the fuckin' Audi?"

"There must be a mechanic in Steinkopf. We buy a dozen cans of paint. We change the plates, paint the car and it might just get us as far as Morocco. Morocco—hell! With a bit of luck, it could get us to London."

He grunted. "We got time to paint a car and steal plates?"

"I don't know. You tell me. What did Jim say? Also, we don't need to steal plates, we just take them from the Land Rover."

He nodded again. "OK. Jim had the plans for the reactor analyzed. It is big, real big. It is like four city blocks at the base, as tall as a skyscraper." He shrugged. "It's a small city in one building. We're not gonna bring that down with thirty pounds of C4."

"We knew that day one. So we need to place special demolition charges at key locations…"

He was shaking his head. "Stop talking. Listen. That is not what instructions we got. Underneath, there is like an inverted pyramid, OK? So you got one pyramid sitting on top of another upside-down pyramid in the ground. You can visualize that?"

"Yeah, I can visualize that."

"Good, so, then in the center, you got a big chamber shaped like a ball. They are just beginning to build that now, so it looks like a circle. That's the big ring we saw, right? In that ball is where the reactor is gonna be."

"OK…"

"All around that ball you got passages—a whole network of passages goin' this way and that way, up and down…"

"I get the idea."

"And then right at the bottom, at the lowest peak…"

"The lowest peak?"

"You know what I mean, man. The point of the upside-down pyramid, right there, there is a chamber, twenty foot across, and the whole fuckin' weight of the whole fuckin' structure is resting on that one point."

I frowned. "It also has the whole planet supporting it. That chamber is going to be about eight or nine hundred feet underground."

"Sure, but the structure, all the floors above, the pillars and columns, and especially the spherical structure that will hold the reactor, all of that is putting downward pressure on the walls of the building, and all of that pressure is meeting in that chamber. Don't argue with the experts, man. These guys know their stuff. So that is where we put the bomb."

I shook my head. "That had better be one hell of a bomb."

"It is. It has a yield of one point five, maybe two kilotons."

"*What?* That's…"

"I know. And he ain't gonna parachute it in, either. We have to go get it."

"How the hell are we going to transport a thing like that? How the hell are we going to get it *in there?* Has he gone out of his mind?"

"Take it easy. It's not that heavy. Maybe fifty kilos, one hundred and ten pounds…"

I went cold all over and I felt the hair on my arms and head prickle. "It's not that heavy…? One hundred and ten pounds…?"

That could only mean one thing. He shook his head. "No, it's not so heavy. It's in a backpack. We have to go collect it."

"It's a tactical demolition nuclear device. It's the only thing capable of releasing that much energy that you could carry in a backpack."

"Yeah, that's what it is."

"Where the hell did he get something like that from?"

"That doesn't concern us…"

"Bullshit!"

"We have to deploy it, Lacklan. Omega cannot be allowed to build this thing."

"Where did he get it?"

"I don't know. I think Russia. We are meeting the delivery guys in Springbok."

I leaned forward and pointed at him. "With a yield of two kilotons, that bomb will flatten everything in a radius of two miles. The blast damage and radiation will go well beyond that. It will wipe out the town of Goodhouse and probably kill the inhabitants of Steinkopf into the bargain!"

"You're not thinking."

"I am thinking, goddammit! I'm thinking about the men, women and children who will be killed by this device!"

He held up a hand, then closed his fist but for one finger. "One, the plateau between the mountains where the reactor is being built is the size of the blast radius, so it will be contained by the mountains. Goodhouse is on the other side of the mountains…"

"That's bullshit! What about the contamination to the River Orange?"

"Let me finish, and focus on what I am telling you, Lacklan. Second, and to answer your question about the river, the blast is gonna be *eight or nine hundred feet below ground level*, in a bunker designed to *contain* the heat of a fusion reactor. The whole fuckin' building is gonna collapse down on that bomb and seal in the radiation."

I closed my eyes and shook my head. "Sweet Jesus!"

"We got to do it, Lacklan! If you are worried about poison and damage, just imagine a world where Omega owns and controls the only source of energy for the whole fuckin' planet."

"We're talking about a damned atom bomb, Njal! How close do we need to get to the enemy before we become him?"

"I don't do philosophy, Lacklan. Omega's godda be stopped, and I'm going to stop them."

"The end justifies the means?"

"Dude, you sit here and ask existential questions. Meanwhile, I'll go and stop Omega."

"Listen, pal, I just came back from murdering ten men and a woman in the name of this cause...!"

"You gonna do it or not, Lacklan? Discuss your conscience with Jim, or your fuckin' therapist. I ain't cut out for philosophizing. You think it's wrong, don't do it. I respect that. But you gotta have the brains to see there is no other way to stop these bastards from building a fuckin' fusion reactor. You gonna let them do that, or you gonna stop them?"

I sighed and rubbed my face with my hands. "You're right."

"You said yourself, dude, the only thing with that much power that we can transport quickly is the suitcase bomb. So that's what we gotta use."

I wanted to ask where it would end, how far we had to go to stop the enemy before we became that enemy. Instead, I said, "All right. Where do we pick it up?"

"Springbok, at the El Dago Restaurant."

I stared at him. "The *what?*"

"What can I tell you? This is South Africa."

"Who are our contacts?"

"Two Russian backpackers. We get into conversation with them, offer them a ride to the airport. They catch their flight and leave us with the backpack."

"Russians. Russian Mafia."

"I don't know, man, but it ain't the kind of thing you can go shopping for and say, 'oh, I'm not gonna buy my atom bomb from the Russians because their packaging kills polar bears,' you know what I'm saying?"

"Back off, Njal."

"So gimme a break with the moral angst, will you? You think I enjoy this shit? It's tough, but we gotta do it."

"When do they arrive?"

"Tomorrow, lunch time. We be there at one."

"So how do we get the damned thing into the building site?"

He shrugged. "I have some ideas, but I was chilling, taking some sun, you know, waiting for you to get back. You the soldier, right? I'm just the fuckin' Norwegian bastard." He grinned.

I sighed. "OK, you fucking Norwegian bastard, you made your point. Now pay attention and learn. This is Introducing Nuclear Devices into Fusion Reactors, one-oh-one."

"We gonna use the thirty pounds of C4, the RPGs and those TEA rockets, right?"

"You know it. We go in tomorrow night. We take the Land Rover and we approach around the rocks along the river. We take the device, the C4, grenades, rockets—the whole lot, plus two gallons of gasoline. We leave the device at the foot of the western face of the rocks above Goodhouse, then we take fifteen pounds of C4 each and the gas, we mine the site office and the buildings surrounding it and we strategically position the gasoline. We use cell phone activated remote detonators.

"Now, here is the smart bit. Before we detonate them, we detonate one small charge on the southeastern side of the fence, enough to blow a hole in it. Ten seconds later, we detonate the rest. All hell breaks loose along the eastern side of the site, the buildings start burning and we sprint like hell for the hole in the fence. That gets us into the site. From there on in, it's up to you to get us to the chamber. You have a map?"

He nodded. "On my cell. But it is simple. There are two high-speed elevators. We plant the bomb in the chamber and then we need to get out."

"OK, so we when we arrive, we plant a charge at thirty yards from where we leave the Land Rovers. When we're leaving, we blow a hole in the fence and that's how we get out."

"OK, cool. Now tell me why you want to go in on the southeastern side."

I nodded. "Because it's the most direct route to the entrance to the building, and it's close to where we'll be setting the charges to start the fire, so we don't have to waste a lot of time running back and forth."

"OK. Makes sense."

"So, this afternoon we buy the paint for the Audi and we change the plates. After we plant the device, we get the hell out of here, take the Land Rover to where we have left the Audi, and head for the border with Namibia."

"OK, it's a plan. Now you need to sleep. I'll call you in two hours and we go into Steinkopf to get the paint. We also need sticking tape and paper, or plastic sacks, to cover the windshield and the chrome."

I nodded, then smiled. "OK, Njal. Tomorrow night we'll be on our way home."

He smiled, but I could see that his eyes were worried. "You gonna hold it together till then?"

"Don't be stupid. You know I will."

"Sure."

I SLEPT like the dead for two hours. At two fifteen PM, Njal woke me and we drove into Steinkopf. There we found the only mechanic in town. Attached to his workshop was a kind of glorified hardware store-cum-car parts shop. The owner watched us with steady, curious eyes as we bought all the stuff we needed, including the large refuse sacks, rolls of masking tape and two dozen cans of white spray paint. It was the kind of attention we didn't need, but there was nothing we could do about it. All we could hope for was that nobody would come asking questions, at least until after we were across the border.

When we were done, we drove back, taking a different route across the desert toward the rocks, to avoid leaving too many fresh tracks in the same place. When we got back, we spent the rest of the afternoon masking the windshield and the chrome and spraying the car into a nondescript color that, with a bit of luck, nobody would notice.

After a couple of hours or three, when it was done, I told Njal, "We drive as far as Angola, then we decide."

"Decide what?"

"It's about five thousand miles from here to Morocco. Do we drive? Or do we risk getting a flight? Or is there another option?"

"I agree, we decide that tomorrow or the day after. But first we call Jim, maybe he can arrange an extraction."

"I have a contact in Cameroon if we need it, but that's still six hundred miles from the north of Angola, and well over a thousand from Namibia—and a good two thousand miles from where we are now." I sighed and shook my head. "We need to be aware, Njal. This isn't like the operations we did in Europe and South America, or even back home in L.A. There we crippled them financially. We broke them and they couldn't come back at us. But that's not what we're doing here. We've cut off the head, and we are destroying their reactor, but their corporate infrastructure and their finances remain intact. The body is capable of growing another head. Somebody will take over, and there will be people hunting for us. Not only that, Africa is their stamping ground and they will know how and where to look."

I stared at him while he poked a cigarette in his mouth and lit up, then threw me the pack. I caught it and said, "They'll deduce where we crossed. They'll check what vehicles went over during the relevant hours. They'll narrow it down to a handful of cars, one of them will be the Audi, and they will go after those cars systematically until they find us."

He took a long drag and spoke as the smoke emanated from his mouth. "So we get to Namibia. We abandon the car in the desert, we go to ground and we call Jim on the number he gave us."

I shook my head. "Jim is powerful, but there is a limit to what he can do. He can't send in an army to get us."

He snorted. "He can get hold of a tactical nuclear device!"

"Which he bought from Russian contacts. He pays and they deliver. The Russians have resources for that. It's not the same as organizing an extraction from a foreign country. You need some kind of local infrastructure for that."

"So, what?"

I thought about it. "We take the plates from the other Land Rover too. It's still parked up in Springbok. We buy more spray paint. As soon as we're over the border, we drive into the desert and find a place to lie up. Then we change the plates again and repaint the car. We bury the old plates, the paint tins—everything—and move on."

"We need new IDs."

"I know, Jim should have thought of that. But it's too late, that's not an option now. We're going to have to improvise. Maybe we can charter a yacht in Namibia and sail to Morocco."

He puffed out his cheeks. "That's shit, man."

"This is what they drummed into us in the Regiment, Njal. Plans need to be thorough. Plans made on the go like this one are dangerous plans. We came in without an extraction strategy." I shrugged. "Now we're stuck. That's as close to suicide as you can get without putting a gun in your mouth."

He sighed and nodded. "OK. So we cross, change the plates and paint the car, drive north as far as Windhoek, then go west to the coast, find a nice port town with tourists, yachts, all that shit. There we charter a yacht." He pulled out his cell and started to look. After a moment, he said, "Maybe Walvis Bay, directly west of Windhoek. It's got a nice harbor, big port."

I nodded. "It's our best chance. If Omega are looking for us, they'll be focusing on borders and airports."

"We hope."

"Yeah, we hope." I shrugged again. "Like I said, it's our best hope."

FIFTEEN

Springbok might have been a town in some remote part of Arizona, or New Mexico. It looked like the kind of town Stephen King might have written about, positioned on the edge of a trans-dimensional portal to hell. We approached on the N7, from the north. There is no simple way off the N7 into Springbok, it's like the engineers who built the road didn't want to go there, so we ended up taking a long detour through the desert on a track called Inry Street, which eventually took us into town.

The town was stark, desolate, with low buildings widely spaced on broad, largely empty streets. We didn't see many people, and those we did see looked like they wanted to be somewhere else. There was a listless, hopeless feeling which hung like an invisible pall over the town. After Inry Street, we turned into Luckhoff Street, which made Njal snort.

"It is more like Fuckoff Street."

"That what passes for subtlety in Norway?"

"Luckhoff."

I did a bad imitation of his accent. "I know one choke. Luckhoff is sounding like fuck off. Dat is funny."

"Right, because Americans are real subtle. You know all about irony, right?"

"Mine axe vonts to heff one meeninkful exchange off ideas mit you."

"Yuh, you funny. And you accent is German, not Norwegian."

"Mine axe vonts to get inside your head."

"Funny."

Finally, we turned down Lodge Street and into Voortrekker Street. El Dago was on the bend. I pulled over, parked and we swung down from the cab. The restaurant was a red brick cube with eight steps up to a glass door, and a small, crude terrace on the left. We climbed the steps and pushed inside. It was plain and unremarkable, with red gingham tablecloths, wooden floors and a counter at the end with a smiling woman behind it. A couple of the tables were occupied by people who looked indefinably local. They glanced at us when we came in, then carried on with their food. But the two guys sitting by the window watched us carefully as we looked around. They were big, lean and had a predatory alertness about their eyes. I noticed beside their table, up against the wall, there was a large rucksack. The guy sitting next to it was in his mid twenties, with short blond hair and pale blue eyes: a true Russ. The guy opposite him was shorter, swarthy, with dark hair and Slavic features.

We took the table next to theirs and the waitress approached us, smiling, and asked what we'd have.

Njal picked up the menu, but I said, "We'll have a couple of ostrich burgers, and a couple of beers."

She went away. We talked for a few minutes, then Njal looked over at the two guys, who had returned to their food and were talking quietly in Russian. He gestured at the rucksack.

"You been far?"

The blond guy studied him a moment before answering. "Here and there. Is good visiting places you don't know. You are from South Africa?"

"Germany. You been to Cape Town?"

He nodded. "Cape Town, Jo'burg, Pretoria."

"Cool. Where to next?"

"Now we go home. We need get to airport."

"Yuh? Where you flying to?"

"We fly to Jo'burg, then London, then Moscow."

"Man, that's a long journey. Is your pack heavy?"

"Is heavy, man. We like to get rid of it."

The waitress came over with the burgers and the beer. She set them down, I paid her and picked up my bun. "We'll give you a ride to the airport. What time is your flight?"

He gave me the dead-eye for a moment, then looked at Njal. Njal nodded. "Sure, we give you a ride. We got the Land Rover outside."

"Flight is in couple of hours. I am Gregor, this is Vlad."

Njal leaned over and gave Gregor a complicated handshake that involved at least five different ways of gripping each other's fists, then sat back. "I'm Peter, this is Bob. We travellin' around, looking for work."

I finished my burger in a couple of large mouthfuls, then drained my beer. Njal looked at me curiously. There was something nagging at me and I couldn't pinpoint it. The other customers were ignoring us. So was the waitress, but I couldn't have been more uncomfortable if my chair had been on fire. I looked at Njal.

"OK, let's go."

He looked at his food and his drink, then at me. "You in a hurry?"

"Yeah, I'm in a hurry. Let's go."

Vlad muttered something at his pal. Gregor looked from me to Njal. "You gonna give us ride to airport, right?"

"Yeah, sure."

I said, "Yeah, we'll give you a ride, but we need to go now."

There was some sighing. Njal drained his glass, picked up his burger and stood. The two Russians stood and Vlad shouldered the hundred and ten backpack like it weighed a couple of pounds. He was obviously the muscle of the outfit.

I stepped out and moved to the Land Rover, scanning the street up and down. I couldn't see anything that looked wrong, but I still felt it. Njal and the Russians followed down the eight steps and crossed the sidewalk. As they approached, I pointed to the back of the truck.

"Put your rucksack in back. Vlad, you ride up front with me. Gregor, you ride in back with Peter."

He frowned at me. "Is there problem?"

I held his eye for a second. "Not if you don't make one."

He drew down the corners of his mouth and shook his head. "We don't make a problem, man. We cool."

"So get in the back with Peter." Vlad slung the rucksack in the back, then climbed in beside me up front. Njal and Gregor climbed in the back and the doors slammed. I fired up the big diesel, did a 'U' and followed Voortrekker up the hill, under the

N7 flyover and out into the desert along the N14, toward the airfield. As we left the last few houses behind us and wound into the arid hills dotted with gnarled shrubs and rocks, Gregor spoke up and I knew suddenly what it was that had been troubling me.

"I got message from back home. Pakhan say we need change the arrangement."

I glanced at him in the mirror. He was watching the back of my head. Njal was staring out the window. I said:

"Change?"

"Price gone up. Is big risk, bringing package here. Value of package gone up. So price must go up also."

I took my eyes off him and looked at the road ahead. "How much?"

"Two hundred fifty thousand U.S. dollar."

"You're out of your mind. You think we have that kind of cash on an operation like this?"

"You make call. Your commander make transfer. I give you bank details."

I sighed like he was a pain in my ass, but I had no choice and glanced in the mirror again. Njal was still looking out at the desert.

"This is your department, Pete. Can we do it?"

He didn't answer for a moment. Then he made a big show of pulling his cigarettes from his pocket and lighting up. "We don't got much choice, right? We need go back to camp." He looked at Gregor and his face wasn't friendly. "You gonna miss your flight."

"Yeah, is OK. We change flight."

Njal looked at me in the mirror. "OK, we go back to camp."

I turned at the intersection with Kokerboom Road and looped back onto the N7, headed north. Then I hit the gas. There was hot anger welling in my gut, and it was turning to an ice-cold rage. We passed the village of O'Kiep on the right and then we were out in the wilderness, twenty-five miles from Steinkopf. Soon after that, we came to a turning on the right of the road, a dirt track that wound up into the hills. It was barely wide enough for the truck, but I slowed and took the turning. It was as good a place as any for what we had to do. Vlad was looking worried and turned to Gregor. He said something in Russian and Gregor said, "Where your camp is?"

I spoke without feeling. "Relax, it's in back of those hills up ahead."

"Don't try nothing stupid. You don't want make enemy of Pakhan."

"Chill, friend, don't start throwing threats around. You've complicated things enough already. The last thing we need is a vendetta with the Russian mob. You'll get your money."

He seemed to relax. I followed the track for a couple of miles around the back of the hills, then pulled into a narrow valley between two large rocks. There I killed the engine and climbed out. Njal climbed out the other side and the Russians clambered down after us, looking nervous. Gregor started to say, "Where is..."

I interrupted him and spoke to Njal. "You want to get your laptop?"

As I said it, I pulled my Sig from my waistband and put two slugs through Vlad's two-inch brow. They erupted out the back of his head, spraying what brains he had over the pale sand.

Gregor's reaction took me by surprise. It was instant. He seemed to levitate and his right foot lashed out and kicked at Njal's head. Njal weaved back and raised his arms, but it wasn't enough. The kick connected and Njal went down.

The Land Rover was between us. I took aim and fired, but he had already ducked and rolled toward the back of the truck. I ran to intercept him. As I got to the rear, he sprang at me in a roundhouse kick. I ducked. He landed and instantly spun into a back kick that caught my wrist and knocked the gun from my hand. He didn't pause. He lashed out again in two front kicks that forced me back. Then he dropped and spun and knocked my feet from under me. I crashed onto my back, knocking the wind from my lungs, and my chest went into a spasm of pain. Gregor didn't wait. He sprang up, dropped his right knee on my chest and drew his fist back for the death blow to my head.

I didn't think. Wheezing for breath, I grabbed a handful of the dry, gray dirt and threw it in his face. He snarled and his hands went to his eyes. I smashed my fist into his balls and as he staggered back keening, I struggled to my feet, drawing deep, painful breaths. He was still blinded, half running backward, trying to get the dirt from his eyes. I went after him. He heard me and as I drove my fist into his jaw, he weaved. I caught him a glancing blow. It didn't put out his lights, but he went down on his back. I pulled my knife from my boot, stepped on his left hand and dropped my knee on his chest. But he wasn't an easy kill. As I rammed the Fairbairn & Sykes through his esophagus and out through his jugular, he rammed his own hunting knife into my thigh. The pain was intense and I let out an involuntary cry. As he coughed and gurgled and the death spasm shook his body, I staggered to my feet and stumbled back, clutching at my leg.

I wrenched out his knife and stood, with my right leg trembling violently, and hobbled back toward the Land Rover. The wound wasn't spouting blood, so I knew he'd missed the major blood vessels, but twice I fell when my leg refused to hold my weight. Eventually, hopping and cussing, I made it to the hood of the truck and leaned my weight on it. Njal was on all fours, vomiting into the dirt. I watched him a moment as he tried to stand, feeling the dull agony of my wound throbbing up my leg and into my brain. I could not afford to lose consciousness. We had to get back to camp, and Njal was concussed and probably couldn't drive.

I said, "You need to kick dirt into that vomit," and knew I wasn't thinking logically.

After a moment, he raised his head to look at me. "What?"

"You need to degrade the DNA."

He nodded and pulled himself to his feet.

I added, "Can you drive?"

"Why?"

"I don't know if I can use my right leg. He stabbed me."

His eyes were dull and unfocused. "You left any blood?"

I shook my head. "No. I got the knife and so far it's all sticking to my pants. But we need to get out of here. I'm not focusing. Not thinking straight."

"Yeah? I can't see straight. Motherfocker had a hell of a kick."

"OK, I can drive. Get in, Njal. We have to go now."

He pulled open the passenger door and I limped around to the driver's side. We hauled ourselves in and sat for a moment. I could feel myself going cold and starting to shiver and I knew shock was setting in. I could not afford that. I pointed at the glove compartment.

"Get the whiskey."

He grunted and nodded, pulled the bottle out and handed it to me. I took a large slug and it helped. I pulled the cigarettes from my pocket with shaking hands and lit up. Then I took off my shirt, bound it around the cut and between us, we pulled it as tight as it would go, then knotted it. After that, shaking badly, I fired up the truck, turned it around and headed back toward the N7.

We didn't talk again until we'd left the road and we were approaching the camp. Then Njal said, "This complicates things."

"We can still do it."

"Of course…" But he didn't sound very convinced.

We got back to camp, hid the Land Rover and staggered out of the cab. Njal found the first aid kit, cut away my trouser leg and exposed the gash in my thigh. He inspected it and glanced at my face. "It is deep. You are lucky he missed any major veins or artery. Two inches down and you are dead."

"Thanks."

"Take some more whiskey. I'm gonna put some surgical spirits on it."

I took a swig and he poured the spirits on. It hurt like hell and he started wiping it with cotton wool. I swore violently under my breath and he pulled the sutures from the box.

"I'm gonna stitch it. It's gonna hurt."

"I know," I said malevolently. "I've done this before a few times."

He worked fast and efficiently. I tried to keep my yelling under my breath and got through half the bottle of whiskey. When he was done, he smeared the wound with antiseptic cream and bandaged it. Then he gave me a handful of painkillers to take on top of the whiskey, and told me to go and sleep.

"It is two thirty. You got nine hours. If you're gonna live through the week, you godda be functioning tonight. So sleep. I'm gonna go get sick in a hole. Then I'm gonna sleep too. I'll call you at twelve. Then we go do this, and go home."

I nodded. "Yeah, OK, thanks, Njal."

He walked away. I heard him digging, then I heard him retching, and after that there was nothing.

I WAS ALREADY AWAKE when Njal came to get me at twelve. I was sweating and shivering, and by the way he looked at me, I must have been pale and sickly too. Before he could ask, I said, "I'm OK."

He handed me a flask of hot coffee and some chocolate, and we loaded the truck with all the stuff we were going to need and clambered into the Land Rover. My leg was stiff and I was getting powerful shooting pains that either meant I was healing or getting gangrene, but whining about it wasn't going to help and I needed Njal focused on the mission, not on me.

It was three miles as the crow flies from our camp to the site, but driving around the huge rock hills where we were hidden, some of which were two thousand feet high, turned those three miles into just over eight. And the going was slow, over deep sand and sudden rocky outcrops that meant taking further detours. The moon was already setting by then, and we dared not use the headlamps. So poor visibility was an added difficulty.

After just over an hour of creeping, picking our way between the vast hulks of rock and grinding and sliding over loose, white sand and gravel, we finally came to the river. There we slowed and climbed down to inspect the terrain. We found to our surprise that there were fields of crops running along the riverbank, and, to our relief, there was a long, straight road of beaten earth skirting the fields. We followed the road for three miles east, keeping to a steady twenty-five MPH, and skirted two huge headlands—two black behemoths rising against the dark, turquoise sky—with the river glinting black and silver on our left.

But after ten or twelve minutes, the road simply vanished into the river. We had a vast, black wall of stone on the right, and the river on the left and in front of us. Our path was cut off. We climbed out again and walked to the river's edge. The pain in my leg was excruciating and I could feel a warm trickle of blood on my thigh. I ignored it, knowing I had no choice but to hold it together until we were across the border, and tried to think.

Njal walked on and waded out into the black, slow-moving water. The dying light of the moon lapped around his inky legs and the stars danced on the small waves. He looked back at me. "It feels solid." He waded on a few paces more and the water swirled around his shins. It was less than knee-deep. He stood looking for a while, then turned and came sloshing back. The light of the moon was dull on his face, casting his eyes into black shadow.

"Underneath the water, it is the road. The river is a little flooded, but the ground is hard. It is maybe half a mile, then we have road again. We take it slow and careful, we'll be OK."

I nodded and we returned to the truck, climbed in and pulled the doors closed. He put it in gear and we rolled into the water. For ten or fifteen minutes, we proceeded slowly and carefully, sometimes as much as three feet deep in the river, but after about a quarter of an hour, it started to grow more shallow and the steep, rock face on our right began to recede. Then the path emerged again. Njal slowed to walking pace and we began to curl inland, around the massive, black headland. Finally the huge, sandy esplanade opened up on our right: two miles of flat, white dust, and at its center the eerie, half constructed form of the power station. But it wasn't as we had expected to find it. Because the entire site was floodlit and the place was crawling with armed guards in pairs, patrolling the inside of the perimeter fence.

Njal spun the wheel, pulled in close to the rock face and killed the engine. We both sat for a moment, staring. Outside the perimeter fence, the darkness seemed deeper, darker, by contrast with the spotlights inside the perimeter. This at least could be to our advantage. But once inside, there would be nowhere for us to hide. We would be spotted instantly.

After a moment, Njal sighed and said, "We should have foreseen this. They increased security because of the hit on Knysna."

"We did foresee it, Njal, there was just fuck all we could do about it."

I glanced over at the river, then touched his arm and pointed. In the blackness I could just make out a form, darker than the darkness, resting on the water. "What the hell is that?"

He frowned, squinting. "A boat?"

"It's a damn big boat. The river's not deep enough for a boat that size... And how the hell did it get here? The river's not navigable."

He shook his head. "I can't make it out."

Then it dawned on me. I got a flash in my memory and saw it clearly, flying over my head, over the mansion and into the lagoon. "It's a sea plane."

"A sea plane...?" He stared at me. "Shit, what does it mean?"

"I don't know. It flew into Knysna when I killed Pi and Ro. I don't like it."

We watched it a while longer. Eventually, he shrugged. "It is not doing anything. Maybe it brought some of these guards. Either way, we got a bigger problem, Lacklan." He looked back at the floodlit site. "It's gonna be almost impossible. We are maybe six hundred yards from the reactor building. A mile from where you want to blow an entrance on the far side of the fence, half a mile from the buildings and the site office you want to burn. The whole goddamn place is floodlit and you can hardly walk. We need to rethink how we do this."

I stared at the enormous, illuminated area, surrounded by chain link fences and barbed wire, with the guards patrolling inside. I shook my head. "The time and place of our death was decided long ago by the Norn, remember? If it is tonight, then it will be tonight, whatever we do. So we man up and if we go down, we go down fighting."

He nodded. "I like that. But I also want to blow this fuckin' place."

I nodded. "OK, we won't go down easy. Here's what we do. When this pair of guards passes, you crawl up to the fence and you place a whole two pounds of C4 against the vertical support. That's going to be our point of ingress and egress, close to the truck. So we leave the rucksack here, in the truck, instead of on the south-eastern side as we had originally planned."

"OK..."

"Then, between us, we take the C4 down along the riverbank, under the cover of the reeds, and we move in, behind the site office and the buildings, when we are out of view of the guards at the perimeter fence. You still with me?"

"Yuh, makes sense."

"We place the charges and the gasoline at the back, out of sight, and return the way we came."

"OK, it might work."

"So, this is the sequence: we detonate this near charge at the fence and follow up with the RPGs and your TEA rockets, until we have blown a hole big enough in the fence—a few seconds—then we blow the buildings on the far side and set fire to them. It will look like the main attack is there and that will draw the guards; *then* we go in *in* the Land Rover..."

He grinned and started to laugh. "I like this one. Yuh, that's good. Come on, let's do it."

So we did.

SIXTEEN

It was slow, difficult and painful.

The first step was for Njal to inch his way very slowly to the perimeter fence while I kept him covered with the 416. He was aided by the fact that the glare from the spots on the site made the darkness outside the perimeter almost impenetrable by contrast. And by the time he was within the area of light, he was concealed by the large rolls of barbed wire. He positioned the two cakes of C4 as best he could and managed to crawl back without being seen.

Then we shared out the remaining twenty-eight pounds of explosive and two gallons of gasoline, and ran down to the river—Njal ran, I hobbled. The pain in my leg was intense, but I had no choice but to assimilate it and go with it. When we got to the riverbank, the going was a little easier, and we had the cover of dense bulrushes and what looked like thick sugar cane plantations.

We covered about a mile in just over twenty minutes and approached the site office and the outhouses from the rear, with the cover of the rocks that rose up to about one and a half thousand feet behind them. There was a total of six buildings all together, all constructed of wood: the main, two-story site offices, and then a cluster of small office buildings, sheds, storehouses and one large, hangar-like construction which I figured housed machinery and perhaps fuel.

We took a minute to rest, then we distributed the C4 to maximum effect. I placed two pounds against the back wall of the hangar, hoping it would ignite any fuel on the inside, and we placed the two gallons of gas against the wall of the office building, with enough charge to ignite it but not completely vaporize it.

By the time we'd finished, I was exhausted and I could barely move my right leg, but we hobbled back under cover of the stone hills and back along the river, in the shelter of the cane and the reeds.

Finally, we got back to the Land Rover and pulled the HK416 RPG launcher from the back of the truck. I felt I was going to pass out and took a minute to lean against the hood, feeling the cold night air on my face and listening to the ripple and splash of the river. The moon was gone. I wondered if I was going to die that night. It seemed likely.

Njal appeared by my side, holding the M202 FLASH rocket launcher and a bottle of whiskey. I took a long pull and it seemed to help. I handed it back to him. He toasted me and said, "See you in Valhalla, my friend. It has been an honor."

"Yeah, you too, Njal."

He took a swig and put the bottle back in the cab. I took out my cell and we watched the brace of guards approach the corner of the perimeter fence. Njal got on one knee and took aim. As the two men drew level with the two pound charge, I dialed in the code and it exploded instantly, ripping a big hole in the fence, dismembering the guards, but hardly affecting the barbed wire at all. That was a problem. I heard Njal swear and pull the trigger on the launcher. The four rockets erupted from the box, scorched across the darkness and exploded in white-hot flames into the fence. He loaded another clip and fired again, and then a third time. Meanwhile, I kept up a steady bombardment of RPGs. By now the wire was incandescent with white-hot flames. He fired a fourth volley and stood, throwing the launcher into the back of the Land Rover.

I dialed again and across the vast esplanade, beyond the building site, the wooden offices erupted. A fireball exploded through the office building, and a moment later the hangar erupted in a vast ball of black flames and smoke two hundred feet high that engulfed the entire row of buildings. I figured there must have been fuel there after all.

Njal had the engine running. I swung in and slammed the door, and we thundered toward the incandescent hole in the perimeter fence.

There was a flash of heat and the screaming, rending sound of steel and wire tearing against the chassis of the Land Rover. Then we were through, in the glare of the spotlights, tearing across the sand toward the fifty foot wall of the base of the pyramid. I had expected a hail of lead, a rain of fire, to be unleashed against us as we burst into the compound, but as we sped toward the eastern face of the building, toward the entrance, all we saw was two dozen guards running away from us, like all hell was breaking loose on their asses. But they weren't running away, they were running toward the inferno that was the site office and the surrounding buildings. I snarled at Njal: "Slow down, keep behind them."

"I got it."

They had the gate open at the far end of the compound and were streaming out, shouting instructions at each other. Njal swerved right and rounded the corner of the building, accelerating toward the gaping entrance to the vast site. It was about twenty feet across and within the gap, on the inside, all I could see was acres of concrete, steel girders, cement mixers and all the chaos and paraphernalia of a building site. I heard the brakes complain and we swerved again, ducking inside the enclosed area.

I swung out of the cab, ignoring the stabbing and throbbing in my leg, ran to the back of the truck and hauled out the rucksack. Njal snapped, "I take it. Your leg will slow you down..."

I went to pass it to him, but outside there was a shout. We looked and against the huge, dancing flames of the site office, we saw the two dozen stenciled forms of the guards running back toward us, shouting. Njal stared hard into my eyes.

"OK, it is now," he said. "Go! I hold them. *Go!*"

I pulled the rocket launcher from the truck, fitted a clip and threw it to him. Then I turned and ran toward a twenty foot square hole in the floor, over on my right, that I knew from the map Njal had shown me was the access to the maze of tunnels and rooms that lay beneath the surface. Behind me, as I ran, I heard the spit and hiss of rockets, and moments later the quadruple explosion of the TEAs, and immediately after that, the spit and stutter of the Heckler and Koch.

I pulled the night vision goggles down over my eyes and plunged into the black hole that was the ramp leading down into the bowels of the pyramid. The floor was raw concrete covered in dust and grit. My feet slid from under me and I fell, sprawling and rolling twenty feet to the floor below. Shafts of pain stabbed through my leg. I staggered to my feet. My brain was numbed and dulled by the pain, but I struggled to focus and searched the eerie, black and green subterranean world. Tall columns towered above me, supporting the ceiling and the floor above. Fifty feet away I saw what I needed: the cargo elevator that would take me deep down, eight hundred feet into the bowels of the desert, to the chamber where I was to leave the rucksack, the bomb that would destroy this place forever, and with it Omega.

And probably me, too.

I half ran, half limped across the fifty feet of raw cement, hearing the stutter of fire up above. It was good to hear because it meant that Njal was still alive, but I wondered how long he could last, how long he could hold out before they overwhelmed him by sheer force of numbers.

I arrived at the elevator, punched the button and the large, steel doors hissed open. Then I was struck by a ton of bricks and hurled to the ground. My leg kicked in spasms of agony. I struggled to get to my feet, but the hundred and ten pounds of backpack held me pinned to the ground.

A hand wrenched the goggles from my head. I covered my face with my forearms and felt two powerful fists slam into my arms. Before a third could land, I reached up with my right and grabbed a handful of his face, searching with my fingers for his eyes. I found one with my thumb and he screamed, backing up and pulling away from me. I rolled, pulled the Sig and fired blindly in his general direction, then struggled to my feet, searching the floor with my hands for the goggles. My fingers closed on them and I backed away toward where the elevator was, pulling them down, over my face.

Again the eerie world of inky black and green. I scanned the vast hall of arches and pillars, but could not find my attacker. Upstairs, the shooting had become sporadic. I heard the engine of the Land Rover roar, then the screech of brakes. I checked the elevator. He was not there. I stepped in and hit the red button. The doors slid closed and we began to descend.

I had not killed my attacker. I had heard no scream when I opened fire, and I was pretty sure I had not seriously hurt him either. There was no doubt in my mind that he had figured out what I was trying to do and had retreated because he planned to attack when I reached the bottom of the shaft. The car rocked and rattled as it sped down, the cabled clanged and clattered, and I tried to foresee in my mind's eye how he would attack. There was another cargo elevator, I knew that. Was he going down ahead of me? Did he already have men waiting for me down there? If he knew I was coming and knew what I was going to do, why had he been alone? Why had there not been a whole squad of them, armed with rifles?

I felt the car begin to slow, un-slung the rucksack from my back and flattened myself against the wall beside the door. It slowed to a halt and stopped with a jolt. The doors hissed open, I dropped to my belly and sprayed the empty blackness with fire and an RPG for good measure.

I lay, listening to the violent echoes reverberate and die away among the blackness, until there was only ringing silence. Then I scrambled painfully to my feet, grabbed the backpack and hobbled out of the cage to lose myself in the shadows outside.

The only light was what little spilled from the elevator. I fitted my goggles and leaned against the side of the elevator shaft. My leg was trembling and the pain was making me faint. I slid down the wall till I was sitting, scanned the area and tried to regain my strength.

The ceiling was high, maybe fifteen or twenty feet. There were massive columns supporting it, and roughly thirty feet away, there was a steel door which I knew led down to the chamber which was my final destination, and probably my grave, too. Aside from that, the place was featureless. There was no sign of my attacker, but he could be hiding behind any one of the sixteen columns I could see. I slipped off the backpack, got to my feet and crept to the back of the elevator shaft to peer back toward the other side of the space. It was much the same, except that, fifty or sixty feet away, it contained another elevator shaft. Aside from that, there was nothing. I returned, heaved the rucksack onto my back and limped to the nearest pillar. I didn't get shot and nothing happened. I gathered my strength again and half-ran to the next, and then the next. One more and I was a short run from the steel door. Something like hope was beginning to smolder in my gut. I pulled my Sig from my waistband and made the last run, turned my back to the locked entrance and scanned the room behind me. There was nothing, no one. I was alone. I turned and blew the lock out of the door.

Inside, a staircase descended to the left, but the blackness was total and not even the night vision goggles could penetrate it. I unhooked my flashlight from my belt and descended, following the dancing beam. After nine steps, the flight turned left for three steps, then left again and another nine steps down. The space was narrow and smothering. I am not claustrophobic, but I could feel the first writhings of panic twisting in my belly as I went deeper. I could feel the vast weight of the edifice above me, of the nine hundred feet of earth and rock above me, of the enormous depth to which I had descended and of the tiny space into which I was compressed.

At the bottom of the second flight, there was another door. Again I blew the lock and the report, and the clang of lead on steel, was deafening in the tight, cramped space.

The door swung open and I played the beam of the flashlight through the opening. Another short flight of nine steps, straight down, with no banisters or rails, into a room that was square, supported on four massive pillars. In the center of the room a cube: a slab of rock, four feet by four by four.

I descended the stairs, feeling I would collapse and fall from them before I reached the bottom, and staggered the last few steps to the rock. It had the appearance of highly polished granite and was featureless but for a large circle engraved into the center, enclosing the omega symbol: omicron enclosing omega. No doubt it had some powerful philosophical meaning.

I heaved the rucksack on top of it and opened it,

exposing the digital pad that was the timer and the start button. I knew I would not get out—could not get out. I knew my fate, as Njal would call it, was to die here, in this vast, anonymous tomb, vaporized nine hundred feet below the surface of the planet. Still, you don't stop fighting until you're dead, do you? So I took a moment to try and calculate how long I needed to get out, to get back up to the surface. I had no idea, so in honor of Jim and Njal, and Odin, I punched in nine minutes and my finger hovered over the ignition button.

"Do you know what you're doing?"

I knew the voice. I went cold all over and my hair prickled. I turned and shone the flashlight toward the stairs. He was sitting on the third step from the bottom. I couldn't see his face because he was wearing a hoodie, but I knew who it was.

"Yeah," I told him. "I am going to vaporize the last residue of your sick organization."

"You are doing more than that, Lacklan. You are fulfilling the prophecy engraved on that stone. This pyramid is omicron. Your bomb is omega. Omicron is the seed, omega is the life that erupts from it. You, the instrument of your world and your society, try to suppress us, but we are the life that explodes from your repression. You have no idea who you are, Lacklan Walker, but you are the instrument of destiny. You are fated to enable Omega."

"You're full of shit. How are you here, anyway? I killed you."

"You broke my heart, brother."

I turned back to the bomb.

His voice continued. "It's the same bomb, you know. The one you disarmed at the United Nations."

I began to laugh. "Hoist with your own petard, huh?" I pressed the button and the hundredths of a second began to race. I turned back to the stairs. He was gone and somewhere in my mind, I realized I must have been hallucinating. Ben was dead.

I dragged my trembling, useless leg toward the stairs. I felt suddenly very cold and sleepy. The stairs looked steep and narrow, and with no banisters to hold onto, I knew I could not make it. I knew I would not make it to the top, but I had to try. I had to try because you don't stop fighting till you're dead.

One at a time, feeling vertigo as I climbed, hearing my breathing loud in my own ears, feeling the sweat running on my face, I crawled through the door and looked up the next flight. I had not left myself enough time, and it was too late now to go back and change it. I stood and dragged myself, achingly slow, up the next nine steps. The pain in my leg was a piercing, ripping, stabbing in my brain that made it impossible to think of anything else. Through it, somehow, I climbed one more step, turned the corner and started all over again, one step after another, impossibly slow, with the timer spinning at the speed of light beneath me.

I wondered why I should struggle. It would be easy to lie down, go to sleep. I would not even notice the explosion. No more fighting, no more killing, only eternal stillness in a vaporizing flash.

I smiled as I dragged myself up one more step; only five to go. That had always been the problem. I had never known how to lie down. Lying down was a skill I had never learned. I slept awake, listening for the demons who came in the night. I began to laugh. I had killed so many demons that they had learned to fear me. Lacklan Walker, the demon killer.

I pushed through the door and pulled down the goggles over my eyes. The green and black world rocked sickeningly and I fell hard on the concrete floor. I got up on my hands and knees, then to my feet. I wondered how many minutes I had wasted. In my mind, I saw myself running to the elevator, and then, for agonizing seconds, did not know what was my imagination and what was real. I looked around, saw three ink-black columns between me and the elevator shaft, and dragged my leaden, half-paralyzed leg toward it. My breath was loud, like a bellows in my ears.

Then I was at the elevator. I stood on the threshold. The buttons were a long way away. I reached for them and fell again, hard. My whole world was pain: severe. A serious voice in my head told me, "This is serious." Nausea overwhelmed me. "This is where you give up, pal. You've done what you came to do. Now lie down."

I curled, reached up, sat, fought to stand.

"Lie down."

He was in the doorway, tall, narrow, lanky, inky black; his arm was outstretched, pointing at me. I laughed. "Plenty of time to lie down when I'm dead."

I gripped the rail and pulled myself to my feet. The pain was a tearing of live tissues in my leg and I may have screamed. I pounded the red button with my fist and the elevator began to rise. But I knew it was too late. I knew the fireball would be chasing me up the shaft, reaching up to burn me, to enfold me, to consume me and drag me down where I belonged: in Hell.

SEVENTEEN

I HAD STOPPED MOVING. THERE WAS A NOISE. IT was a noise I knew well. It was the noise that had defined my life for over a decade. It was the spit and stutter of automatic fire, and the thud and whine of rounds impacting and ricocheting off rocks and walls. The sound was distant, then close: the sound of answering fire.

I lay, knowing I had to stand, but not sure how. I rolled on my side, one hand on the floor of the elevator, pushing, but not moving. My eyes closed. I wanted so badly to sleep.

Plenty of time for sleep when you are dead. Perhaps now was the time. Time to die, time to sleep.

Then the roar of a Heckler and Koch. My heart surged and I pushed, struggled to a kneeling position. A voice in my mind roared, *Lacklan Walker does not kneel!* I roared and, my leg screaming with the pain, rose to my feet. The elevator door was open and a tall, inky, lanky figure stood staring at me. I thrust the Sig out in front of me with both hands and stared into Njal's face.

He squinted into my eyes, ducked into my gut and lifted me over his shoulder. Then turned and ran. Hot lead rained on us like a hail storm. Njal's voice, roaring incoherently, filled the caverns of the building. Then we stopped and I was hurled into the back of a Land Rover. The door slammed. The glass in the windows shattered around me. The driver's door slammed. The engine roared and the wheels screamed, Then we were hurtling, lurching and bouncing into glaring light.

Adrenaline pumped, burning in my gut. We cornered and I rolled on my belly, then dragged myself toward the front seats. Swearing and cussing at Njal for throwing me in the back, I somehow dragged my useless leg with me and clambered into the passenger seat, shouting with pain and trying to see where we were.

We were hurtling across sand toward the gap we had blown in the perimeter fence, and there was a Jeep on either side of us and a Toyota truck behind us.

Njal looked at me, handed me his 416 and grinned. "You are one hard son of a bitch. We gonna die tonight, my friend! Tonight we go to Valhalla!" Then his face flushed, his eyes went crazy and he bellowed like a crazed demon, *"Odin! Odin!"* He spun the wheel, drifted on the sand and careened toward the Jeep that had been on our right wing. I began to laugh like a maniac. I could see their faces in luminous relief, their eyes wide, their mouths gaping and shouting. I knew what Njal was going to do and put the 416 to my shoulder. He spun the wheel again and we passed them within maybe a foot. I didn't give a damn if they killed us or not. I was with him. Today was a good day to die, and if we went down, we'd do it in a way to make the Valkyries hot and wet.

I opened up and sprayed the Jeep with three hundred rounds in two seconds. It was a storm of fire and lead that shattered windows and windshield, ripped open chests, exploded skulls and destroyed the four men in the vehicle.

Next thing, we had come around and the second Jeep was ahead of us. I blew out the windshield of the Land Rover and opened up again into the back of the Cherokee, seven short bursts of four rounds through the back window. The car swerved, fishtailed and rolled over.

Then we were hurtling for the gap in the perimeter fence. The Toyota had fallen back behind us. We exploded through the fence and out into the dark.

Njal was headed for the track along which we had arrived, but I pointed straight ahead. "Make for the river."

"What?"

"Change of plan. We are flying out of here!"

"You can fly?"

"Of course I can fly! Head for the river and let's get the hell out of here!"

He veered and hurtled crazily toward the mass of sugar cane that masked the river. I knew he remembered, as I did, that on the other side there was a track and then the water. What neither of us knew was that before the track there was also a ditch. A ditch almost three feet deep, out of which the cane was growing. We hit it at forty miles an hour and smashed to a juddering halt. The impact sent both of us crashing through what was left of the windshield, sprawling, dazed and winded on the path.

I opened my eyes and looked up at the mantle of stars above. All kinds of pain were throbbing and piercing my body, my entire being. I could hear water, and feel it lapping at my face and my head. In that moment I truly wanted to die, just to stop the pain.

Somewhere I could hear a diesel straining, and voices shouting. Then Njal, wide-eyed and panting, blocked out the stars above. He reached down with his long, lanky arms and dragged me to my feet. "Run!" he snarled.

I couldn't remember how to run, but I did my best, and in a couple of strides, I was wading knee-deep in water with sludge sucking on my feet. Then the darkness was flooded with light. Ahead, forty or fifty feet away, I saw the plane. I recognized it as a King Air 350. I saw Njal dive and sink beneath the water. For some reason, instead of doing the same, I turned and stared, and for a timeless second, everything froze.

Then the world shook. I staggered and fell to my knees, struggled to stand again but failed. The water splashed and rose in waves. There was a deep thunder, and the earth seemed to groan. Away in the compound, I heard the massive crash and rumble of the vast construction collapsing in on itself, and in the darkness I saw an immense, billowing cloud rise up above the sugarcane, shrouding everything, under-lit by the spotlights at the site.

At the bank of the river, there was a red Toyota truck. Above the cab there was a bank of spotlights that were glaring and half-blinding me. Behind the spots, I could just make out two men in silhouette, and a fifty cal. mounted machine gun. The men was gazing up at the cloud, clinging to the sides of the truck. There were armed men standing beside the truck, too: three on my right, two on my left, and they also were staring up at the billowing black mushroom.

But in front of the truck there was one man, and he was

staring at me. I could see him with clarity, though his face was in shadow. He was tall, six two, in his early thirties and dressed in khaki; and he was pointing at me, screaming, "*Kill him! Kill him!*"

It is a little known fact that bullets disintegrate on impact with water, and the higher the power of the round, the less it penetrates before it disintegrates. I fell. The last thing I saw before I sank into the wet blackness was the flaring fire of the weapons as they opened up. I dragged my aching body deep into the cold, soothing water and swam: one big pull, another stroke and another, a third and then a fourth, until my lungs were screaming for air; and then I kept going a little farther. Finally I broke the surface, wiped the water from my eyes and looked around. I could hear voices screaming, shouting, distant. I could hear splashing and thrashing. But I could not see the plane. I turned and found myself staring at the port float, five feet from my head. Then there was Njal's voice hollering at me, "*Get up, they are coming!*"

I looked up. He was on the float, reaching down for me. I grabbed his wrist and he mine, and he hauled me up. Then the door was open and we were clambering in. Bullets were smacking the fuselage, whining out into space, and my brain, body and my hands went into automatic. The engine was coughing, the props were turning, the plane was shaking and vibrating and we were moving down the black snake of the river, accelerating, churning up great waves of white foam. Njal was hooting like a cowboy on steroids and then the tone of the engine dropped, we lifted and suddenly all about us was the darkness of space and the stars as we rose up, higher and higher, banking south. We were flying.

I did one circle above the enclosure, its bright lights and the burning buildings now obscured by the massive, spreading cloud of dust. Then I turned to starboard and we rose, up into the pre-dawn sky, away from the carnage and the inferno, heading north, for home.

I looked at the fuel gauge. It told me she was full. I looked at Njal. He had his head thrown back and his eyes closed.

"If we're lucky, we'll get two thousand miles out of this crate."

He opened his eyes and looked at me. "That will get us to the Gulf of Guinea."

"It will get us to Cameroon."

"You got a friend in Cameroon."

I nodded. "Billy."

I pulled my cell out of my pocket and dialed the number Ian had given me. It rang three times and a voice that sounded like Hugh Grant at a vicar's tea party in Oxford said, "You'd better have a bloody good reason for phoning me at five in the fucking morning."

I smiled. "Good morning, Billy. What the hell are you doing in bed at this time? It's almost midday."

"Good Lord! Is that you, Lacklan? Ian said you might call. Given that you have, I assume things haven't gone according to plan."

"There was no plan."

"Super."

"In about three hours we'll either be landing in the jungle in Cameroon or ditching in the sea in the Gulf of Guinea. I await your instructions with interest."

"Judging by the racket, you're flying."

"King Air 350."

"How far can you get?"

"I could probably make it to Nigeria, but then we'd crash."

"Good. No, don't do that. The Nigerians don't take kindly to Western soldiers crashing into their country. Put her down at sea, just outside the Baie de Malimba. I'll make a call so you don't get shot down, and come out to meet you in the yacht."

"That would be very kind of you."

"Where are you headed after Cameroon?"

"Boston."

"By way of…?"

I tried to think, but my brain ached. "London, I guess."

He made a discouraging 'Hmmm…' sound, then said, "OK, I'll see what I can do. I can probably get you as far as Spain, or Morocco."

"That would be very much appreciated, Bill."

"What friends are for, old chap. What's your ETA?"

"About three hours."

"Of course, you said. Super. Nice to hear from you. Glad you're back on the scene."

He hung up and I turned to Njal. "I don't suppose you rescued the whiskey from the Land Rover?"

He answered without opening his eyes, with his head still thrown back like he was sleeping. "Yuh, I did. I grabbed it from the glove compartment as I was being propelled out of the windshield. Because, I thought, Lacklan is gonna ask me for this as we are flying over the fucking Namibian desert."

He opened his eyes and turned his head. "We left everything, man. I ain't complaining. We got out with our lives, which I did not expect to do. But we left behind the Audi, the weapons, the Land Rovers... You got your papers?"

"Yeah, I got my papers. You?"

He nodded. "I always keep my papers on me. But everything else, man."

"They'll trace us."

"I know, but we destroyed the fuckin' reactor, you killed the cabal, and we got out alive. That's good. We did good, man."

"Yeah, we did good."

But I was thinking about the hallucinations I'd had in the chamber, when I was setting the bomb, and about the guy I'd seen in front of the truck at the river. "I want to know who arrived in this plane." I looked at Njal. "I want to know who it was. He arrived at Knysna when I killed Pi and Ro, and he arrived at Goodhouse when we destroyed the power station. It's too much coincidence. I want to know who it was."

"You say that like you think you know already."

The plane droned on. Outside the window, the horizon was turning gray and, far below, we moved over the Namibian shoreline and out over the south Atlantic, where small, luminous white crests appeared as though by magic on the tiny waves as they broke in the dawning light.

"I don't know," I said at last. "There was something familiar about him."

"You OK?"

"I'll live."

He jerked his head at the controls. "Put it on autopilot. I

stay awake for a couple of hours. You sleep. I want you awake when you bring this thing down."

I nodded, put the crate on auto and staggered back into the fuselage. There I found a sofa, lay down and passed out.

IT SEEMED I had only been sleeping for a few seconds when Njal shook my shoulder. I opened my eyes and wondered if I was going to be able to move. My body felt ossified and everything hurt a little more than everything else. He handed me a cup and I sat up and took it.

"I found a coffee machine and a minibar. Good morning."

I took the cup and drained it. "Is there more? What time is it?"

"Eight. We have not much fuel left. We are approaching the Gulf of Guinea."

I dragged my leg back to the cockpit and climbed behind the controls. It was a bright morning and I could see the coast of western Africa over on my right, and a few miles away, the broad mouth of the Wouri Estuary and the southern headland of the Baie de Malimba. I began my descent.

Long before we had hit the water, I had already spotted his yacht speeding toward us. It was a blue and white Princess Y88 motor yacht. We hit the surface of the ocean in a shower of foam, skipped three times and began to slow. The yacht slowed too and came about to keep pace with us, and as the engines died and we came to a halt, the yacht began to close in.

I could see Billy on the flybridge, dressed in white with a peaked sailor's cap, and that was Billy Beauchamp all over. He waved to us and a couple of guys on the main deck dropped a dinghy on the waves and powered over to us. They pulled alongside the starboard float, one of the guys stayed at the wheel and the other, a big hulk with a broken nose and a cockney accent, called up, "Come aboard, I'll take care of the crate for ya!"

We clambered down, he swung up into the cockpit, and while we were ferried over to the yacht, the engines roared into life and the plane took off, flying east toward the coast.

As we staggered aboard the yacht, filthy, bruised and bleeding, Billy came down from the flybridge, smiling genially as though we had just arrived at his cocktail party. "Lacklan, my dear fellow, how are you? Come and sit down, have some coffee." He turned to Njal and held out his hand, "Bill Beauchamp, how do you do?"

They shook and he led us inside to a comfortable lounge where coffee was laid out on a table set before a sofa and two leather armchairs. We sat and as he poured, he spoke.

"Ian just gave me the sketchiest of details. Obviously, I have had to pass them on to Her Majesty's Home Office. That's the name of the game at the moment, I'm afraid. I can take you to Malaga, which will take us about five days, and from there you can make your way back to Blighty, L.A., Boston or wherever you need to go. But HMG would like to hold onto the plane, and they'd also like me to debrief you."

Njal's eyes were hooded. "What if we don't want to be debriefed by you?"

"Then the best I can do, old chap, is ferry you ashore to

Douala, offer you some cash and food and a place to sleep for a few nights."

I spoke up before Njal could answer. "I have no problem telling you where we've been and what we've done, but I need to know who you're going to tell about it."

"My superiors at the Home Office, obviously. Aside from them, nobody."

"The Home Office is a big place, Billy, with lots of departments."

"MI6, African Office."

"You got a cook on this excuse for a boat?"

He raised an eyebrow at me. "Uncouth American, could you not have taken after your mother, instead? She is a fine woman, you know? Yes, I have a cook. What do you want?"

"Bacon, eggs, mushrooms, kidneys, toast and a gallon of coffee."

Njal was nodding. "Yuh, for me, too."

He sent the order to his onboard chef and called the skipper to instruct him to set a course for Malaga. Then he said to me, "So, Lacklan, what have you been up to?"

"You ever hear of Omega?"

He shrugged. "Rumors…"

I reached down and pulled my knife from my boot, then cut away the leg of my jeans. The bandage Njal had applied was caked with blood, which had seeped out and run down my leg. I saw Njal wince. Billy Beauchamp was too English to show much emotion, but he raised an eyebrow and said, "You need a hospital."

I shook my head. "I need you to listen carefully, and I need you to make your superiors listen carefully to you. This…" I pointed at the caked blood. "This is not rumors.

This is fact. I got this stealing a two kiloton nuclear device from the Russian Mafia, so I could plant it under what was going to be the world's first fusion reactor, on the border of Namibia and South Africa, at a town called Goodhouse, on the Orange River. The device detonated nine hundred feet below the surface and destroyed the building. That much you can get your techs to confirm. Now, get comfortable, Billy, and I will tell you a story that you are not going to believe..."

I told him the whole story, warts and all, partly because I trusted him as much as I trusted Njal, and at least as much as I trusted Jim, but also because I wanted MI6 and the British Home Office to know about Omega. I wasn't sure why yet, but I knew it was important. While I was talking, he got his first aid guy to clean my wound and dress it, and check me over generally. After I had finished my story and he had finished cleaning me up, I walked in a kind of trance to my cabin, fell on the bed and slept like the dead for the next twelve hours straight.

For the next five days, Njal and I did little other than eat, drink and sleep, and in between discussed Omega, and how all that was left was Omega 5 in China, and the remains of Omega 4 in Africa. Njal was convinced we had not done enough yet to destroy them. And I found that increasingly, I didn't care.

On the fifth day, we sailed through the straights of Gibraltar at dawn, with the sun rising over the eastern Mediterranean, and as we stood on deck drinking coffee, Bill asked me, "You and Njal have your tickets?"

I nodded. "He's going back to L.A. I'll go via London and Oxford."

"Marni?"

I nodded again.

He sighed. "You always were besotted with her. I don't know why you've taken so long to act on it." I didn't answer, so he went on. "I can't promise you what HMG will do with this information, Lacklan. There may well be representatives of Omega in the department, you appreciate that?"

I nodded. "I'd be surprised if there weren't."

"You needn't have told me everything, Lacklan. Why have you? What are you hoping to achieve?"

I thought about it. "A year ago, Omega was the favorite to win the race for global power. Anyone seeking power would have been wise to back them. Now they are crippled, in disarray. If Western governments, like the U.K., become aware of them now, instead of backing the winner, maybe they'll hunt down and destroy the loser."

He nodded. "A tad cynical, but probably true." He frowned, and after a moment asked, "But what of their predictions? What of their concerns about overpopulation, climate change...?"

I looked up at the looming mass of Gibraltar, towering over the ocean. Three hundred years earlier, a handful of Royal Marines had snatched it from the might of the Spanish empire and held it till now. Sometimes, I told myself, the Davids of the world won against the Goliaths.

"I don't know, Bill. I don't understand it. Western alliances can mobilize a million men to go to war against a dictator who snatches a few oil wells from his neighbor, and will invest trillions of dollars in such a war. But faced with a crisis that threatens to cause famine and death on a global scale, they sit and talk, question the validity of the evidence, discuss economics and blame, have conferences and recommend recycling plastic bags..."

"You sound like a spokesman for Omega."

I stared at him for a long moment. He raised an eyebrow at me and I sighed. "That's the real tragedy of this story, Bill. Nobody is wearing the white hat. There is no good guy, only bad guys and worse guys."

He grunted. "That's why they invented religion."

I offered him a smile that was skeptical. "To teach people morals?"

He laughed. "No, so that the worse guys could exploit the bad guys."

Shortly after that, Njal and I thanked Bill and disembarked at the port of Malaga. He promised me he'd visit me in Boston to tell me what he could about his superior's reaction to the debriefing.

Later, Njal and I sat in a café on the port and called Jim on the burner he'd given us. Njal put it on speaker.

"Where are you?"

"Malaga."

"Were you successful?"

"In everything."

"Do you need help?"

Njal glanced at me. I shook my head. He said, "What do you want us to do?"

"Come to L.A. We'll talk here."

I said, "I'm done talking, Jim. I'm going to Oxford and then I'm going home to Boston. I'm through with this."

"It's not that simple, Lacklan. There is still China."

"You take care of it, Jim. I'm out."

"Let me know when you get back. I'll come and visit."

I sighed. "Anytime, Jim. But you come as a friend and guest, not as a colleague. I told you. I'm done."

"OK, Lacklan. I'll see you in a week or two. Take it easy."

He hung up and Njal and I sat in silence, not thinking about Jim or China or Omega, but feeling the warm sun healing our wounds and bruises, listening to the lapping of the sea in the harbor, the chatter and laughter of normal people, and the gulls wheeling overhead. It was good, therapeutic, but after a while, their cries became ominous. To my ears, it sounded as though they were crying war.

I went with Njal to the airport. He gave me one of his complicated handshakes and grinned when I got it wrong. "You gotta learn this shit, man."

We embraced and as he turned to go I gripped his hand again, as though I were going to Indian wrestle him. He stopped. "What is it, Lacklan?"

"Thanks, Njal. For getting me out of there. I was finished."

He shrugged. "What friends do. I'll see you Stateside. Be lucky with your girl."

I watched him till he was through security, then spent the rest of the day in town, replacing my clothes and killing time till my evening flight to Gatwick.

EIGHTEEN

I had called Marni from the airport to tell her I was on my way. She had sounded pleased and told me not to hire a car. So it wasn't a surprise to see her waiting at arrivals, but it still gave me a kick. We stood for a long time just holding each other, with the crowds jostling and pushing around us, enjoying the closeness; enjoying being together.

Eventually, we let go and stood a while smiling, looking at each other in a way that was probably nauseating for onlookers, but was nice for us. Then we walked, arm in arm, to the parking lot where we got in her Mini and she drove us through the long English summer twilight, to Oxford.

We didn't go to her apartment. It was late and we went instead to a pub on the high street that had a dining room at the back. There we had steak and kidney pie and good English beer, served as it should be, at room temperature. When we had finished the food and the waitress was clearing away the plates, I asked her for a cheese platter and two double Bushmills, no ice. When she'd gone, Marni reached across the table and took my hand.

"You look tired."

I nodded. "I am tired."

"You want to go home?" She smiled. "I mean to my apartment."

"Not yet. I'm enjoying this. It's the first day of the rest of my life."

She narrowed her eyes, but there was pleasure and amusement in them. "You say that as though it has a special meaning."

I squeezed her hand. "It has."

"That sounds serious."

"I'm done, Marni. I've told Njal, and Jim. This last job…" I shook my head. "It was too much. I'm not doing that anymore."

She sat forward and added her left hand to her right, holding mine. Her eyes were bright, but uncertain. "What are you telling me, Lacklan?"

The waitress came with our whiskeys and a wooden board with a variety of English cheeses on it, and a basket of crackers. She set them down and gave us both a secret smile, like she knew what we were talking about and she approved.

I took a moment to put some Wensleydale on a cracker, eat it and sip some whiskey. English cheese and Irish whiskey is a combination that would make the gods weep with envy.

"Marni, I have loved you since I was a kid. You were always the only girl for me, and you still are. I thought—I hoped—that Abi would make me forget…" I shook my head. "But I never did."

I saw tears in her eyes, but she was smiling. "I never forgot either, Lacklan."

"When you told Gibbons about the job in Europe, I thought—I *hoped*, again—that that would cure me. But it didn't. You are the only thing that makes sense to me in this world, Marni. I got into this whole business with Omega because I thought you were in danger. I went to find you. It's what I've been doing all my life, looking for you."

She frowned, reaching for my hands again. "But why, when I came to London, what was it, seven years ago now? Why did you send me away?"

"Because I was stupid, Marni. Because I was trying to protect you from what I had become. Because I didn't want you to be a part of what I was. But that is all over now. I'm done with it, and the fact is, Omega is finished. There is no way they can recover from what we have done to them. So I'm done, and I want to do something different with my life now, Marni."

Her eyes were bright and she was smiling. "What do you want to do?"

"I want to stop destroying and killing, and I want to start creating, and giving life. I want you to come back to Boston with me. I want you to be my wife. I want to have children. And together I want us to think of ways that we can make a difference." She closed her eyes and squeezed my hand and I saw a tear trickle down her cheek. For a moment, I felt a stab of anxiety. "Will you do that?"

She opened her eyes, gave a small, wet laugh and nodded. "Yes."

"You know, Ben always criticized me, both of us, because we attacked Omega, but we never had anything to put in its place. We offered no solution, no alternative. So, now that they are broken, maybe we, with Cyndi and others, maybe we can start to work on a solution, a way of offering hope…"

She reached across the table with her right hand and put her finger to my lips. "One step at a time. First, let's heal a bit, spend some time, you and me, together, building a home; not fighting any wars, but enjoying each other and being happy."

"See? That's why I need you in my life."

She laughed. I laughed too and it felt good. We finished the cheese and ordered another round of Irish and talked about our plans. She clung to my hand again with both of hers. "Don't go back yet! Stay with me for the month while I wrap things up. Call Kenny in the morning and give him the news…"

"He'll be happy. He always wanted it to be you."

"Bless him! We'll get a shipping company to send my stuff over. Then, Lacklan, let's go by boat! To New York! We'll take a cruise! And then we'll drive up to Boston!"

"That sounds perfect…"

"And we'll get married at the church, in May! Please?"

The church where Ben and my father were buried. I put the thought from my mind and smiled. "Anything you want, Marni."

She was quiet for a bit, smiling back at me. Finally, she said, "All I want, all I have ever wanted, was you. We've both made mistakes in the past, Lacklan. But this time we are going to get it right."

"Yes." I reached across now and took her hand. "Come on. Let's go. I want to tell you things I can't tell you in public. I need to whisper them." I winked and her cheeks colored.

I called the waitress for the bill and while she was getting it, Marni became pensive. "Lacklan, do you remember a long time ago, in Colorado, when this whole business began, I gave you my diary?"

"Sure. I still have it."

"And I kept telling you to do your reading..."

I frowned and thought about it. "Yeah, I guess you did say that a couple of times."

"Did you ever do it?"

"My reading?"

"The diary! Did you ever read the diary?"

I shrugged. "I read bits..."

She shook her head and smiled. "Son of a gun..."

"Why?"

The waitress came with the bill. I paid and looked at Marni, waiting for an answer.

She shook her head. "Come on, I'll tell you on the way home."

We stepped out into the warm evening air. I stood on the outside and she clung to my arm with both of hers. We started to walk along the old street, with the amber streetlamps washing the blacktop and the ancient buildings. "You remember there was a whole business about my father's research? Everybody was searching for it high and low. Omega were crazy to get their hands on it..."

"I remember. I thought you and Gibbons got hold of it, when you arranged the conference at the UN."

She leaned against me slightly. The cars sighed as they past. We dodged a couple of people, strolling, taking our time. "Not exactly." She laughed. "All of his research was contained in the diary!"

I frowned at her. "What?"

"It's crazy. I didn't realize it for a long time. He was a very clever man. He wanted me to have it, and he didn't want anybody else to get their hands on it. So he put it in the diary."

"How?"

"That was the thing. He left a letter with his attorneys, to be posted to me on that particular date, telling me where —and how—to find it. It was…"

Her eyes became abstracted, her smile a little rigid, looking down the street, ahead of her. I followed the line of her gaze. About twelve or fifteen feet away, there was a man walking toward us. His head was down and he was walking quickly, on a collision course. I stepped aside and pulled Marni with me. By then, he was just two strides away. He changed course too, still looking down at his feet. I said, "Hey pal, look where you're go…"

And he looked up. For a fraction of a second, I saw him as I had seen him last, floodlit from above by a bank of spotlights, with the red Toyota behind him. For a moment, I felt the dark water lapping at my legs, heard the rumble of the earth as the bomb detonated nine hundred feet below, heard the shouting voices and the stutter of automatic fire. And then I was back in Oxford, with the traffic hissing slowly past in the amber streetlight. He was staring into my face, holding my eyes with his. He spoke softly. His accent was strongly South African.

"You made a mistake, Mr. Walker."

A soft sound, like a soft hiss of gas, and he had shouldered past us. I looked after him, watched him disappear among the crowds on the sidewalk. Marni was heavy on my arm. I looked at her and saw that she was sagging. Her hands were clutching at her belly, with thick, dark blood oozing between her fingers. She looked up into my face and there was fear and panic in her eyes.

"Oh, God, Lacklan... I've been shot..."

She went down on her knees. People stopped, gathering around. A voice was shouting, screaming, *"Get an ambulance! For god's sake! Somebody call an ambulance!"*

I was on my knees by her side, holding her hands, stroking her face, weeping, begging her to stay with me, fumbling for my cell. Somebody was holding my shoulders, telling me the ambulance was on its way. Sirens wailed across the night. There were people gathered around her. Somebody said he was a doctor. Her eyes were on mine, glazed, out of focus. Her skin was pale, cold and pasty.

Then they were lifting her onto a gurney. Men and women in reflective clothes were pushing me, jostling me, telling me to let them do their job, that I was in the way, that she was critical and I was not helping.

And then the ambulance was pulling away and I was running, running like a maniac though the traffic, trying to keep up, calling her name. Men in uniform surrounded me, gripping my arms, telling me to stop, to calm down, to focus. A big, broad face with a broken nose, piercing eyes staring into mine. "Sir! Sir! Look at me. Look at my eyes. Listen to me." The crackle of radios in the night. "She's going to the hospital. We'll take you. I'm a police officer. My name is Sergeant Hogben. I'm going to take you to the hospital. Do you understand me?"

My breathing, loud, trembling, slowing. "Yes. Please."

"And then I'm going to need to know what happened."

"She was shot."

"Yes," he said. "I know."

BLACK WINDOWS INHABITED by cold ghosts. Chairs made of cold vinyl and cold steel, reflecting the cold strip lighting from the ceilings. Sergeant Hogben had gone. He had gone to get coffee. I didn't know how long he'd been gone.

Marni had been rushed into the operating theater. She was bleeding out. She'd been shot in the gut with a 9mm round at point blank range. You don't survive that kind of wound. That is an execution with malice, making an example. It is one of the most painful ways to die. Mercifully, she had become unconscious. She would die in her sleep.

A surgeon appeared at one point. He seemed to be standing in another, parallel reality, separated from my reality by a sheet of impenetrable glass. He stared into my eyes as he spoke, like he was trying to read my face to see if I understood him.

"She'll be in surgery a while yet. We are doing everything we can. You should go and get some rest."

I told him, "We got engaged tonight. Home... we were going home together."

He said something about seeing the nurse, about being sedated. Then he went away. Slowly, my thoughts began to take shape. I didn't go to see the nurse. I didn't want to be sedated. I called Billy Beauchamp.

"Lacklan. Twice in just a few..."

I cut across him. "They murdered Marni."

He was silent for a moment. "I am so sorry."

"On Oxford High Street. They shot her in the belly."

"What do you want from me? Anything..."

"Get the cops off my back. I have a Sergeant Hogben asking me questions. Get him off my back."

"I'll make the call."

I hung up and called Jim.

"Lacklan, where are you?"

"In Oxford. They shot Marni. She's in surgery, but she won't survive."

"I'm so sorry."

"I'll wait till she dies. I'll bring her home and bury her at Weston. Then I'm going to hunt them down. I am going to kill every last one of them. I am going to destroy Omega, burn their buildings to the ground, annihilate their companies, their bank accounts, everything they have, I will destroy. I will crawl inside their minds and their dreams and I will destroy them too. I will destroy everything, until not even the memory of them exists."

He was quiet for a moment. "Welcome home, Lacklan. I will be right there with you, my friend. I'll be right there with you."

Don't miss DEATH IN FREEDOM. The riveting sequel in the Omega Thriller series.

Scan the QR code below to purchase DEATH IN FREEDOM.

Or go to: righthouse.com/death-in-freedom

NOTE: flip to the very end to read an exclusive sneak peek...

DON'T MISS ANYTHING!

If you want to stay up to date on all new releases in this series, with this author, or with any of our new deals, you can do so by joining our newsletters below.

In addition, you will immediately gain access to our entire *Right House VIP Library,* which includes many riveting Mystery and Thriller novels for your enjoyment!

righthouse.com/email

(Easy to unsubscribe. No spam. Ever.)

ALSO BY BLAKE BANNER

Up to date books can be found at:
www.righthouse.com/blake-banner

ROGUE THRILLERS
Gates of Hell (Book 1)
Hell's Fury (Book 2)
Ice Burn (Book 3)
Judgement by Fire (Book 4)

ALEX MASON THRILLERS
Odin (Book 1)
Ice Cold Spy (Book 2)
Mason's Law (Book 3)
Assets and Liabilities (Book 4)
Russian Roulette (Book 5)
Executive Order (Book 6)
Dead Man Talking (Book 7)
All The King's Men (Book 8)
Flashpoint (Book 9)
Brotherhood of the Goat (Book 10)
Dead Hot (Book 11)
Blood on Megiddo (Book 12)
Son of Hell (Book 13)
Merchant of Death (Book 14)
Extinction C-14 (Book 15)

HARRY BAUER THRILLER SERIES

Dead of Night (Book 1)
Dying Breath (Book 2)
The Einstaat Brief (Book 3)
Quantum Kill (Book 4)
Immortal Hate (Book 5)
The Silent Blade (Book 6)
LA: Wild Justice (Book 7)
Breath of Hell (Book 8)
Invisible Evil (Book 9)
The Shadow of Ukupacha (Book 10)
Sweet Razor Cut (Book 11)
Blood of the Innocent (Book 12)
Blood on Balthazar (Book 13)
Simple Kill (Book 14)
Riding The Devil (Book 15)
The Unavenged (Book 16)
The Devil's Vengeance (Book 17)
Bloody Retribution (Book 18)
Rogue Kill (Book 19)
Blood for Blood (Book 20)
The Cell (Book 21)
Time to Die (Book 22)
The Reaper of Zion (Book 23)

DEAD COLD MYSTERY SERIES
An Ace and a Pair (Book 1)
Two Bare Arms (Book 2)
Garden of the Damned (Book 3)
Let Us Prey (Book 4)
The Sins of the Father (Book 5)
Strange and Sinister Path (Book 6)

The Heart to Kill (Book 7)
Unnatural Murder (Book 8)
Fire from Heaven (Book 9)
To Kill Upon A Kiss (Book 10)
Murder Most Scottish (Book 11)
The Butcher of Whitechapel (Book 12)
Little Dead Riding Hood (Book 13)
Trick or Treat (Book 14)
Blood Into Wine (Book 15)
Jack In The Box (Book 16)
The Fall Moon (Book 17)
Blood In Babylon (Book 18)
Death In Dexter (Book 19)
Mustang Sally (Book 20)
A Christmas Killing (Book 21)
Mommy's Little Killer (Book 22)
Bleed Out (Book 23)
Dead and Buried (Book 24)
In Hot Blood (Book 25)
Fallen Angels (Book 26)
Knife Edge (Book 27)
Along Came A Spider (Book 28)
Cold Blood (Book 29)
Curtain Call (Book 30)

THE OMEGA SERIES
Dawn of the Hunter (Book 1)
Double Edged Blade (Book 2)
The Storm (Book 3)
The Hand of War (Book 4)
A Harvest of Blood (Book 5)

To Rule in Hell (Book 6)
Kill: One (Book 7)
Powder Burn (Book 8)
Kill: Two (Book 9)
Unleashed (Book 10)
The Omicron Kill (Book 11)
9mm Justice (Book 12)
Kill: Four (Book 13)
Death In Freedom (Book 14)
Endgame (Book 15)

ABOUT US

Right House is an independent publisher created by authors for readers. We specialize in Action, Thriller, Mystery, and Crime novels.

If you enjoyed this novel, then there is a good chance you will like what else we have to offer! Please stay up to date by using any of the links below.

Join our mailing lists to stay up to date -->
righthouse.com/email
Visit our website --> righthouse.com
Contact us --> contact@righthouse.com

- facebook.com/righthousebooks
- x.com/righthousebooks
- instagram.com/righthousebooks

EXCLUSIVE SNEAK PEEK OF...

DEATH IN FREEDOM

CHAPTER 1

She didn't die, but she didn't live either.

Marni lingered in a coma, somewhere between life and death. At first, the hours dragged past through empty hospital corridors: bright lights on black glass, doctors and nurses, and listless cleaners making their rounds, while I waited for her to die. But morning broke, pink and yawning among cold birdsong, and Marni was not dead.

So then the days began to drag by, in a relentless procession to and from the hospital, walking the same ancient, sandstone streets, seeing the same morning faces, nodding as they became familiar, meeting day after day with doctors who always told me the same thing: we had to wait and see, she might live and she might die.

And gradually the days became a week, two, three, and one morning at the end of the fourth week, I awoke in her bed and realized that the crisis and horror of that night, when she had been shot, had surreptitiously become a way of life. She might continue for months, or even years, in a near permanent vegetative state. She might open her eyes at any moment, or she might die that very day.

Either way, it was time to take her back to where she was born, to where we had spent our childhoods together, reading comics, playing board games on rainy days and battling countless enemies in the New England forests when the sun shone. So I arranged an air taxi and a private nurse and a doctor to attend to her during the flight, and I took her back to Weston. She had three paths she could take: live, die or linger. Whichever one she took, she would take it at home, with me by her side.

I put her in the room next to mine, arranged twenty-four hour care seven days a week, a doctor to visit her regularly and a physiotherapist to keep her muscles moving and the blood flowing. And so we settled into a new life.

When Kenny, the butler I had inherited from my father along with his house, had begged me to return home and settle, this, I am pretty sure, was not what he'd had in mind. But when I'd said this to him and Rosalia, my cook, standing in the kitchen drinking coffee with them, she had flung her arms around me and wept.

"We know you and Marni all our life. You like our own children," she'd said. Then she'd stared into my face, her cheeks shiny and wet. "She gonna be OK, *hijo mío*, you gonna see! She gonna be OK."

Shortly after that, Jim Redbeard had come to see me. In a world where the majority believe that the smartest thing you can do in life is mortgage yourself to a bank, take on the responsibility of kids so you can't afford to pay that bank what you owe them, and then teach those kids to do the same stupid thing you did—Jim Redbeard was the craziest person I knew. Which made him pretty sane by any other standards. He looked like a Viking and behaved like a Viking, with a vast appetite for food, wine, women and life. His creed was 'do as thou wilt shall be all of the law,' and he lived by it.

He had been a professor of philosophy at UCLA and was an expert in Norse mythology. He described himself as an anarcho-capitalist and had made a fortune writing self-help best sellers. Now he devoted his life, as I had, to bringing down Omega. And between us, we had almost managed it, but the price had been high. The price had been Marni.

During his visit, I had avoided the subject of Omega, but on his last night, sitting in front of the fire in my study, drinking old Irish whiskey, he had said to me:

"Lacklan, you have paid the ultimate price, but the job isn't done. If you give up now, they will have won."

"I have no intention of giving up, Jim. I told you I am going to hunt each one of them down and kill them.[1]"

"When?"

"When Marni dies... I am not leaving her side till then."

He'd sighed and sat back, crossing one vast leg over the other. "That could be years, Lacklan. Hell, she could outlive you."

"I am not leaving her side."

"So they win." He waited. I didn't say anything. "They win, and she goes unavenged. Are you sure that's what you want? You destroyed Omega here in the States, you destroyed them in Europe and Latin America, and you crip-

---

1. See *Kill: Four*

pled them in Africa. But in China and Russia they are strong, Lacklan, and they could grow back to become more powerful than ever.[2] And if they do, I don't need to tell you that they will come after you, *and* Marni. They will punish you."

I had stared into the flames, hearing the crackle of the wood, feeling the warmth on my face. I knew he was right, but it was a truth I did not want to face.

"If I go and, while I am gone she dies…"

He sighed. "You're like a surgeon, cutting out metastasized tumors. You've cut them all out, but you've left one, for fear that while you are removing it, your patient will die." He had leaned forward then, with his elbows on his knees and the orange flames dancing in his glass, wavering on his face. "If you don't destroy them, she will certainly die their victim. If you finish the job, she has *some* chance of living."

Then he had drained his glass and stood. "I am returning to L.A. tomorrow morning, Lacklan. Tomorrow is Wednesday. I'll expect you there on Saturday at the latest, to discuss our plan and our strategy. We have to finish the job. There is no other way."

And he had gone up to his room.

I had spent most of the next day with her, talking to her, though the doctors had told me she couldn't hear me. I explained to her why I had to do what I had to do, why I had to go, even though she couldn't understand. I had sat by the open window, smelling the coming fall on the cool breeze, watching her and remembering our childhood together, and

---

2. See *Kill: One; Kill: Two; The Omicron Kill and Kill: Four* respectively.

our teens, our first adolescent kiss. We had always known we were supposed to be together. But the gods had not agreed.

Finally, I had packed a bag, climbed into my Zombie 222 and headed for Los Angeles.

It was a forty hour drive and I did the whole thing like an automaton, driving by the numbers, barely aware of my environment or what was going on around me. I kept my eye on the mirror and on the sky, to make sure I was not being followed, and I slept twice for four hours. Otherwise, the journey passed in a kind of blur.

At ten o'clock on Friday night, I pulled up outside his house on Paseo de la Playa, at Malaga Cove, and killed the engine. As I climbed out of the car, Jim came down the garden path to greet me. Behind him, warm light was spilling from his open door into the dark garden, silhouetting the palms and the yuccas that fronted his house. In the background, there was the heavy sigh of the ocean at the foot of the cliff.

He took my hand and slapped me on the shoulder. "I'm glad you came."

I slung my bag over my shoulder and closed the trunk.

"I didn't have much choice."

"You could use a drink."

"Yeah, I could at that." I walked past him, up the path to the door. "Is Njal here?"

"No." He followed after me. "He doesn't believe you should be here." I stopped in the hall and turned to face him as he closed the door. He held my eye and added, "He thinks you're spent."

"I'm not spent."

"Leave your bag on the couch. Mioko will take it up. Go ahead out to the terrace. I'll bring out the drinks."

I stepped out onto his broad terrace, with the gardens running down to the cliff edge and the luminous, moonlit ocean beyond. I sat at the big, oak table he had there and he followed me out with a bottle of Bushmills and two glasses. He poured two generous measures straight up and sat.

"He didn't like the way you handled things in South Africa.[3]"

"The job was impossible, we had no preparation and we had to improvise. It was suicide. It was a miracle we got out alive. You know it and he knows it."

"He said you became emotional, erratic, unpredictable. He said you lost perspective."

I drained my glass and put it down. "Then what the hell am I doing here?"

He shrugged. "I'm telling you why he's *not* here. I am more pragmatic. You're right. You went into a mission which was all but impossible and you both came back alive. To my mind, *res ipsa loquitor*, the facts speak for themselves. But I respect Njal. He's damn good at what he does and his judgment is sound, so I think you ought to be aware of what he's thinking."

I pulled my cigarettes from my jacket, flipped my old, battered brass Zippo and took my time lighting up. As I let out the smoke, I said, "OK, so I'm aware of what he's thinking. I go to China alone."

He shrugged again, more elaborately. "We need to formulate a plan, see who we're dealing with, what's

---

3. See *Kill: Four*

involved. Besides, Njal's a good friend to you. Don't write him off too soon."

"What's that supposed to mean?"

He sighed and picked up his glass, but instead of drinking, he squinted out at the ocean, where a vast sheet of moonlight lay fractured on the water.

"His refusal to be here was not because of a lack of trust in you. It was more concern. He thinks you need a break. He believes you're burned out and need time with Marni."

"He's right."

"I know." He turned back to face me. "But we can't afford that luxury. We—all of us—need you to go into China and Russia and finish the job, and you have to hold it together till the job is done."

We watched each other a moment. Finally, I gave a small laugh. "You're a ruthless son of a bitch, aren't you?"

"Yes." Then he echoed my laugh. "I believe you're the president of that club, aren't you?" He sipped and set down his glass. "Believe me, Lacklan, if I had your skills, I would do it myself. But I haven't and we both know—all three of us know—that you are the man for the job. Nobody knows Omega as well as you do. Nobody has the experience you have. We have no choice. It has to be done and you have to do it."

I nodded, then heaved a deep sigh. "I know. So what are we dealing with?"

He reached over and took my pack of Camels. He shook one loose, stuck it in his mouth and lit it, then inhaled. He spoke with a trail of smoke issuing from his mouth.

"Omega Five covers not just China, though that is where the heart is, it covers also Russia, Japan, southeast Asia and all the islands. Their cabal..." He paused, studying my face, then repeated, "Their cabal, I don't know if you remember this, is Phi, Chi, Psi, Omega... and Alpha."

I went cold and felt my hair prickle. "Alpha was Ben. I killed Ben."

"He may have been replaced."

I refilled my glass and said, apparently contradicting myself, "I saw him, Jim. In Africa, in the pyramid, when I was placing the bomb. I saw him."

"You thought you did, Lacklan. You said yourself it was an hallucination."

I sighed and rubbed my face. "Maybe Njal is right. Maybe I'm losing it... mentally."

"Or maybe they're just fucking with your head. The texts, the hints..." He shook his head. "You told me you shot him..."

"Twice, in the heart. He was dead, Jim. I know he was."

"Then they're fucking with your head. It's what they do. It's what they specialize in. How many programs of theirs have you come across that were all about mind control? The Richard John Erickson Institute, the Sun Beetles, the lab at Cosalá... Don't let them get to you."

"How could they make me hallucinate that?"

"Hallucinogenic drugs pumped into the air, coupled with the suggestions they had already implanted in your brain... Hell! Even holograms." He spread his hands. I helped myself to another shot of whiskey and thought about it. It made sense, up to a point.

"Why would they want to do that to me? How does that benefit them?"

"You got me there, Lacklan. But if you'll forgive me saying so, I think the question is irrelevant. We need to destroy them and kill them. It doesn't matter why or how they did it. You killed him. He's dead. Now we have to kill the rest of them."

I nodded. "Yeah, you're right. But this operation can't be like the last one, Jim."

"It won't be."

"I aim to come home alive. Marni needs me and I am going to be with her till she dies."

"She may recover, Lacklan."

"No. She won't. But I plan to be with her at the end. So we plan this out thoroughly, in detail. I want a separate identity for each hit. I want a workable extraction and an identity for that extraction. No improvising, no last minute plans, no escaping by the seat of my pants."

He shook his head. "It's your show. You plan it, you design it, you tell me what you need. I'll use what influence I have to make it happen. You want me to talk to Njal, see if I can change his mind?"

"I don't give a damn. But if he wants in, he needs to decide before I start making my plan."

"He'd be useful."

"Sure, and in China we'd both stick out like a couple of neon dildos at a vicar's tea party."

"Only part of your mission would be in China, and you would pose as visiting businessmen, I assume." He paused, tipping his empty glass this way and that. "Part of Njal's concern was that you were responding emotionally to situations where you should have been dispassionate…"

"Like feeling bad about murdering a woman in cold blood? Or giving three innocent hookers the chance to get away? The day I stop doing that kind of thing is when you need to start worrying." I sighed. "Sure, he's useful and I know he's got my back. I think I've proved I have his too. If he wants in, I'll be glad to have him along. If he doesn't, I don't care. I'll do the job either way."

"OK, let's look at the outline of the plan. I'll decide after that whether to ask Njal to join you. You want some food?"

I shook my head. "I need to sleep. But before that, tell me who Phi is."

"Gregor Ustinov. He lives in Moscow. Former director of the KGB, now a private industrialist, billionaire, not surprisingly with ties to the Russian Mafia." I didn't ask, but he pressed on. "Chi, Haruto Kobayashi, head of the Kobayashi corporation, lives outside Tokyo. Psi, Liu Wang—or as they would have it, Wang Liu—one of the new billionaires, remarkably young at thirty-two, has ties to the Chinese Communist Party. Omega, Abba Roth..."

"Abba Roth? That's an Anglo-Jewish name."

"Indeed. In Omega Five, things are a little different. The last shall be the first, Jormungand, the worm Ouroborus."

"Spare me the mysticism, at least till tomorrow. Who is this guy?"

"There is very little information available on him. He lives in Moscow, but travels a lot to China and Mongolia. A dot com billionaire, but has since invested heavily in armaments, nuclear energy and lithium-ion technology." He waited for me to say something. I didn't, so he went on with the list. "Alpha, Benjamin Walker, your brother, dead and buried in the family graveyard. As far as I know, Alpha has not been replaced."

I stood. "OK, Jim, thanks. Let me get some sleep now. We'll talk in the morning."

He raised his glass to me. "You got it. Rest."

I went up to my room, lay down on the bed and passed out.

CHAPTER 2

I slept eight hours, rose at seven and had a long hot, cold, hot shower. Then I went down to the terrace, where Jim was sitting at his oak table being served coffee and hot bread by Maria, his Latina, live in cook-cum-housekeeper. He watched me sit with inquiring eyes as he sipped his coffee. Maria smiled.

"What can I get you, Captain Walker?"

"Black coffee, Maria, and rye toast with butter." I had given up telling her I was not a captain anymore. She poured me a demitasse of strong, black brew and hurried inside to get my toast. I sipped and spoke as I set down the cup. "OK, if Njal will come in on this, I'd like to have him along. You can tell him this operation will be well planned, down to the fine details, no improvising, no hallucinations, no rogue action."

"Good, I'm glad to hear that."

"Step one, we go into China and take out Liu Wang. We can't make it look like an accident."

"Why?"

"Because they'll know, as soon as he winds up dead, whatever the apparent cause, that we're coming after them and they'll go to total lock down."

He frowned. "So what are you suggesting?"

"He has to go on holiday, on a trip, to his country house—whatever—and he has to remain in contact, sending messages, Whatsapps, emails… That will afford us an opportunity to go after Phi, and Omega in Russia."

Maria came out with a basket of toast, which she set beside me, and patted me on the shoulder. Jim broke a croissant and as he buttered it, he said, "Spell it out for me, Lacklan. I'm not following you."

"We take him out, kill him, but we make it seem he's on holiday."

His eyebrows rose on his forehead. "OK, what about Kobayashi in Japan?"

I nodded and started spreading butter on hot rye. "We are going to lure Kobayashi into a visit to Wang in China, or we'll lure Wang into visiting Kobayashi. Either way, it works. We get the two of them together in a private meeting—on a trip, a yacht, a country house, it doesn't matter at this stage—somewhere isolated. That will justify their relative silence and their absence and give us time to hit Ustinov and Roth in Moscow."

"That means getting you from China or Japan to Russia very quickly."

"Can you do it?"

"I'll have to."

"We haven't much choice, but we can nail down the details later. We're going to revise this plan a hundred times before we go in." I bit into the toast and spoke with my mouth full. "In Moscow, we take out Ustinov and we interrogate Roth. I want two things from him: one, access to their computer network…"

Jim nodded. "Good."

"I am going to need Philip Gantrie in on this operation, from the beginning."

"The neutron bomb guy."[1]

"I'll need him to set up the meet between Kobayashi and Wang, to hack their private phones and computers, send out messages on their behalf. And when we have Roth, I'll need Phil to take control of their network."

He frowned. "Take control?"

I studied his face a moment. He looked worried. "Long enough to make sure they haven't spawned a baby Omega somewhere. When we destroy that network and wipe out their funds, I want to know that we are annihilating Omega for good."

He looked relieved. "OK, that's fine. It's a tall order for Gantrie. Are you sure he can do it?"

"No." I shook my head. "But if anybody can, he can. He was recommended to me by my father. Don't forget, my father was Gamma, so Phil must have some knowledge of Omega, and how they work."

He raised an eyebrow. "Can you trust him?"

I shrugged. "He designed the cyber bomb that brought down Omega Europe, you tell me."

"All right. Can you arrange a meeting?"

"I'll talk to him. He's tricky and shy, but I think I can

---

1. See *Kill: Two*

persuade him. Meantime, we are going to need IDs to get into China, IDs to get from China to Russia, IDs to get out of Russia, and two spare IDs in case things go south."

He shook his head. "You can't travel around with all those IDs. If you get stopped..."

"No, they'll have to be left at collection points, banks, attorneys' offices, PO box, left luggage at the airport... You know the drill."

"OK, for now we'll get them made, then we'll think about how we get them to you. What about hardware?"

I thought about it, gazing out at the brilliant turquoise ocean. "How hard is that going to be?"

He made a face and shrugged. "Hard. I can get you a couple of Sigs and a Glock that you can collect at the U.S. embassy in China. Otherwise, it means crossing over the border from Myanmar or Vietnam. If you make the hit in Japan, it's easier."

I shook my head and drained my cup. "We don't need a lot of hardware for the first hit. Couple of hand guns, some tracking devices, bugs. How about Russia?"

He smiled. "You upset those boys when you killed their couriers."

"They upset me. They almost screwed the operation."[2]

He chuckled. "I know. I told them that, but I need to build some bridges. We'll see how it goes. Either way, Russia should be easier than China. What will you need?"

"I don't know yet, but I don't think we'll be blowing up the Kremlin. Probably just handguns and electronic surveillance equipment." I paused. "There is something else,

---

2. See *Kill: Four*

Jim. I want Senator Cyndi McFarlane briefed on the operation."

"Are you out of your mind?"

"Think it through, Jim. OK, we go in, we finally destroy Omega, Omega is no more, then what? You know as well as I do that Omega was only ever a symptom, it was never the original cause. So when we bring Omega down, what are we going to put in its place? The Bilderberg Group? The Illuminati? The Fourth Reich? Islam? The Sinaloa Cartel..." I shook my head. "The problems that brought it into existence are still there."

"OK, I get it. And I agree. But how the hell do you think Cyndi McFarlane can help?"

I sighed, poured myself more coffee and looked back at the vast, placid Pacific. I wished vaguely, irrationally, that I could be like that: placid and still.

"I detest what Omega were trying to do, Jim. Or at least, I detest the way they were going about it: the two tier world with the elite sipping Martini while the obedient, lobotomized masses served them, happy prisoners in their own, unquestioning minds. And you know I would fight to the death to stop that. But that was just their *solution*. What we are fighting is their *solution*."

"I'm not following you, Lacklan."

"What we have consistently ignored, from the start, is the *problem*—the problem they were trying to solve. They were proposing a solution to a problem, and that problem will still be there after they are gone. It will still have to be addressed, and solved. I want Cyndi McFarlane involved because I trust her, and when Omega come down, I want her picking up the pieces."

"How will she do that?"

"You need to talk to her. That's your department. I kill people, you philosophize. We need people in the White House. You need to start exerting influence in the legislature. We need people in place who we can trust, who are willing to tackle the problems Omega is tackling; and we can do that through Cyndi."

"You're beginning to sound like a politician."

"Yeah, I love you too. I just don't want to spend the rest of my life fighting Son of Omega and Grandson of Omega. Omega existed for a reason. You and I, and Njal, we can destroy Omega, but we can't destroy the reason they exist. Senator McFarlane might, if she can muster enough support."

He spread his hands and made a face. "OK, I can't argue with that. But nobody else, Lacklan. The risk is too high. You, me, Njal and Cyndi. That's it. A cabal of four."

I nodded. "A cabal…"

We spent the rest of the morning discussing details, giving the plan some shape and looking at possible ways it could be carried out. We decided provisionally that it made more sense to lure Wang to Japan, partly because two westerners would be less conspicuous in Japan than they would in China, and partly because it would be easier to get black market hardware there if we needed it. Exactly how we would lure Wang to Japan was a moot point which we would need to discuss with Philip Gantrie, the cyber wizard, but our thoughts were running along the lines of covert messages purporting to be from Kobayashi himself.

As far as the hit in Russia was concerned, I favored the idea of drawing Ustinov and Roth together, so I could take them both down at the same time, and we explored several ways that could be done.

By lunchtime, we'd gone about as far as we could and Jim sat back in his chair and looked at his watch.

"We can't proceed any further until we know for sure that Njal is onboard."

I nodded. "We also need to be sure of Phil, and I want to talk to Cyndi."

"Take a flight. Go to Washington and meet with her. Meantime, call Phil, arrange a meeting with him. While you're in D.C., I'll have a talk with Njal, discuss the plan with him. I'm sure he'll agree. But you need to reassure him too."

"I'll take the car. I need to go via Wyoming."

He frowned. "*Wyoming?*"

"Yeah, there is something I have to pick up there. It might be important. If it is, I'll let you know. On the way, I'll call Phil and Cyndi and arrange to meet them. I'll see you back here in a week."

"What's in Wyoming, Lacklan?"

"My old house. There is something there I need to pick up. It may be nothing, but it may be important," I repeated. "If it is, I'll tell you."

He smiled and shook his head. "Have it your way."

We talked some more over lunch and at two o'clock, I climbed back into the Zombie and headed east toward Corona, to pick up the I-15 toward Nevada and Utah. On the way, I called Phil on my hands free. He answered in his characteristic way.

"Amtrak customer services, how may I direct your call?"

"What are you going to do if one day it really is a wrong

number and somebody really does want Amtrak customer services?"

"Can you say something else, please?"

"Hello, Phil, this is Lacklan calling, I would like to talk to you. What did you do, run me through voice recognition?"

"Yes, and stress detection. In answer to your question, I can patch you through to Amtrak if I need to. That is child's play. What do you want to talk about?"

"We're going to finish the job."

"Dear God... Your father never imagined..."

"I need your help."

He was quiet for a long moment. Then he said, "What kind of help?"

"We need to meet."

"I don't like meeting."

"I know, but we haven't much choice, Phil. You want to meet me at my house?"

"In Boston?" He sounded alarmed.

"No, in Boulder, Wyoming."

"Oh..." I heard him swallow. "I guess..."

"I'm on my way now. I figure I'll get there in twelve to fourteen hours. I could meet you there tomorrow."

"Yes, I guess..."

"Come on, Phil. This is serious. I can't do this without your expertise. Just come over and we'll talk. You want me to pick you up somewhere now?"

"No!" Then again, more softly, "No... I'll make my own way. I know where it is. I'll see you there tomorrow PM."

"OK, thanks, Phil. I appreciate it."

He hung up without answering and I called Cyndi.

"Well, if it isn't the Lone Ranger. I just know you're not calling to ask me on a date."

"Y'all ain't wrong, farm girl, and you ain't right neither."

"Did you learn to speak like that in your Boston prep school, or in the British Army?"

"I need to talk to you, Cyndi. We are finishing the job."

She was quiet for a while. I could hear her breathing. Finally, she said, "What does that mean?"

"It means what you think it means. It also means we need to talk face to face, and not in D.C."

"OK, where?"

"I'm on my way home now. I have to stop for a day in Wyoming..."

"My god, you are becoming a cowboy."

"Yes, ma'am. I'll be there a day, then I'll head home. So you could come to Weston, day after tomorrow. Come for dinner. Stay over. We have a lot to talk about."

"Do you know you are very bossy?"

"I'm used to giving orders and being obeyed." I let the smile show in my voice. "But it's more fun with senators than with grunts. Can you make it?"

"I'll clear my schedule. It is really what I think?"

"Yeah, it is really what you think. But I need you to be thinking about what happens after..."

"Yes, I see. It's very sudden."

"Important change usually is."

She sighed. "Yes, that's true. How is Marni?"

"The same."

"I'm sorry. It's taken its toll on you, hasn't it?"

"Yeah, well, you know how it is with life, Cyndi. Sooner or later, it'll kill you."

"That's not funny, Lacklan."

"No."

"I'll see you in Weston in a couple of days. Stay safe."

"You too."

I hung up and ten minutes later, I pulled onto the I-15 headed north and opened up the massive twin engines under the Zombie's hood. In absolute silence, we streaked into the desert at a hundred and thirty miles per hour under the midday sun, with nothing but dry wilderness stretching out before me.

Wyoming.

It must have been no more than a couple of years ago, though it seemed like another life. Marni and I had stayed there together for six months, as man and wife. They had been the happiest six months of my life. Then she had left for Oxford, for Gibbons and her work—her father's work. After that, we had drifted apart. I had married Abi and Marni and I had rarely spoken. But when we had, she had asked me several times the same question—had I done my reading. It had never registered at the time that she was urging me to read her diary: the diary she had given me, the diary she had left in Wyoming, the diary she had told me, just before she was shot, contained all of her father's research. It was that research that had driven Omega to have him killed. It was that research that had driven Marni to go on the run, and caused my father to beg me to find her, protect her, and bring Omega down.

Nobody had ever found that research, and all along it had been in Marni's diary. That raised a lot of questions: why had she not simply come out and told me before? Why had she left it in my hands in the first place? Why had she and Gibbons not accessed and used that research, if it was so damaging to Omega? But she had been shot before she could tell me.

We had been together six months in Wyoming, with the diary, and she had never mentioned it. Then she had left, and left me with the diary. Why?

The diary was still there, in my bedside drawer. And before I did anything else, I planned to find the answers to those questions.

CHAPTER 3

I DROVE THROUGH THE HOT, SCORCHED DAY AND into the evening, and by the time I reached Fillmore, in Utah, the sky was on fire on my left, and on my right it was engulfed in darkness, seeping in over the Pahvant Mountains.

I didn't pause to rest. I had coffee and sandwiches in the car, which kept me going, and my mind was wide awake.

At ten, I skirted Salt Lake City and started to climb into the Wasatch Range, following the I-80. I figured I was four hours from my house in Boulder, and in my mind I kept going over the damned diary, entry by entry, searching for the clue as to how he had inserted his research in among those pages. I hadn't read the whole thing. I had dipped in here and there, but at the back of my mind, something was troubling me.

At about midnight, it dawned on me that I wasn't sure where I was. A while back, I had passed a turn off for the town of Kemmerer. I should have been on highway 230, but nothing looked familiar and I cursed myself for obsessing over the diary when I should have been paying attention to the road.

Within twenty minutes or half an hour, the road had degenerated and it was clear I was no longer on any kind of highway. I came to a bridge over a creek that was engulfed in dense mist. I slowed to a crawl and crossed the bridge with the window open, leaning out to see, because the windshield was misted up. I couldn't hear any water.

I followed the road for another ten miles and came to a second bridge, bigger than the first, that spanned a broad canyon. Here I could hear water splashing below, and there was a sign at the entrance to the bridge that read 'Welcome to Freedom.' Beside it was another sign that read 'Barge Creek.' I knew Barge Creek and I knew it fed into the Green River. I was not too far from the highway, and probably no more than two or three hours' drive from home.

I crossed the bridge and followed a winding road up through steep hills, west along a deep valley, and then started to climb again. I had emerged from the mist, but the darkness was still intense and the stars above me were brilliant in a black sky. After a couple of miles or a little more, I began to see lights ahead. I checked my watch. It was one AM and I was beginning to get tired.

Five minutes later, I passed a gas station sitting in a pool of listless, yellow light. I glanced at my display and saw my batteries were almost spent. A moment later, I was in among a sprawl of pretty houses with large front lawns and ample backyards. The town was dotted with abundant gardens and the roads were lined with plane trees, cherries and almonds. It looked prosperous and cared for. Pretty soon, I found myself in the town square, looking at the town hall. It was a handsome, 19th century building in brown stone. The clock said it was one fifteen, and beneath it two flags hung, Old Glory and next to it a white flag bearing a green ash. I pulled into the parking lot beneath the flags and killed the engine, then climbed out to look around.

I was in a broad square, with a large garden at the center. There were scattered trees and flower beds crisscrossed by paths that radiated from a bandstand at the center. Beyond, there was a row of shops, a restaurant and, next to it, a small hotel. All the windows and shop fronts were dark. The only light came from the old, iron streetlamps and the clock on the town hall façade. The stillness and quiet was absolute, but for a small, red fox who loped across the road a hundred yards away, stopped at the intersection with Main Street, with his shadow stretched long across the blacktop, and stared at me a while. Then he turned and went on his way.

The glow from a set of headlamps illuminated the spot where the animal had stood a moment before. The traffic lights turned red and a Ford F10, bearing the sheriff's shield on the door, pulled up. Sitting at the wheel, I could see a man in a khaki shirt wearing a cowboy hat, with his arm resting on the door. He was watching me. I rested my ass on the trunk of my Zombie, pulled my Camels from my pocket and lit up while I waited for the lights to change.

He wasn't that patient. He gave his siren a single blast, crossed the lights on the empty street and rolled up alongside me. He took his time looking at me some more while I took a drag. He didn't say anything, so as I let out the smoke, I said, "Evening, Deputy. I seem to have got lost. I'm on my way to Boulder, in Wyoming. But I seem to have taken a wrong turn somewhere."

I showed him the pack of Camels. He gave his head a single shake. "Where you coming from?"

"Los Angeles."

He gave a single nod. "You took a wrong turn at the intersection with the two-forty. It happens. You'll have to go down to La Barge to pick up highway 89, via Calpet."

"Somewhere I can rest up till morning? Also…" I gestured at the hood of the Zombie. "I need to charge her up. Is there somewhere I can do that?"

He let his eyes run over the car, then looked at me.

"Charge her up? That's a '68 Mustang, Fastback. You must'a seen the gas station on your way in."

I smiled. "The chassis's a '68 Mustang. Under the hood, it has twin electric motors and lithium-ion batteries."

He raised an eyebrow. "Well, that right there is crime."

I gave a small laugh and gave my head a small twitch. "She'll do naught to sixty in one and a half seconds, top speed of two hundred miles per hour, eight hundred horsepower."

He whistled through his teeth. "That so? What's its range?"

"Five hundred miles."

He nodded a while, eyeing the beast. Then he shrugged. "Guess you'll have to talk to Jonah in the morning. He runs the gas station and the garage. He'll fix you up. Meantime, I'd best wake Missy for you. She runs the diner and the hotel 'cross the way." He jerked his head toward the establishments I'd seen earlier. "She'll give you a bed for the night. You can be on your way tomorrow."

"Appreciate it, Deputy."

Missy eventually came down and unlocked the door after the deputy had hammered on it and rang the bell for about ten minutes. She was in her late thirties, with cute, short blonde hair, scrunched up on her head by her pillow, and squinting eyes that might have been blue or green. She was wrapped in a robe and her face said she didn't know whether to be mad or confused or both. She stared at me and then at the Deputy.

"What the hell, Hank?"

Hank smiled for the first time and made a rumbling noise which I figured was a laugh. "We got ourselves a stray lamb, needs a bed for the night. Mr..." He glanced at me.

I said, "Walker, Lacklan Walker."

"Mr. Walker here took a wrong turn down at the intersection, found his way here. Car needs charging up..."

"*Car* needs *chargin'*..."

"Ne'mind that, Missy. No doubt he'll explain it to you over breakfast if he sees fit. He needs a bed for the night, and I need to get back on my rounds."

I thanked the deputy and he made his way back across the square while Missy closed and locked the door behind him. She led me to a small reception desk beside a door that stood open onto a dark living room.

"We don't get many folks passin' through Freedom."

She spun the old-fashioned register and pushed it toward me with a pen. I smiled at her and signed it. "I gathered."

"How long you stayin'?"

"Just till morning. Charge up my car and be on my way." She narrowed her eyes at me. I explained, "It's electric."

"'Lectric car? Can't be no good. Need gas in a car, not 'lectric."

I wasn't going to argue. "As long as it has a shower and a bed, any room will do."

She pulled an old chub key from a hook behind her. It had the number 14 on it. "First floor. Fourth door on the right, overlookin' the square. Breakfast's at eight. Not nine, not seven. Eight. I can do a full American breakfast—or you can have a continental."

She said all this leaning with her elbows on the counter. Her face said what she thought of a continental breakfast.

"Full American sounds great. I'll be down at eight sharp. Shall I pay you now?"

"You can pay when you leave. You ain't got nothin' to pay for yet…"

After a moment she smiled, then gurgled, to indicate she'd made a joke. I gave a small laugh. "I'll be going up then."

"You sleep well now. See in the mornin'."

The room was twenty feet square with an en suite bathroom. The walls were plain white with two small paintings of flowers hung over the bed. There was a small table with two bentwood chairs. The carpet was beige and the duvet was white with big red flowers. Heavy blue drapes hung over the window.

I dumped my bag on the table and brushed my teeth, reflecting that men make plans and the gods have a good laugh. Then I undressed and sat on the bed, meaning to send Phil a message that I might be late the next day, but there was no signal. So I put my phone on to charge, got under the duvet and fell instantly into a deep, dreamless sleep.

I was up at six-thirty, trained as best I could for an hour in my room and had a cold shower. Missy served me a full American breakfast in the dining room, where I sat alone and ate it with a pot of coffee to myself. When I was finished, I stepped out into the morning sunlight and drove the half mile to the gas station on the outskirts of town with the windows down, enjoying the cool morning breeze. I was struck as I passed the well-kept houses, parks and gardens, by how prosperous the town seemed. The people I passed were friendly; all recognized a stranger and most nodded or smiled.

I found Jonah in the shop at the gas station. He was leaning on the counter doing a crossword and looked up when I stepped in.

"Was eaten, worried and drunk, eight letters, blank, blank 'N' and five blanks."

"Consumed. Are you Jonah?"

He stared at me, then down at his paper. "I'll be darned! Not drunk as in... dog*gone!*" He sighed and filled in the word, taking care over each letter. When he'd finished, he looked up. "I thought it meant drunk, as in, in-he-bree-ated. Never thought... Yeah, I'm Jonah. You must be Mr. Walker, got lost last night. Sheriff told me you'd be droppin' by."

"The sheriff?"

He smiled, revealing an absence of teeth. "He ain't the sheriff, but we call him the sheriff. Sheriff of Lincoln County is a good thirty-five mile nor'west from here, as the crow flies, double or triple that if you're drivin'." He wheezed a laugh, like he'd thought of something funny. "He don't never show his face 'round these parts! No, Hank keeps the peace 'round here. He's a good man."

I gave a single nod. "Can you charge my car? I have the cables and the transformer. I just need a supply."

He shrugged. "I got the supply if that's all you need, but how'll I know how much to charge ya?" He didn't wait for me to answer. "Sure there's nothin' else wrong with your car? That there chassis is all of fifty year old. You want me to look at the brakes? I could look at the suspension. I don't know nothin' 'bout 'lectric cars, but I figure the suspension and brakes got to be the same."

I smiled. "No, it just needs charging up. Shouldn't take more than half an hour."

He wheezed his laugh again. "Half an hour? Don't take more'n thirty, forty seconds t' fill a gas tank!" He creased up his face and laughed some more. "Bring it on into the garage, we'll plug it in!"

I spent the next twenty minutes going over the car with him, showing him how it worked and persuading him it wasn't going to blow all his fuses. He finally plugged it in and told me to return in an hour, because he had some errands to run. By the time I got back to the town square, it was almost eleven and I went into the restaurant to find Missy behind the counter, serving coffee and pie. There was a handful of tables occupied: two elderly couples, a table of three women who looked like office workers, a mother with two kids and a guy in his late twenties or early thirties sitting alone. There was an agreeable hum of chatter, and a clatter of cups and plates. Missy saw me come in and smiled.

"Sit down, honey, I'll be right with you. Coffee and pie?"

"Sure. Blueberry. No cream. Black coffee."

I took a seat by the window, spent some time gazing out at the near empty streets, thinking about China, Russia and

Marni's diary, and then spent some more time taking in the other customers in the restaurant. I noted that the guy who was sitting alone looked tired, maybe stressed. He was eating apple pie and drinking coffee like it was his last meal on Earth, and kept glancing out the window. It occurred to me absently that he looked intelligent; maybe too intelligent. The kind of intelligent that makes you neurotic because you keep asking questions nobody can answer. Or the kind of intelligent that drives revolutionaries to get shot.

I blinked and sighed myself out of the reverie and checked my phone to see if I had signal and Missy leaned over me with a large wedge of blueberry pie, a jug of coffee and a cup dangling from her baby finger. The saucer was in her apron.

"You won't get no signal up here, Mr. Walker. This is the back end of beyond, here. Ain't nobody got a cell phone in Freedom. Closest place you'll get a signal is La Barge."

She set down the pie, then put the cup and saucer in front of me and filled it up to the brim. She winked and smiled. "I remember you like it black and hot, but not sweet."

She sashayed away back to the bar. I smiled and settled to eat my pie. Outside, I saw the deputy pull up in his Ford. He swung down from the driving seat and three more men got out with him, all dressed in khaki shirts with cowboy hats. They all bore deputy badges and they all headed for the restaurant. Their faces said they were not coming for pie and coffee. They were here on business.

I glanced around the room. Everyone had gone quiet. They were all focusing hard on their coffee, except the young man who'd been sitting alone. He was staring out the window and he had gone very pale. I looked for Missy, but she had gone in back.

The door opened and a bell clanked. The boy stood and started yammering, like he was trying to say, "No." He had his hands held out in front of him and he took a step back. His chair shifted and squeaked on the floor.

Hank said, "Now, don't give us no trouble, Noah."

"No, Hank. Don't, this is crazy…"

The three deputies who'd come in with Hank circled around behind Noah and seized his arms, and suddenly he was thrashing like a hooked marlin, kicking his legs, trying to wrench his arms free, twisting his head around in every direction, screaming in a shrill voice, "*Hank! Don't! No! Don't do this! Please!*" Then he was appealing to the other diners, screaming at them, "*Don't let them! You can't just sit there! Don't let them!*"

Nobody looked up. The deputies dragged him out the door and into the street. I watched through the window as they pulled him, stumbling and thrashing, across the sidewalk and tried to shove him in the truck. He resisted, hollering and planting his feet on either side of the door until Hank drove his fist into the boy's belly and he folded up, retching onto the blacktop. When he was done, they bundled him in and drove away.

I sat staring at the empty space where the truck had been, wondering what the hell had just happened. Missy came out and her voice made me snap out of it. She was saying, "Well, who'd like some more pie? I have a fresh apple right out of the oven!"

She stepped over to my table and I frowned at her. "What the hell just happened?"

"I offered you somethin' sweet."

I pointed at the empty chair at the table where Noah had been sitting. "That young man, the deputies just dragged him out. He was hysterical..."

"Noah? Is he in trouble again? That boy ain't never gonna learn! Now who's gonna pay for his pie and coffee?"

There was a murmur around the room, and after a moment, people started to rise from their chairs and make their way toward the door, smiling at Missy and waving goodbye.

"See y'all tomorrow!" She turned back to me. "Now, you want some hot apple pie?"

I shook my head. "No, thanks. I have some things I have to do before I get back to Jonah's garage." I stood and dropped some money on the table. "Where is the sheriff's office, Missy?"

She picked up the money off the table and sighed. "It's 'round back of the town hall, but don't you go getting involved in Freedom business, Mr. Walker. Hank knows what he's doin'."

I nodded, said, "Sure," and I left.

Scan the QR code below to purchase DEATH IN FREEDOM.
Or go to: righthouse.com/death-in-freedom

Printed in Dunstable, United Kingdom